OF ENVY AND EMPATHS
THE GODDESS'S DAUGHTER
BOOK I

WARD PARKER

Mad Mangrove Media

CONTENTS

CHAPTER 1

SOPHIE

Before I sent the crossbow bolt into his heart, the vampire was snoring like a buzz saw. I hadn't known that vampires snored. It made him seem more, well, human.

He also had a smile on his bearded face, as if he were dreaming of a happy incident centuries ago. Perhaps it was a wild-game hunt when he was still human, or courting his lady love.

I stopped my mind from wandering and put up a mental firewall. The empathy in me had to be disabled, or my task would be impossible. Already, my stomach was burning from anxiety and self-loathing.

Why was I becoming so crippled by empathy? I never used to worry much about the feelings of others. It wasn't a useful trait when you were forced to serve as an enforcer for the Executive Council of the Guilds.

Fortunately, the vampire's face reminded me of one of the vampires who had held me captive as their blood slave all those years ago, when I was in drug recovery and highly vulnerable.

The anger and hate that surged into my chest strengthened my resolve to complete my assignment.

The crossbow's trigger clicked, the bowstring sang, and the bolt carved from ash wood, tipped with steel, plunged into his upper chest, just to the left of his sternum.

The vampire's eyes fluttered open, but he began the rapid deterioration process before his eyes registered awareness of what had happened to him.

Of what I had done to him.

It was a quick and merciful death, I told myself. But I felt a deep sense of loss for this vampire I didn't even know, though I could tell he was an exceptionally old one with countless memories.

I was hit by a wave of guilt for destroying him. Even though he was a member of this vampire nest that so flagrantly flouted the rules and risked drawing the attention of human law enforcement.

Feeling the emotions of my targets was why I had quit this job. There was no way I could cold-heartedly punish supernaturals when I could see inside them and sense their life experiences. No way.

But the Council forced me to do this one last assignment.

I turned away from the pile of dust that had once been the vampire. There were still three more in the nest who needed to be destroyed. I knew they were there, and their approximate sleeping locations, thanks to a magic spell that alerted me to supernatural energy.

You see, I'm also a witch—a water witch who harvests energy from the nearby Atlantic Ocean. My self-image is wrapped up in my magic, not in being able to experience the emotions of others.

My sleep spell was why the vampires' human guard was

currently dozing on the floor of the Victorian home's front porch. My magic was powerful enough to destroy the vampires, but I had vowed not to use it for harm. I only used magic to kill when it was for self-defense.

Speaking of killing, I reloaded my crossbow and headed upstairs to where the other three vampires were sleeping.

The wooden steps of the nineteenth-century stairs creaked alarmingly. I had cast my sleep spell over all the occupants of the home, not just the human guard, but magic didn't always work on vampires. If they woke up, I would be in a world of hurt.

Several squeaks later, I reached the top of the stairs and found the nearest bedroom door locked. I muttered a curse and cast a quick spell to unlock it.

The lock was old-fashioned, with a large bolt that clicked loudly as it slid. I held my breath, listening for the sounds of anyone stirring. The house was silent.

I opened the door and entered the bedroom. The room was pitch-dark, like the last one had been. Heavy drapes covered the windows and didn't allow any light to penetrate.

It would be tempting to yank the drapes open and allow light to flood the room and fry any vampire in here. But I couldn't do that. The vampire would probably scream, waking the others. Even if there was no screaming, the others, though sleeping, would sense the invasion of sunlight into their nest.

Fortunately, I had my night-vision goggles. And good thing they were infrared and not the thermal-imaging variety, since my target's undead body was significantly lacking in body heat.

The woman slept on her side, facing away from me, sparing me the sight of her face and the empathy it would stir up. I fired the bolt through her back, and she decomposed instantly and, I hoped, painlessly. It happened so quickly there was no chance to feel any empathy, or even sympathy, for her.

Do vampires have an afterlife? The ones I've spoken to believed they don't, but I'd like to think otherwise. I'm kind of sentimental that way.

I removed my night-vision goggles and left the bedroom. Two more vampires to go. Two more bedrooms with closed doors faced me across the hall in the less-than-complete darkness up here, with a bathroom in between. I glimpsed the edge of an antique claw-footed tub and a modern shower curtain with an illustration of a famous cartoon mouse. A vampire, I was pretty sure, had not purchased that shower curtain.

I chose the bedroom on my left and put my goggles back on. This time, the door was unlocked, so I opened it slowly with my left hand while holding the cocked crossbow in my right, steeling myself for an ambush.

The bed was empty, and the room appeared to be, too.

This didn't mean I could let down my guard. Some vampires chose odd places to sleep, so I got on my knees and checked under the bed. Nothing but dust bunnies under there.

Glancing around the room, I realized the vampire had to be in the closet. Its door was narrow, which indicated the closet was small. Homes over a hundred years old didn't have walk-in closets unless they were mansions—and this one wasn't. Or if they'd been remodeled—and this one hadn't been.

Was the vampire sleeping while standing? Or maybe it was hanging upside down from the clothes rod like a bat?

Sophie, I told myself, *get the vampire clichés out of your head and get to work. You're just procrastinating.*

My crossbow was at the ready when I opened the closet door.

There was nothing but moldy old suits inside. Where was the vampire?

The remaining two residents must be sharing the third bedroom. They must be lovers, I reasoned.

When I left the bedroom and removed my goggles, a skittering, metallic sound came from the bathroom. The mouse shower curtain was opening.

A male vampire wearing a red hoodie and jeans stood in the tub. He snarled at me.

"Why aren't you asleep?" I asked just before he leaped from the tub and charged me.

He flew toward me so fast my eyes barely registered the movement.

Somehow, I got a shot off. Somehow, the bolt struck him, but it was lower in his torso, nowhere near his heart.

I ducked just in time to avoid him slamming into me. He landed, cat-like, in the hallway just beyond me.

As I said before, I don't use my magic to kill unless it's in self-defense. Now was the time to do so.

The vampire, a tall, powerful Black man, backhanded me, sending me crashing into the wall. My crossbow slid away across the hardwood floor. But I didn't need it.

I pulled my broadsword from the scabbard strapped to my back and pushed all the magical energy I could muster into it. My sword, named Alfie (don't ask), was what had given me the reputation of a ruthless killer. A reputation that now filled me with shame.

The vampire sneered at the sight of my sword, but he stepped backward, out of its reach. His eyes fixed on mine and his pupils dilated. A woozy feeling came over me.

Jeez Louise, he was trying to mesmerize me so he could control me.

Not gonna happen. I avoided his eyes and concentrated on the magical energy I was brewing.

I feinted a thrust of the sword, and the vampire took another step backward, smiling with mockery. His fangs were longer than most I'd seen.

He surely figured he could move quickly enough to avoid my blade, but my plan wasn't to stab him just yet.

I activated my magic, and purple lightning arced from the point of the sword, striking the vampire and enveloping him in an aura of deadly energy.

He screamed and writhed. Wisps of smoke rose from his jeans and red hoodie.

I rushed him, thrusting the blade toward his heart, but he slapped the flat side of the blade, and it missed him. My forward momentum sent me into his danger zone.

He captured me in a bear hug and went for my throat.

Just as the points of his fangs touched my skin, I kneed him in the groin. You'd be surprised that such a tactic could work with a vampire, but it did.

All my magical energy had gone into my lightning, so I hadn't used a protection spell on myself. It was too late to cast one now. With his arms still around me, I hacked at his back with my sword, sending more lightning into him.

We both shuddered as the current hit me, too. Amid an audible crackling, I freed myself from his hug, falling on my butt as I absorbed the lethal energy back into my body.

Before the vampire had recovered enough to return his attention to me, I shot another bolt of lightning into him.

I caught the smell of burned hair and used both legs to kick his ankle. Because he was still off balance from the energy I had blasted him with, he staggered.

And I leaped to my feet and made a two-handed swing of the sword at his neck.

The vampire still had faster reflexes than I. He dodged just enough that the sword struck the side of his skull instead of his vulnerable neck.

While the blade was still in contact with him, I sent another blast directly into him. He gurgled and smoke poured from his ears. Yeah, just like in a cartoon.

But it was no laughing matter. He teetered on his feet, putting all his attention into his supernatural self-healing power. Leaving himself vulnerable to more injuries.

"No more cuts, burns, and bruises for you, big guy," I said.

I drove my blade into his chest.

His eyes went blank. He crumpled to the ground, where he became a pile of dust under a red hoodie.

Even his blood on my sword dried up and fell away from the steel.

That was too close for comfort. I still felt a tingling on my neck where his fangs had nicked my skin.

The adrenaline surging through my veins, and my instinct for self-preservation, seemed to have quashed any feelings of empathy for my victim. For now, at least.

I was panting and exhausted, but I still had one more vampire to take care of. The problem was, the noise of my battle had probably roused him or her from sleep, even if my sleep spell had worked. I briefly considered casting another, but it would be weak since I didn't have visual contact with the target.

I needed to find the vampire before they escaped. Or attacked me.

But before I could do it, the muffled crying of a human came from downstairs. Her sadness swept through my heart, and I had no choice but to help her.

THE REASON THE EXECUTIVE COUNCIL HAD ORDERED ME TO destroy this nest was because the vampires were known to hold humans captive. The prisoners were an easy supply of blood, like keeping cows for their milk. No hunting required.

This was a crime according to the laws of the vampires' guild, the Clan of the Eternal Night, because a group of missing humans would attract a horde of law enforcement agencies, which would increase the odds that the vampires would be discovered. Thanks to the Great Unmasking, that would be a calamity.

Nowadays, fake videos of vampires were all over the internet. But if vampires were proved to exist, the species might be hunted to extinction, never mind how powerful they were. And the same could happen to all the other supernatural creatures.

Werewolves had already experienced this, here in San Marcos, Florida, though spending most of their time in human form had saved them from being wiped out so far. Accusing people of being witches was becoming popular, putting me in danger.

The Executive Council of the Guilds, which administered all the supernatural guilds, wanted to prevent any more species from being unmasked. Naturally, they delegated the dirty work to me, despite my protestations.

Exploring the ground floor, I cast a spell that enabled me to sense any living creatures nearby. That ruled out the vampires, of course. There were insects and rodents aplenty here, the human guard who still slept under my spell on the front porch, and, in a room off the kitchen, two young women.

My spell unlocked a door across from the range. The faint light leaking into the kitchen through the blinds revealed a windowless, unfinished room with a washer and dryer.

And the two captives huddled together on top of a sleeping bag, crying.

"Don't be scared," I told them. "I'm here to free you."

They were too afraid to move, so I entered the room and squatted in front of them.

"My name is Sophie. What are your names?"

"I'm Paula," said the older one with a shaved head covered with stubble. "This is Soon Lee."

Soon Lee was petite, with short black hair and a tear-stained face. She shivered, unable to speak.

Both women had recent fang marks on their arms and necks. Vampires secrete enzymes in their saliva to prevent blood from coagulating, but also to heal the punctured skin quickly. This, along with mesmerizing their victims to forget the attack, allows the predators to hunt them again for future feedings.

The vampires in this nest had been too lazy to conceal the evidence. After all, they didn't need to hunt for their meals.

"Are you two strong enough to walk out of here?" I asked.

"Hell yeah," Paula said, shakily getting to her feet. She obviously suffered from anemia.

I helped Soon Lee stand. She practically weighed less than my sword.

"Please try to be as quiet as possible as we leave the house," I whispered after we left the laundry room.

One vampire remained in the house. He or she would have difficulty fleeing in daylight without the help of humans. Now, however, I had lost the advantage of surprise, so the vampire would have the advantage when I went to finish the job.

"I'm going to walk you to the park at the end of the block, and someone will pick you up there to take you home."

The women flinched when we stepped out into the sunlight, as if they were already on their way to being turned. I pushed them to walk as fast as they could with their unsteady legs over the cobblestone sidewalk, my unfinished job weighing upon me.

When we reached the small park, I had them sit on the nearest bench.

"Everything will be all right now," I said. "You no longer have anything to fear."

Their physical and psychological trauma made me fight tears. What I felt was more than sympathy, more, even, than empathy. I wasn't experiencing their emotions—I was reliving my own trauma.

I'd been in their same situation before. My captivity as a milk cow for vampires had been years ago, and I'd managed to block the memories.

Until today.

"What's wrong?" Paula asked. "You look frightened." She glanced behind her for threats.

"Everything's fine."

I forced my mind to clear as I gathered my energies to cast a forgetfulness spell on Paula and Soon Lee. They would have no memories of the vampires or where they had been confined. It was my way of protecting the Equilibrium, the state of affairs that allowed humans and supernaturals to live together, the former blissfully unaware of the existence of the latter.

I guess I couldn't accept that it was too late. The Great Unmasking was yanking supernaturals into the open.

After I activated the spell, both women looked at me without recognition. I smiled and walked away, texting an admin working for the Council to give the women rides home.

THE DOOR TO THE REMAINING BEDROOM WAS LOCKED, SO I had to waste time picking the lock with my magic. The room was completely dark like the others, of course, so I put my night-vision goggles back on.

A vampire stood at the end of the bed, facing me.

"You've come to destroy me, too, I presume?" he asked. Vampires prefer the word "destroy" rather than "kill" when it refers to their own kind. After all, they're not technically alive.

Like the previous vampire, he, too, was Black, though he was smaller and more muscular. He had closely cropped hair and wore a large hoop earring.

Yikes! My heart stopped as I realized I knew him. He was Diego Fernandez, restaurant owner and resident of San Marcos since the 1500s, when the city was a tiny military garrison.

Diego was also a member of the Memory Guild, to which my mother belonged. He'd been an ally of ours in many endeavors.

And he was pretty darn cute for a vampire, I'm not afraid to say.

How could I bring myself to kill him? I mean, forget the cute part. This vampire was practically a member of our family.

"Diego, it's Sophie," I said in a soft voice.

"I recognized your scent, but not your face beneath that silly contraption you're wearing. How are you? It's been forever since I last saw you, though time passes so quickly for me."

"I've been better. Why are you staying here and not with Lethia?" I asked, referring to his lover, the leader of the Clan of the Eternal Night.

"Oh, we have some problems to work out. You know how it is."

I did, though I'd never dated a vampire and had no desire to. The ones I'd met were insufferably arrogant, cynical, and decadent. Diego was the exception, though he did have a touch of snobbery.

"Why are you living in an illegal nest?" I asked. "These are dangerous times. It's not cool to flout the rules. Too much is at stake."

He made an exaggerated grimace. "*Stake?* You should be more careful with your vocabulary."

"Answer my question."

"I had nowhere else to stay. Lethia rules this city's vampires with an iron fist. She forbade anyone from taking me in. Only these losers would do so, though I paid a pretty penny. Have you destroyed them?"

I nodded.

"So, are you going to destroy me next?" Diego asked. "Assuming I allow you to?"

"I don't know. I truly don't know."

CHAPTER 2

DARLA

I pulled a baking sheet of scones from the oven, enveloped in heat, the intoxicating buttery scent briefly calming me. Guests loved my scones, no matter how I varied the recipe. Today, it included blueberries. My varieties were usually butter-based—cold pieces of butter worked into the flour—though sometimes, I made more cake-like cream scones with no butter or fats added.

You can't run a successful bed-and-breakfast without a decent breakfast, and I prided myself on serving meals that were simple to prepare while being hearty and delicious. My visitors preferred to explore the historic city of San Marcos on a full stomach.

But first, I needed to serve it to them. And my daughter, Sophie, wasn't here as she was supposed to be to help me set up the buffet.

I scooped scrambled eggs and chives into a chafing dish, trying to control my frustration. Sophie had always had her, shall we say, issues. But of late, she'd been behaving responsibly for the first time in her life. She helped me out here at the Esperanza Inn and studied magic in her spare time, joining the Magic Guild to fulfill the destiny that came with the magic gene that ran in the women of my family.

The gene skipped a generation with me. But I didn't need any witchy abilities, thank you. My skills as a psychometrist, which awakened when I reached middle age, were a handful in themselves. My psychometry enabled me to read people's memories when I touched an object they had touched. I was invited to join the Memory Guild before I realized how much responsibility that entailed.

Psychometry wasn't my only power. Others were given to me by an ancient earth-mother goddess named Danu who had been gradually taking over my life. Why she chose me to be her human vessel was a long story. But right then, I had an inn to run. I needed to make breakfast before my guests showed up in the dining room.

My husband, Cory, walked past the open door of the kitchen.

"Cory," I called.

His face appeared in the doorway.

"Have you seen Sophie?" I asked.

"I was up early and saw her leave the inn just before dawn. She said she'd be back in time for breakfast."

I sighed. "Well, she isn't."

"She had her sword with her," Cory said. "Maybe she had some enforcer stuff to do."

Because Sophie excelled in attack magic, she was occasionally enlisted by the Executive Council of the Guilds to intimidate members who failed to pay dues or broke the many rules of behavior, risking exposure. Now, it was more critical than ever for supernaturals to hide their natures from the public. Their survival depended upon it.

She had told me she was planning to quit working as an enforcer. I didn't know why she would take another assignment.

"Her responsibilities at the inn should be her priority," I said. "This is our livelihood."

"She's really been stepping up for us lately," Cory said.

As my second husband, Cory was Sophie's stepfather but loved her—and defended her—as fiercely as if he had fathered her.

"You know," he added, "she's had to take over for you a lot during your . . . episodes."

My family called these episodes "freezing" or "going away." They happened when I was possessed by the Goddess and was off somewhere, in another time and place, doing goddess stuff. My body was left behind, unmoving and unresponsive, if only for a matter of seconds, no matter how long I was truly absent.

The fact he brought this up darkened my mood.

"Here, help me bring these trays into the dining room," I commanded. "You're taking over for Sophie today."

"I have a leaky faucet to fix."

"It can wait. Breakfast can't."

AFTER BREAKFAST, AND THE DRUDGERY OF CLEANING UP BY myself, I texted Sophie yet again. No response. I double-checked that she wasn't in her room, then visited the one inhabitant of the inn who always knew what was going on.

In the front parlor of the nearly-300-year-old house was a fireplace featuring a Medieval-era mantel imported from England in the late 1800s. Supporting it were four stone gargoyles.

One of whom was a supernatural.

"Archibald," I said. "Please wake up. I have a question for you."

As usual, the stone face, carved to resemble a demon, remained immobile. Archibald would animate only when he felt like it.

"Please, I need to find Sophie."

He remained as impassive as, well, stone. It was time to trigger him.

"Oh, Archie? Wake up, Archie-boy."

His stone face shimmered, and soon I was looking at a living creature the color of stone.

"You know better than to call me that," he said, his haughty English accent brimming with anger.

"You gave me no choice. I need to know where Sophie is."

"I am not your daughter's keeper."

"You're a nosy busybody who knows what everyone in this inn is up to. You're brilliant about it. Now, tell me where Sophie is."

"Of course, I don't know exactly where she is this morning," he said, his mood slightly improved. "But I do know she's on a mission involving unsavory characters."

My heart sank. Years ago, Sophie had a substance-abuse disorder, and I always feared a relapse.

"Tell me what you know," I said. "Is she hunting these characters as an enforcer, or is she involved with them?"

"Well, a little of both, I would say."

"Will you stop stonewalling me? Pun intended."

"She's doing a hit job for the Executive Council. Some rogue vampires."

"Why is the Council killing supernaturals?" It was very rare for their enforcement decrees to require killing.

"If you ask me, the Council has gotten out of hand,"

Archibald said. "Yet no one asks me." He was a fellow member of the Memory Guild.

"Sophie has killed monsters that slipped through the Veil into our world, but I can't see her killing guild members, even if they've gone rogue. She told me even intimidating them was too much for her anymore. She's devoted to all supernaturals, even the zombies."

"I would hypothesize that the Council has some sort of leverage over her and is forcing her to do its bidding."

I shook my head in denial. "This frightens me."

"I'm sorry I didn't tell you sooner, Darla. I wasn't one hundred percent certain of this, and I didn't want to intrude into your family matters."

"You are a part of our family."

"How kind of you to say. I would be happy to help you speak to Sophie about this."

"Yeah. This calls for an intervention."

Shouting came from the street just outside of the parlor's oaken exterior door that had once been the front entrance when this was a private home. Several voices were filled with fear and anger.

Moving aside the heavy drapes, I peered through the window at an altercation of some sort on the narrow, cobblestone-paved Hidalgo Avenue. A tourist trolley, a tractor that pulled a string of open-air, train-like trailers filled with passengers, had parked crookedly across the street, blocking traffic.

Tourists were pouring from their seats, surrounding a pedestrian like an angry mob.

"He's a werewolf!" a woman shouted.

"Kill him!" bellowed a man.

"Um, folks, can you please return to your seats?" the young

male guide and driver asked in a squeaky voice over the intercom.

"Kill him before he turns into a wolf!"

The crowd was no longer *like* a mob; it was a full-fledged mob out for violence.

I rushed outside and pushed my way through the rabble. The participants weren't expecting a feisty, petite fifty-something woman to yank them aside like a bouncer breaking up a bar brawl.

"Leave him alone, or you'll be arrested!" I shouted.

As I got closer to the victim, I sized him up. He was a balding guy in his forties and dressed for running, in shorts, sneakers, and no shirt.

Having the paranormal in my blood allowed me to spot anyone who was secretly supernatural. Right off, I could sense this guy wasn't a werewolf. He didn't have any lycanthropy in his blood, nor anything supernatural.

What he had was an overabundance of testosterone; the guy had the hairiest chest and back I had ever seen. Getting them waxed was out of the question. It would be as traumatic to the esthetician as it would be to him.

"I'm not a werewolf," he said, cowering. He already had a black eye from one of these moronic tourists.

"He's not a werewolf," I said to the mob when I reached the man's side and put my hand on his hairy shoulder. "He's my neighbor. I can vouch for him. He regularly attends church and doesn't even eat meat. He's just a little. . . hairy."

Even though I had completely invented knowing this man, I was pleased to notice the mob had been cowed by my shouting.

But not for long. Some among them were still hungry for violence.

"He's a werewolf!" insisted a fat man with a southern accent. "I'm a minister, and I feel his evil in my bones."

And I could sense the restless energy building again in the mob. Those on the fringes of the crowd began pushing toward him, moving the innermost people closer to the runner and me.

The collective energy turned darker. And I knew what could follow. Just last week, a woman had been killed by a mob in a nearby town. She, too, had been accused of being a werewolf. Others had been killed throughout Florida.

This was just the tip of the iceberg of the Great Unmasking, as my fellow members of the Memory Guild called it. A local TV station, which grew its ratings with crime stories and other sensationalism, claimed to have proof of supernatural creatures.

A viewer supplied a video of a wolf attacking his chickens. Mind you, there were no wolves in Florida, so the video of a wolf here would be newsworthy alone. But after eating the chickens, the wolf shifted into a human.

The video went viral. Yes, I saw it, and the shifting part was dark and blurry. But I'd seen werewolves shift before, and that's what this was. The video going viral was alarming.

In the past, when cops or other public officials came across evidence of the supernatural, they would cover it up and convince themselves they hadn't seen what they had seen. Anything to keep this knowledge away from the public. Anything to keep the populace from panicking and society from breaking down.

And fear was what we now had. The fear made the TV ratings and internet clicks spike, but it also made the public vulnerable to being manipulated.

It also led to a flood of additional videos, photos, and memes that allegedly chronicled the supernatural: vampires attacking, witches using magic, corpses rising from graves. They spread quickly all over the internet.

I would guess most, if not all, of this content was fake. But it was freaking everyone out. A few social media influencers were building careers out of hunting for supernatural creatures and spurring on the hysteria.

"Someone please call the police," the runner cried. His phone had obviously been taken from him.

A crazed woman crossed the tiny ring of space separating the runner and me from the mob. She kicked him in the knee, causing the crowd to surge toward us with bloodlust.

I had to do something to save this innocent man.

After the Goddess Danu began using me as her human vessel, I discovered I had the power to kill certain monsters who were abominations of nature and didn't belong in this world. The people in this mob, though they were intoxicated by hate, were only monsters in the metaphorical sense. I couldn't—and wouldn't—kill them.

But I had other tools in my tool belt.

Despite the surrounding chaos, I cleared my mind and went into a meditative state. I breathed deeply and felt calmness spread through my insides.

I concentrated on the Goddess and called her to me. In many ways, she and I were one, but I was still a separate being, in a human body that could be temporarily filled by her. For now, at least.

Heat spread, radiating from my abdomen throughout my body, as the Goddess poured into me.

I broke into song. It was an ancient Celtic tune that had not been heard on Earth for thousands of years. Yet somehow I knew it, as well as the strange lyrics in a language I couldn't comprehend.

A couple of people in the crowd laughed, but it was nervous laughter. To them, I wasn't some kook; the song was affecting them.

People stepped away from the jogger and me, their postures relaxing. The violent energy of the mob was ebbing—I could sense it disappear.

Though I didn't know the words of the song I sang, I knew they were instilling in these people a simple but powerful emotion: empathy.

One by one, they turned away from the jogger they had almost killed. They looked chagrined as they shuffled toward the tourist trolley and climbed back into their seats.

Faces turned away from us in embarrassment. The driver/guide, realizing his opportunity, drove the tractor forward with a jerk.

"Folks, on the right is the historic Esperanza Inn, built around 1736 by a Spanish military officer as a home for his family. In the late 1800s, it was turned into an inn. It's said to be haunted."

Haunted, yes. But fortunately, he didn't mention the inn had a vampire and gargoyle as residents, as well as two witches and a psychic who was the human vessel of an ancient Celtic earth goddess.

He didn't mention us, because our supernatural natures were still secret.

For how long, I didn't know. And though this particular mob had been tamed, I was still fearful of our secrets being revealed and a different mob coming after us.

"Th-thanks for saving me," the man said to me. "What was that song you sang?"

"Oh, just a little Celtic folk song to calm down those nuts."

"Do you think they would have killed me?"

I thought they would have, but I shook my head no. "Hope-fully, that's only a shiner you got," I said, "but you should have your eye looked at just in case. Oh, and wear a shirt from now on when you're jogging."

When I returned to the inn, I learned that Sophie still hadn't returned. My witch daughter was running around with a sword and crossbow. I was confident she could take on rogue vampires. But if frightened people saw her in action, would she survive them?

CHAPTER 3

SOPHIE

"Who hired you to kill us?" Diego asked me.

"It wasn't a hiring. I was forced into it. I'd quit being an enforcer until they made me do it, anyway. It seems I can't get rid of my reputation as an effective killer."

"The Council forced you?"

"Yes. Because your nest had captive humans here that you used as livestock. That violates several rules of your guild and the Council. I had no idea you were here, Diego."

"They kept the humans because it's too dangerous for us to hunt nowadays," he replied. "I would wager that Lethia wanted retribution against me and influenced the Council to go after this nest."

"She ordered the entire nest destroyed because of your lovers' quarrel?"

"Not just that. To make an example of us and instill fear in our guild and all the others. She's more than the leader of the Clan of the Eternal Night. She influences the entire Council."

"The Council is made up of the leaders of all the guilds. Baldric is the president. They vote on every matter and rule by consensus."

Diego smiled bitterly. "No. Lethia has Baldric in the palm of her hand. You served her well today."

"I hadn't realized it was her orders I was following. The Council uses go-betweens to give me assignments."

My steely resolve I had needed when destroying the vampires was fading fast, replaced by feelings of remorse. That was the most unfortunate emotion an enforcer could feel.

"I sense you destroyed all my nestmates and removed the humans, except for our guard," Diego said.

"Right now, the guard is fast asleep."

Diego snickered. "Because of your magic, no doubt."

I nodded.

"So, you accepted this assignment because of what you believed was a righteous sense of justice?"

"Partly. You said nowadays it's too dangerous for vampires to hunt, but it's even more dangerous to kidnap humans and risk being found out by the police. Right?"

He shrugged. "Vampires must feed, one way or another."

Diego had the arrogance of a highly successful businessman, enhanced by the sense of superiority from having maintained this success for centuries while we humans came and went. His dark skin was perfect except for a centuries-old scar below his left eye, on his high cheekbone. His black hair was cut short. When he was alive, the Spaniards called him a Moor, but his ancestry was much more complicated.

The angles of his face made me, out of nowhere, desire to draw a quick charcoal portrait of him. There had been a time when I fancied myself an artist and carried my sketchbook with me everywhere.

Now, I carried medieval weapons.

"I was forced to come here because of extortion," I told Diego.

"What do you mean?"

"The Council threatened my mother if I didn't do what they asked. She's become so vulnerable, as if she were ill."

"Did they take her captive?" he asked with alarm.

"No. But they're watching her always now."

"She's a strong woman, especially with the power of the Goddess."

"She's not herself anymore. The Goddess is taking her over more and more, leaving her catatonic. And the Goddess doesn't have the power to fight corrupt guild leaders."

"It sounds like it's time for you to join me and rise up against the Council," Diego said with a subtle grin.

"First, I have to decide if I will kill you."

Diego's grin faded, but he kept it going as he stood at the end of the bed, unable to relax with me aiming my crossbow at him.

"You're truly that beholden to the Council?" he asked.

"I just explained to you that my mother is at risk if I don't complete my assignment."

"Why hasn't she gone into hiding?"

"Because that's totally not her style. And to be honest, I'm not sure she fully appreciates the danger she's in. Or maybe she doesn't care. I'm afraid she's losing interest in her human existence."

"We can protect her."

"Who is 'we'?"

"There are others like me in the clan who want to get rid of Lethia and Baldric. And we have allies in many other guilds who are unhappy that their leaders have been corrupted."

"This sounds like a family affair," I said. "You vampires need to get rid of your leader."

"It's more complicated than that. You're a member of the Magic Guild, yes?"

"Of course."

"Your leader, Orlena, might be compromised, too."

"I see no evidence of that."

"You don't understand the danger we are all in," Diego said with frustration. "You and so many other supernaturals are sleepwalking into your own destruction. We can't have a corrupt Council. The guilds must be focused on protecting us from the Great Unmasking."

"They are."

"Executing our own members is not the way to do it."

He paused, glowering. Guilt swept through me, then a different emotion. Diego's intense feelings of outrage filled me, and they became my own.

"The Great Unmasking will get much, much worse, trust me," he continued. "I was around when the Spanish Inquisition burned witches and heretics based on nothing other than rumor, innuendo, and forced confessions. Today, there are millions of more ways for false information about supernaturals to spread. And a lot of humans would benefit from it financially and politically. The guilds of San Marcos, and supernaturals everywhere, need to stop the Great Unmasking."

"How on earth could we do that?"

"We have our powers. You have your magic and your weapons. Like that crossbow I wish you'd stop aiming at me. Perhaps it would be best, moving forward, if you killed for the right side. For those of us who want to end this spreading rule of fear."

"I don't want to kill at all anymore."

"Sometimes," Diego said, boring his eyes into me, "we don't have a choice if we want to survive."

"Yeah. I guess."

"Several supernaturals have already been killed in Florida for nothing other than TV ratings, internet clicks, and a cynical bid for your governor to get reelected."

"Just because you're a vampire, it doesn't mean she isn't your governor, too."

"I can't vote anymore. When you live for centuries, it becomes impossible to renew your voter's registration."

"And what does this have to do with Governor Witlessin?"

"I'm surprised that I know news of the human world better than you do. Haven't you heard she's called a special session of the legislature to do something about the panic caused by us supernaturals popping up everywhere?"

"Um, no. That doesn't sound good."

"Now all of us will be offered as sacrifices to rally the humans behind the governor. Vilifying the 'other' has always been a way to get the population scared and stirred up. People will gladly vote for anyone who promises to protect them. But the usual 'others' don't scare everyone. So, the media and the politicians discovered new 'others.' We supernaturals, including witches like you. We scare everyone, no matter where you're from or what political party you belong to."

"This all came from a couple of random videos that went viral?" I asked.

"I don't believe this is random. I think someone is encouraging, or even orchestrating, the Great Unmasking. We must stop them."

"How can the guild members of a little city like San Marcos do that?"

"First, we must kick out the corrupt members of the Council. Then we link up with other supernaturals across the state."

"What do you think you're going to do, shut down the media? Make the government fall?"

"We just want to end the Great Unmasking. Get supernaturals out of the news. We hope that once supernatural creatures aren't top of mind, people will eventually file us under superstitions again, like humans did when they became a modern society."

"Isn't it too late to get the toothpaste back into the tube?"

"Humans don't want to deal with supernaturals, and we can easily be forgotten. When they kill us, there's very little physical evidence we existed. Destroyed vampires turn to dust. Dying werewolves revert to their human forms. The dead bodies of other species could be written off as humans with birth defects. Many of the victims have been humans mistakenly identified as supernatural."

"It doesn't matter."

"Sophie, will you join us? You can't simply stay out of this fight. The Council is extorting you into being an assassin. They could harm your mother. And it's only a matter of time before the public discovers you're a witch."

"At the moment, I'm alive and so is Mom. If I become an insurgent, both of us could be dead tomorrow."

"You underestimate your talents."

I finally lowered the crossbow. Diego appeared relieved.

"I'm not going to kill anymore," I said.

"You will have a big fight on your hands, because the Council will never let you just walk away. There will be an enormous price."

"I agree. But that's a smaller step than becoming an insurgent. I'll look into the alleged corruption of the Council, but I have too much work to do at the inn to join your crusade. Take care of yourself, Diego, and stay safe."

I turned and left the room, thumping down the stairs on legs that threatened to collapse as the adrenaline fled my body. After putting my crossbow in its case, I went outside and got into my car parked across the street.

It was a sunny day, and looking around at the Victorian and neo-Gothic homes, it was easy to believe that life was as normal as it had been for hundreds of years. I was tempted to pretend I could return to the inn and do my chores as if I were in my previous life.

But I understood that the new reality was going to bite me on the butt.

Little did I know that it would begin that night.

I CHANGED INTO A T-SHIRT AND SWEATPANTS IN MY BEDROOM on the inn's third floor, a former guest room I had commandeered when I agreed to work for Mom and Cory full time here. I tried not to disturb Cervantes, the cat who was a pet and my witch's familiar, but the curled-up bundle of sleek black fur on the end of my bed stared at me with yellow-green eyes.

Rough day? he asked telepathically, in a Spanish-accented human voice.

"Yes," I answered aloud. "I swear this was my last enforcer mission."

I'm sensing death vibes all around you.

"Sorry. Didn't mean to bring my work home with me."

I sense more than that, but I'm not sure what it is. Treats would make me feel better. The ones that are crunchy on the outside and soft in the middle. Salmon flavored, please.

"Nice try. It's time for bed."

When I shut off the bedside light, I was still pretending that life was normal, that Cervantes and I would sleep soundly, while Mom and Cory slept in their cottage in the courtyard behind the building.

Sure, the inn had a few ghosts, a vampire, and a gargoyle. But they were family, as far as I was concerned. In fact, I trusted they would be as safe as we humans.

I must have been sleeping lightly, because the rattling of my bedroom doorknob made my eyes snap open. The knob twisted a second time, the intruder obviously not understanding the concept of a key-card-activated lock.

Cervantes escaped to his hiding place beneath the bed.

The door was visible in the faint light of a streetlamp seeping through the closed mini blinds. I stared at the door, praying that it would not open, casting a spell to ensure that it would not.

Hopefully, the intruder was just a drunk guest mistaking my room for theirs.

There were no sounds at all, but I sensed a presence outside the door. The prickling at the back of my neck told me that the presence was supernatural. It was my witchy genes that enabled me to identify others of the occult world.

But what kind of creature was it?

For some reason, the door had become more difficult to see. It was as if shadows had increased in front of it.

I glanced at my window. The ambient light from the street-lamp had not dimmed at all.

Returning my eyes to the door, I cast a spell to enhance my vision. It usually helped only modestly. I was still virtually blind compared to having a vampire's night vision.

Still, I could see the source of the darkness. Opaque shadows were literally flowing through the gap beneath the door like black smoke.

And they coalesced to form the silhouette of a large man standing in front of the door.

At a time like this, I should have my sword in hand. Where was it? The scabbard wasn't hanging from my desk chair where I usually put it.

Great. My sword was on the floor in front of the closet atop my cast-off clothes from the day before. But I was afraid to move with the shadow-man standing there.

Two glowing embers appeared where the shadow-man's eyes would be. The realization came to me that this was a wraith.

And it was looking at me.

I dove out of bed to the floor, scrambling across the rug toward my sword, but my ankle tangled in the bedsheet.

You failed in your task, a raspy, barely human voice said in my head. *You refused the order to destroy all the vampires.*

I got my foot free from the sheet and groped for my sword. Who knew, besides Diego, that he hadn't been destroyed? Did Lethia have a psychic connection with him?

You may not disobey.

"I killed three out of four vampires," I said through clenched teeth. Why I argued with a wraith, I had no idea.

And how had Lethia conjured a wraith, anyway? I hadn't realized vampires could do that. There was no time to ponder this as I crawled across the carpet.

You must be punished. One human in this inn will be killed for the one vampire you spared.

At last, I grasped the hilt of my sword and pulled the blade from the scabbard. From my position on the floor, the bed blocked my view of the wraith, but I would have to assume it was still by the door.

"Take me instead," I said.

The other humans in the inn were my family, and the guests we swore to protect. I was the only one who could fight back against the wraith.

With my sword's pommel tight against my chest, I rolled along the floor until my line of sight cleared the end of the bed. I aimed my sword at the door and unleashed a bolt of purple lightning.

The wraith was no longer there. The lightning hit the door and melted the little placard that showed the nearest emergency exit.

You will not be taken because you have more slaying to do.

The voice came from inside my head, not from any particular direction. Still, there was a dark mass beside my bed, opposite the side from which I had dived.

Yeah, I made out the man-like silhouette. The burning-ember eyes appeared as the wraith looked right at me.

Before the human is killed, you will suffer the pain of one who is disobedient.

The wraith moved across the floor, and suddenly, the shadow engulfed me. The darkness was dense, almost solid. I couldn't see. And now, I couldn't breathe.

Searing pain cut through my head and heart. My hands went numb, and I dropped the sword. Was I having a heart attack and stroke at the same time?

Add a migraine, asthma attack, and panic attack. A fever and convulsions, too.

Plus, I really needed to pee.

The pain was so overwhelming that I must have fainted, because the next thing I knew, the darkness in the room was several shades lighter. I could breathe again, and the pain was gone.

The wraith had left my room, but that meant it was elsewhere in the inn, seeking a human victim.

I couldn't allow it to kill an innocent because I had disobeyed an order. Stumbling out of my room into the bright hallway, I despaired at not being able to find and stop the wraith in time.

CHAPTER 4

SOPHIE

My first instinct was to protect my family. My human family, that is. Roderick the vampire and Archibald the gargoyle weren't as vulnerable as mortal humans.

And my mother, though the Goddess Danu possessed her more and more, was still mortal.

I ran downstairs with my sword, hoping all the guests were asleep and wouldn't see the spectacle I created. Mom had always told me not to run with scissors, but never said anything about swords. While I ran, I slipped it into its scabbard that was now strapped to my back.

Bursting outside into the courtyard, I rushed to the cottage where Mom and Cory lived. The door was locked. Too many encounters with evil people and monsters had finally taught them to lock it each night.

"Mom! Are you guys okay?" I asked in a voice loud enough for her to hear me, but not enough to echo in the courtyard and wake the guests.

I knocked rapidly, like a woodpecker.

The door opened a few inches, and Mom's face appeared, puffy from sleep.

"What's wrong?" she asked.

"A wraith came after me. He said he's going to kill someone here tonight to punish me for not assassinating Diego."

She blinked. "What on earth are you talking about?"

"Enforcer business. I'll explain later. We have to make sure the wraith doesn't kill anyone."

"Darla?" Cory called from inside the cottage. "Who are you talking to?"

"You guys appear to be okay," I said. "How do we protect the guests?"

"I've never encountered a wraith before."

"They're like ghosts. But more demonic and a lot more dangerous. So, what do we do? Knock on every guest-room door?"

My panic was finally infecting her. "There's no time," she said, her words tight.

Intense fear suddenly prickled my heart. It wasn't my heightened anxiety, but a terror of imminently losing my life.

I glanced around me, but I didn't see the wraith or feel his presence. My life wasn't in immediate danger.

It slowly dawned on me: the terror I felt was someone else's.

"I think he's in one of the guest rooms now," I said. "I feel their fear. But which room?"

Mom smiled. This wasn't a time for smiling.

"What?"

"Your gift is finally bearing fruit," she said.

"What are you talking about?"

"You're an empath. I saw signs of it years ago. You must have inherited it from me, because my psychometry and telepathy are very specific empath powers."

"An empath? Is that why I've been feeling too much empathy lately?"

"Yes. This is a psychic form of empathy, allowing you to feel emotions much more strongly than a typical person would and easily know what others are feeling. Maybe, even, to *create* feelings in them. You need to harness this ability now, quickly, to find out who is feeling fear."

I didn't have a clue how to harness my supposed ability, but I did know how to use magic to heighten my senses and perceptions.

Meanwhile, Cory had joined Mom at the door, looking over her shoulder, his mop of gray hair disheveled from sleep. Both were staring at me, expecting me to resolve the crisis. I stepped away from the cottage and stood by the fountain where the white noise of trickling water would help me concentrate.

I cast the spell to heighten my senses and focused on the other person's fear that was taking over my brain.

It was a woman who was crying, whimpering, while the man-shaped shadow approached the foot of her bed. Her lips trembled while she recited the Rosary.

I felt her struggle to contain her panic. I felt her draw upon the strength of her religious faith as she tried to convince herself that she was having a nightmare, or at the very least, was hallucinating the figure standing by her bed—that it was just a shadow of the armoire created by the moonlight coming through her open blinds.

When the glowing red eyes appeared, she screamed.

I realized she was a nun in her seventies. Unfortunately, that wasn't enough information, because we had three elderly nuns in three rooms tonight, as they were in town for a bingo tournament.

But as I empathized with her plight, I became one with her. I didn't just feel all her emotions; I tapped into her sensory impulses. Now, I could more fully see what she was seeing: the wraith, the mahogany armoire, the Chippendale chair at the dressing table.

She was in room 201, until tonight one of our non-haunted rooms. Her name was Sarah, though she now went by the religious name of Teresa.

And the wraith was slowly sucking her life force from her.

The window of room 201 faced the courtyard. There it was, above me, with the open blinds.

I'd always been fascinated by the athletes who practice parkour, the urban sport of running up walls and jumping from ledge to ledge. But I'd never thought I'd try it myself, until I cast a spell to send a jet of wind at my back as I sprang forward, my rubber-soled shoes gripping the stucco-covered stone walls of our ancient inn.

Fortunately, I only had to propel myself up one story before my hands grasped the windowsill, and I pulled myself up onto the narrow ledge. Two solid kicks later, and I had bashed through the window, leaping down into the room amid the shattered glass.

Teresa screamed, and the red smoldering eyes of the wraith turned to me.

"Room service!" I announced as I reached over my shoulder and unsheathed Alfie.

Pain flared into my head through my temples, but I was too amped up to let the wraith's attack stop me. The specter was directly in front of me, only a few feet from the tip of my sword.

The purple lightning bolt shot into the center of the wraith's shadow shape.

The shadow and the glowing orbs disappeared.

Well, that was easy.

Too easy. The wraith reappeared on the side of the bed, looming over Sarah.

You accomplished nothing other than forcing me to kill her more quickly, the raspy voice of the wraith said in my head.

I shot another bolt of power into it, narrowly missing the nun, who was paralyzed with terror.

The dark silhouette of the phantasm faded, rose into the air, then grew more solid while it floated near the ceiling, next to the ceiling fan.

Was it even possible to destroy a wraith? They were just spirits, after all. Really powerful ones.

But a spirit, a disembodied soul, was a form of energy. And though I did poorly in my physics class in high school, I knew that energy can't be created or destroyed. It can only be converted into another form.

Yikes! The piercing pain flared in my head again. I needed to shut down this wraith ASAP before I passed out.

An idea popped into my head. It was worth a try.

I aimed my sword at the wraith floating above me, but instead of shooting energy into the phantasm, I cast a different spell. It was like flicking the reverse button on an electric screwdriver. Instead of converting my magical energy into lethal lightning bolts, I drew energy through my sword *from* the wraith.

I accidentally made an empathetic connection to the wraith. I hadn't even realized you could empathize with someone who was dead, and it wasn't pleasant. The wraith was the soul of a man who had experienced a horrifying death, then was forced into servitude by an evil entity. The wraith yearned to be freed.

Yet, it suffered as its very essence was being taken away by my sword.

A horrible wail echoed in my brain as my sword sucked the wraith's energy into it. A wraith had no physical mass, so I essentially just absorbed the wraith into my mighty broadsword.

But now what?

Teresa moaned from the bed as her petrifying fear dissipated.

"What happened?" she asked. "I remember there was an intruder in here, then you broke through my window."

"Just an errant wraith. I took care of it, so everything's fine."

"My window is broken."

"I apologize for the inconvenience. It will be fixed in the morning."

My sword was becoming uncomfortably hot in my hand. It was also vibrating and making a humming sound. I was afraid it had absorbed too much energy. Wraiths must be chock full of it.

"Why are you holding a sword?" the nun asked.

"It's what I used to get rid of the wraith. But I seem to be having a bit of difficulty here."

My sword was now burning my hand and trembling so violently I couldn't return it to its scabbard. And I feared what would happen if I dropped it on the floor.

I yelped as my palm burned. What would happen if the wraith's energy flowed from my sword into me? It wasn't pure, neutral energy. It was evil.

"Ow!" I whined from the pain.

Reflexively, I pushed the energy back out of the sword, which was still pointed at the ceiling.

The wraith-energy flowed directly into the ceiling fan.

The fan turned on with a screaming of its motor. Its blades spun so fast they were a blur, like a plane's propeller. The mechanism wobbled back and forth, threatening to detach itself from the ceiling.

"Turn that off!" Teresa shouted.

The door to the room opened, and Mom came in without knocking. She looked up at the industrial accident about to happen.

"Did you put the wraith in the ceiling fan?" she asked.

"Long story. We need to transfer his energy somewhere else."

"We'll send the spirit where it belongs. To the Otherworld."

"Why not send it to heaven?" the nun asked.

"That's fine," Mom said. "Each religion has its own version of the afterlife, so whatever the wraith believed in when it was a living human. Or whatever kind of creature it was."

"But the wraith is an evil spirit," I protested. "Shouldn't we send it to hell?"

"That's not for us to determine," Mom said. "Our only job is to get it off the material plane."

"I'll pray for it," Teresa said.

"How are we getting it out of the ceiling fan and off the material plane?" I asked in a loud voice to be heard above the deafening scream of the motor.

Mom didn't answer. I could tell that Danu was in her as she stared at the fan with a serene look of bliss on her face. She raised her hands as if she were trying to heal the fan. Good luck with that.

But suddenly, the fan's motor turned off. It took forever for the blades to slow down, but the danger was gone, along with the wraith.

"Did it pass on to the spiritual plane?" I asked.

Mom's expression returned to normal. "Yes. But I want to know who sent it here to kill."

"Why did it want to kill me?" Teresa asked. "Because I won big at bingo tonight?"

"Can you cast a forgetfulness spell on her?" Mom whispered to me.

I nodded. I cast the spell, followed by one for sleeping, and we tiptoed from the room.

"I'll send Cory here to clean up the broken glass," she said as we walked down the hall. "Now, you've got some explaining to do."

CHAPTER 5

DARLA

Dawn, and breakfast prep, would come in only a couple of hours, so there was no point in trying to go back to sleep. I stopped by the cottage to tell Cory that the wraith had been dealt with.

"Sophie is something else, isn't she?" he said before immediately returning to bed.

I went to the inn's kitchen, where I made a small pot of coffee. The coffee for the guests would wait until breakfast time to ensure it was as fresh as possible.

"Thanks for sending the wraith to the Otherworld," Sophie said, entering the kitchen and pouring herself a cup. "Or should I thank Danu?"

"You know that we're one and the same."

"It's not as simple as that. Danu is taking you over."

"Nonsense."

"Mom, you've been freezing more and more."

"I don't like that term. I'm simply unresponsive for short periods of time while I visit Danu's realm."

"I'm concerned about you. The freezing could be mini-strokes, or a cognitive issue."

What was she implying?

"I haven't yet turned sixty. I'm too young for dementia," I said.

"Some people show signs in their fifties."

"Let's change the subject."

"I'm just worried about your health. You say your freezing moments are brief, but they're concerning. Guests notice and think something's wrong."

"I've stopped driving. Does that make you feel better?"

"Barely. I won't feel better until you see a doctor."

"Toot-a-loo!" said a male voice as the kitchen door swung open.

It was Roderick, our resident vampire. His daytime sleeping lair was a crawlspace hidden behind the smaller, older refrigerator, where he'd been magically imprisoned until Mom broke the seal and freed him when she bought the inn.

"You two are up quite early," he said. He wore the same moldy suit coat that was fashionable in the late 1800s when he was alive. He self-consciously wiped a speck of blood from his lower lip.

"Family matters," I said.

"I'll leave you to them. Dawn is approaching, and I'm going to sleep off my blood-sugar high."

Roderick lacked the ability to mesmerize human prey, so he usually fed upon dogs, cats, possums, and raccoons. Though any human tourist foolish enough to pass out drunk within Roderick's range would wake up feeling extremely anemic.

"Sleep well, Roderick," Sophie said.

"I'm sure I will," the vampire said with a smile as he pushed the fridge to the side, opened a small wooden door behind it, and crawled into his hidey-hole.

I rolled the fridge back to its place.

"You've successfully kept the conversation away from you, but it's your turn on the hot seat," I said to Sophie. "Answer me. Why did the wraith come here?"

"I think the Council sent it," she grumbled.

"The *Council?* Whatever for?"

"To punish me for not completing my assignment. I was supposed to take out a nest of renegade vampires who had human captives. I rescued the humans, but I spared one vampire. It was Diego."

I gasped and stared at Sophie for a long moment, unsure of what to say. There was way too much to unpack here.

"You've killed monsters who escaped through the Veil and created problems here on earth. But you've never killed fellow supernaturals from our city. Or have you?"

"Yes." She fought back tears. "As an enforcer, I've run some supernaturals out of town, and knocked some sense into others, but I've only killed two prior to the vampires yesterday."

"Of what species were the two?"

"I don't want to talk about it."

"Why would the Council order you to wipe out the vampire nest?"

"Because of the Great Unmasking. The vampires were breaking rules and flaunting it. Law enforcement would have discovered them any day now."

I shook my head. "This is highly unusual."

"Diego said he thinks Lethia was behind the order. She wanted to get back at him."

"You shouldn't be dragged into their problems. Isn't it time you quit being an enforcer? Now that your empath powers are blossoming, how can you do this work?"

"Yeah, I don't want to anymore. But I'm good at it. And they sent a wraith to kill a guest to punish me."

"I don't know of anyone on the Council who could summon and command a wraith. Perhaps Orlena, but I didn't know her before she became the leader of the Magic Guild."

"I barely know her, either," Sophie said. "Would a vampire have that ability?"

"You mean Lethia? I doubt it, but she's so ancient that she might have powers we've never heard of. Maybe Baldric did it with his Fae magic."

"He used to be my tutor. Why would he do something so cruel?"

I shrugged. "Speaking of powers, we need to train you as an empath."

"Why? Having abnormal amounts of empathy only seems like a burden to me."

"To you as an enforcer?"

"No, to anyone just trying to get by in life."

"Sophie, there are many ways to get by in life that don't require causing or ignoring unhappiness in others."

"Spoken by a true earth-mother goddess."

"I'm serious. Ever since you became a witch, you've focused on battle magic. Why not consider healing magic or other benevolent kinds of spells?"

"Must you always judge me?"

My daughter just turned thirty, and she still acted defensive with me. What was I to do?

"Learning to enhance and control your empathy isn't just about passively experiencing others' emotions," I said. "You can possibly influence their emotions. You could do quite a bit of good that way."

"Or a lot of mischief," she replied with a naughty grin.

"Not that you would ever do that," I said with my own smile.

"How do I learn to control my empath abilities?"

"You could use magic. I believe Arch Mage Bob knows some spells to enhance psychic powers."

Bob, the previous leader of the Magic Guild, was another of Sophie's tutors as she trained to be a witch. Bob had been turned into a vampire by Lethia, but he still had plenty of magic at his command.

"I'll ask him if he can help you," I added. "Call it a gut feeling, but I truly believe you should take advantage of being an empath. These times demand it."

Sophie looked at me quizzically, as if she didn't understand what I meant. But we dropped the topic as the time arrived to prepare breakfast for our guests.

It turned out we would get a glimpse of my meaning sooner than I'd imagined.

AT THE ESPERANZA INN, UNLIKE SOME BED-AND-BREAKFASTS, we didn't serve merely coffee, juice, and muffins. We offered a complete buffet, including eggs, bacon, sausage, and periodic special treats.

And don't forget my famous scones.

I was pulling a second batch from the oven—it turned out the nuns in town for the bingo tournament had an insatiable desire for my scones—when Sophie took a sharp intake of breath.

"I know her," she said, staring at the television.

I always had the morning shows on when I labored in the kitchen, though I rarely paid much attention to them. While I put the fresh scones onto a serving platter, I took in the news program with concern.

". . . our exclusive interview with Paula Jasper, who claims she and another woman were held captive by vampires in San Marcos."

Cut to a video of a pre-recorded interview on the set of our local network-affiliate station.

"They kept us as prisoners," Paula said. "Locked in a laundry room of an old house. They dragged us out every night and fed on us."

"They bit your necks, like in the movies?" the female reporter asked.

"Yes, it was horrible." She wiped away a tear. "They sort of hypnotized us or something. I couldn't move or scream or do anything. I was completely defenseless, and the vampires would bite my neck right here." She ran a finger along her jugular vein. "It hurt really bad at first, before my neck went numb. They bit my arms, too."

"I don't see any scars or marks."

"They have a power to heal the bite wounds so there's no proof of what they did."

A good reporter would be skeptical and push back on sensational claims like these. But this wasn't a good reporter. This was Meghan Whortle, who was a central figure in the Great Unmasking. She had turned material that would normally be fodder for tabloid TV and social media into hard news. She also had a major presence on the internet.

She should have been laughed out of her profession, except for the credible reception her reports received from the powers that be. Namely, Governor Ada Witlessin and other state politicians, who endorsed the stories and amplified them. It wasn't what you'd expect responsible leaders to do, unless they wanted their constituents to be frightened.

"Paula was one of the humans I freed yesterday," Sophie said, astonished. "She shouldn't have remembered any of this. I cast a forgetfulness spell on both of them. What went wrong?"

Paula continued, describing her vampire captors.

"Did they assault you in any other way?"

"You mean sexually? No, they didn't. But they were rough and cruel. They were monsters. They said they captured us because it was too dangerous for them to hunt out on the streets every night. San Marcos has you to thank for that, Meghan. You've brought their existence to light, so we know there are vampires, and we need to be extra careful at night. I guess Soon Lee and I weren't careful enough."

"For our viewers, I should mention that Soon Lee wouldn't come on to talk with us. She says she remembers nothing about her experience."

"That's because of the witch. Is it okay for me to mention her? I don't want your audience to think I'm making this all up."

"Go right ahead and talk about her," Meghan said. "I believe you."

"The woman who rescued us was a witch. She was carrying a sword. Can you believe it—a sword? The police said the vampires fled the house after we were rescued, but I think the witch killed them."

"How do you know she was a witch?"

"Well, along with her sword, she had amulets and mystical tattoos. I think she cast a spell to make us forget her, the vampires, everything. It obviously worked on Soon Lee. I guess it worked on me, too, for a little while. But hours later, my memories came back."

"Why did my spell fail?" Sophie asked me in an anguished voice.

"I don't know. You must have been distracted."

Now, a spokesman for the police department was speaking to Meghan.

"Naturally, we're pleased that the victims escaped," he said. "We're putting all our resources into finding the individuals responsible for their abductions."

"Was there any evidence of vampires living in the house?" Meghan asked.

"I can only comment that male and female suspects were residing in the house. And we will find them."

"If I was distracted," Sophie said, "it was by empathy."

"What?"

"I was overwhelmed by feelings of empathy for the two women as I put the spell on them. It was also empathy that kept me from killing Diego."

"Of course you couldn't kill Diego! He's a friend of ours."

"I hadn't known he was part of the nest. But my orders were to eliminate all the vampires there. It shouldn't have mattered that we know him."

"Of course it matters! You couldn't be that cold-hearted, even if you weren't an empath."

"I'm not sure I enjoy being an empath. Look, it led to a wraith trying to kill a guest. And to this woman going on TV and blabbing about the vampires and a witch, unmasking even more supernaturals. I don't like this one bit."

"You must be patient and explore your gift. I'll reach out to Bob to see if his magic can assist you. And I'll also get you an audience with the Council so you can resign as an enforcer."

"Why are you pushing this empath thing so strongly?" she whined.

"Because as a psychometrist, I think you inherited the empath gene from me. And, frankly, I was never happy with the belligerent turn you took with your magic."

"It's not for you to decide!" she said before storming out of the kitchen.

There I was, watching a rerun of Sophie's adolescent phase. And having to clean up after breakfast all by myself. Once again.

The dining room finally emptied of guests eager to head out and explore the sights of San Marcos. The last to leave were Mr. Humphrey, staying in 203, and the three nuns, stuffing their pockets with scones. Teresa appeared to remember nothing of last night, so Sophie's forgetfulness spell did work as designed in her case.

I carried all the dirty plates and chafing dishes into the kitchen and texted our only full-time housekeeper, Bella, to please vacuum the dining room. Next, I set about scraping dishes and loading the industrial dishwasher.

"Sorry for intruding, but I need so badly to speak with you, and I don't have a phone."

The voice was familiar, but I couldn't place it until I paused my work, turned around, and saw him in his monk-like garb.

"You again? You've got to be kidding," I said.

CHAPTER 6

DARLA

The guy who'd entered the kitchen was tall and thin, a bit stooped in posture. His face was gaunt, with a heavy brow. The top of his head was bald, with a ring of graying hair beneath the bald spot—a tonsure like the medieval monks wore. The tops of his ears had the slightest hint of pointedness.

Truth was, he was not a man. He was a faerie in human form, who served as a priest of his species.

"Daughter of Danu, it has been too long," the faerie said, bowing to me. When he straightened, he squinted as he studied me. "Somehow, I sense there is more of Danu in you now. Should I call you Danu instead?"

"Wilference! It indeed has been a while," I replied, thinking it hadn't been long enough. "You can just call me Darla."

"Your human name? But you're a goddess."

"You know I'm only the human vessel of the Goddess. So, what brings you to San Marcos?"

"I come bearing a message from Her Majesty, the Faerie Queene."

That's what I had been dreading to hear from the instant I saw him at the door to my kitchen. My past involvement with the Fae had been nothing but trouble.

"Queene Ookee the Thirtieth requests your assistance in an endeavor that is extremely important to our people."

He paused. I waited.

"There is a substance called phytolucine that is found in the forests of this planet. Our people require it to complete a major experiment we have embarked upon, one which is of the highest importance to the Queene."

"I've never heard of that stuff," I said. "Why would you think I can help you?"

"You were a favored guest at the Court of Seelie. They would know how to find and acquire phytolucine. Since they are avowed enemies of our court, we cannot simply request it from them. Rather than embark upon a war between our courts, the Queene requests you serve as an intermediary."

The Court of Seelie is another name for the Elves. The Court of Unseelie is another name for the Fae. Some historians call the Elves the Light Elves and the Fae the Dark Elves.

I call them the good guys and the bad guys.

"I'm sure this phytolucine substance will only be used for good purposes," I said, not hiding my sarcasm.

"I do not know. But I was told it will benefit the Fae."

"The Fae that repeatedly tried to kill me in the past."

"The court has nothing to do with the attempts on your life. It was Jaekeree and his followers who wished to send the Goddess back to the Otherworld."

Wilference had never been my enemy in the past, like the evil Jaekeree, whom I had defeated. But I wanted to probe Wilference more to see if he was holding back any information. Fortunately, I had a handy way of doing that.

"How rude of me to not offer you a seat," I said. "Come with me to the parlor, where we're less likely to bump into guests. Can I get you a glass of wine?"

Yes, I know. It was still morning. But Wilference was not one to turn down free food or drink.

"That would be delightful," he said with a smile. "A white wine would be so refreshing in this heat. I can't remember the human names for your grapes, so I'll take whatever you recommend."

I grabbed two glasses and a Chardonnay left in the fridge from last evening's Wine Hour, and led the Fae priest into the parlor. We sat in wingback reading chairs and sipped the wine that I had poured.

Yes, sometimes I, too, can't say no.

"I sense that one of those gargoyles supporting the fireplace mantel is supernatural," Wilference said. "The one on the far right."

"Yes, it's just Archibald. Anyway, tell me more about this phytolucine substance," I said.

"I had thought it was merely folklore, but I was told by our magicians that it is real. It is created by trees, though I'm uncertain how or why. Apparently, humans know nothing about it. Or they call it something else and are unaware of its potential. No other species knows about it, either. Except for the Fae and Elves."

"What do you need it for?"

"That," he said, sipping his wine, "is deemed unnecessary for me to know. I am only the messenger."

"If the Elves know about it, do they already use it in some way?"

"They share the same legends as ours in which it is mentioned. From what I was told, they don't know it can be used as a magical ingredient."

"Ah, so the Fae plan to use it for their magic!" I said triumphantly.

"Oh, did I leave that part out?"

"Assuming the Elves know how to harvest this substance, why would they allow it to go to their enemies?"

"You would persuade them. As a divine being, you'd make the perfect diplomat."

I didn't believe that. And I told him so.

"You could ask Danu to intervene."

"I don't think so."

"Then, perhaps you could take some of the substance without their knowledge," he replied.

"Why would I steal for you?"

"You would be lavishly rewarded. The Queene has plenty of gold. And this inn," he gestured at the walls, "could use a bit of renovation, am I wrong? Until the day comes that you leave the material world and fully become a goddess, you still have a business to run."

My instant reaction was anger, but I hid it. Surely the Fae didn't believe that I could be bought off so easily. Unless they believed the Elves had hosted me to win my favor. The truth was, I considered the Goddess—me included—to be a natural ally of the Elves.

The Seelie Court shared the earth-mother instincts of the Goddess. Whereas the Fae were greedy like humans and all too eager to destroy the earth to enrich themselves.

Still, I sensed there was more to this "partnership" that Wilference was proposing than he let on.

He finished his wine, and I quickly poured him another glass.

"Are you aware of what's going on with humans?" I asked. "The existence of supernaturals being revealed to the public?"

"I am certain the Queene would know, but not I. I'm concerned only with spiritual matters."

Like bribing me to steal from the Elves.

"Aren't you concerned the Fae could be revealed?"

"No," he replied after a gulp of wine. "When we're in human form, humans could never identify us as supernaturals. And humans would never encounter us in our natural forms."

Their natural forms aren't very attractive. I'll leave it at that.

"Is there any chance some Fae magic is involved in revealing the supernaturals? There's a lot of hatred and irrationality spreading through our communities. I know we humans can act crazy on our own, but it seems to be so accelerated and amplified. Like magic is behind it."

"I wouldn't know. I'm sorry." He stood up, a little wobbly. "I must leave now. Thank you for your hospitality. Please consider the request the Queene has made of you, and I'll return another day to hear your decision."

I led him down the hall and out the main door before I rushed back to the parlor to fetch his empty wineglass.

It was time to use my psychometry.

I took the glass with me to the cottage. Cory was doing maintenance somewhere in the inn, so I would have privacy here. I sat in my favorite chair, slowed down my breathing, and cleared my mind.

Holding the wine glass with my fingers atop Wilference's finger smudges, I felt the spark of psychic energy, as an image of—

—*Darla looking more aged than when I last saw her. What a shame for humans that their lifespans are so short. She most certainly has more of the Goddess in her, yet she is still mortal . . . This wine is superb. Not as sweet as Fae vintages and more complex. This is perhaps the only thing humans do better than us. Other than their silly technology. . . Mmm, it's delicious . . . Now, I must present the proposal . . . The offer of gold doesn't seem to excite her as much as I'd hoped—*

I lost his thoughts when he put down the glass. Holding my fingers close to, but not touching, the glass, I found another concentration of psychic energy from when he picked up the glass again and was able to reconnect. He was slightly agitated, as if he was annoyed that—

—she changes the subject to the madness spreading through the humans. I honestly hadn't heard anything about it. Perhaps it's the result of Fae magic, and, if so, bravo to the magicians who used the humans' irrationality against them. I'd always believed the humans would wipe themselves out someday so my people wouldn't have to do it. As a priest, I'm supposed to be against such things. Just as I'm against what they're going to do to Darla if she doesn't fulfill our request for the phytolucine. I suppose, though, there are those who want to kill her whether she delivers or not, the ones who don't want Danu to be active in earthly affairs again. They believe she must be killed in human form before her transformation is complete. . . Oh, look at the time! I've tarried too long—

His thoughts ended as he set his glass down a final time. As I came out of my trance-like state, I reflected on what he'd been thinking.

That my life was in danger. Even if I produced this substance they wanted.

Lest you think that divinity is all fun and games, consider the fact the Fae apparently wanted to kill me to prevent me from becoming a new incarnation of Danu.

Danu had never died. She had only disappeared from the memories, imaginations, and hearts of humans. The Fae were afraid that I would make Danu relevant again.

I didn't know how I would do that. I was just an anonymous middle-aged lady with a moderately successful inn in a historic tourist town. But somehow, I thought the Fae were right, and

Danu was using me to tether her to our contemporary population.

I didn't want to be killed to prevent me from becoming Danu.

Though, in the back of my mind was the fear that I was fated to die in order to become the Goddess.

"YES, I'VE HEARD OF PHYTOLUCINE," SUMMER SAID WHEN I called her. "It has a different name in Elven folklore. I didn't know it actually existed."

The half-elf was a fellow member of the Memory Guild. Her day job was at a nursery and garden center just outside of town. My sole encounter with the world of Elves was thanks to her.

"The Fae apparently believe it's a real substance," I said, "and they want to use it for their magic. I think it's safe to assume that they have bad intentions."

"Why did they speak to you about it?"

"Because they want me to be their go-between and get some for them. Wilference said it was because I'd met your king and queen, but it sounds like they believe Danu would have some clout over the Elves."

"Elves don't worship Danu, but they're fond of her. Still, they would never hand over something that would make the Fae's magic more powerful."

"The Faerie Queene would pay enormous sums of gold."

Summer laughed derisively. "Like the Elves would care about that."

"And my life might be at risk if I don't deliver."

"Is that true?"

"According to Wilference's thoughts."

"That's so unfair! We need to protect you."

"King Aiwin needs to send a message to the Fae that the Elves will never give them any phytolucine. He must put a stop to this before I get dragged into it."

"I'll try to get word to the king. And you should know, we couldn't give away phytolucine even if we wanted to. According to the legends, it belongs to the forest—to the trees and plants. It is not ours to give or to steal."

"That sounds exactly like something the Fae would want to get their grubby hands on."

I DECIDED IT WAS PREMATURE TO WARN MY FAMILY OF THE potential threat against me. It had only been Wilference's supposition that I would be harmed, and I had no intention of becoming involved with the Fae's attempt to acquire phytolucine.

Besides, Cory and Sophie had already endured the threats against my life by Jaekeree and his rogue group of Fae. I didn't want to freak them out again. This would hopefully be nipped in the bud.

"You seem preoccupied," Cory said as we ate a simple dinner in our cottage that night.

I looked into his eyes. He was worried about me already. It wasn't fair to withhold information from him.

"It's not a problem," I replied. "And I intend to keep it that way. You see, it involves—"

Suddenly, I was no longer in our dining nook. I was in a primeval forest of thick, towering trees and a lush undergrowth of saplings and ferns. The air was alive with the chattering of birds, squirrels, and chipmunks. Insects buzzed, but none harassed me. The roar of a waterfall came from ahead of me, though I couldn't see it.

The forest was brimming with life, pure and uncontaminated.

This was the way it usually was when I'd been summoned by Danu.

I threaded my way through the tree trunks toward the sound of rushing water, walking with bare feet on a soft carpet of leaves and pine needles.

The trees thinned out, and I reached a pool in a river, beneath a waterfall that fell from a cleft in a cliff above. In front of where the falling water hit the pool stood a beautiful woman, naked, her long hair covering her breasts.

It was Danu. The earth-mother goddess worshipped by the earliest Celts in Ireland, Scotland, and across Northern Europe. The River Danube was said to have been named after her.

She was so familiar to me, existing in my DNA, pulsing through my blood. But I had only seen her in brief dreams like this.

If I was her human vessel—if I was fated to become her—why did she still seem so mysterious to me?

Her hair was dark and long and straight. Her face was youthful and sharply angled. Danu's beauty differed from that of contemporary fashion models. It was classic and eternal.

When I looked in the mirror, I never saw beauty such as hers. I'd experienced tastes of her power, such as when I calmed the mob outside the inn. Yet I felt so inferior to her, so mortal, so unworthy of her legacy.

Danu smiled when she saw me reach the bank.

"Worry not," she said. "Your future will be unveiled for you when you need to know. Do not think unkindly of yourself. I chose you because you are the reincarnation of my child. And you're soon to be me."

"Why did you summon me here today?"

"Because of the phytolucine you seek. It is the secret wealth of the forests, and it heals the earth. It belongs to them and no one else. You must protect it. Prevent those who wish to exploit the earth from getting their hands on it."

"I don't even understand what it is."

"You will learn in due course."

"Will you help me protect it?"

She smiled. "Of course. But I can only act through you. And you must be vigilant during trying times."

"Trying times?"

"You are my chosen one, but you still must prove yourself to me."

"Well, that's not exactly what I wanted to—"

I was back in the dining nook of our cottage. Cory stared at me with concern as our baked chicken grew cold.

"You're back?" he asked.

"I didn't go anywhere. I mean, physically. My spirit was summoned by the Goddess."

"You froze again. How can we be sure that there's nothing wrong with you?"

"I'm perfectly fine."

"Darla, I'm serious. We need to see a neurologist."

"What are you talking about?"

"You might be having mini strokes. Or some sort of seizures. It could be a cognitive effect caused by aging. We need to get answers."

"I'm being transported into some period of ancient history to talk to a goddess. A doctor wouldn't understand that."

"I'm not denying the Goddess. But you still might have a

medical condition that explains all of this. Maybe she caused the condition. Or the condition allows you to communicate with her."

"Or, I'm just a normal woman being transported to another time, so I blank out for a few seconds."

"More like a few minutes. I'm calling in the morning to make an appointment."

"You asked why I seemed preoccupied. It's because the Fae want me to help them acquire a substance called phytolucine. And the Goddess just now tasked me with preventing them from getting it."

"I'll make it an emergency request for an appointment."

CHAPTER 7

DARLA

I'm not claustrophobic. Well, I wasn't until I lay inside a tube wearing a medical gown, as a demonic monkey banged the tube with a hammer.

I made up the part about the monkey. MRIs involve a lot of loud rhythmic banging, which is absolutely lovely, after the mechanized platform slides you slowly into a narrow coffin—I mean, a tube—and you're told to *not move at all*.

They'd given me noise-cancelling headphones but told me their music system was down today. The supposedly relaxing 1970s and '80s soft rock had offended a patient, and he had taken his frustrations out on the equipment.

I tried to relax. Remember, I'm a psychic, and I'm good at putting myself in trance-like states.

But not during my MRI scan. Not during the *BAM-BAM-BAMs*. Or the *da-DUM, da-DUM, da-DUMs*.

To make things worse, Wilference's thoughts that I had read from his wineglass came back to me, as if he were rapping to the beat of the MRI.

She must, be killed, in hu-, man form, before, her trans-, forma-, tion is, complete.

I heard that hundreds of times while I spent nearly an hour in that freaking tube.

When I was finally released from the coffin, and allowed to dress in my own clothes and put my metallic jewelry and accessories back on, I was sent on my merry way with a CD holding the images of my "brain scan with contrast."

CORY HAD SCHEDULED A NEUROLOGY APPOINTMENT FOR THE following day, when the doctor would tell me what the images of my brain foretold.

Cory drove me to the appointment, and Sophie insisted on coming along. I felt buoyed by their emotional support. But I had to ruin it by informing them about Wilference's visit and his request.

"I'm not helping the Fae get that substance," I said in the car. "Danu doesn't want me to, either."

Cory slammed his hand on the steering wheel. "I don't really care what Danu—"

"Now, now," I said. "No sense in angering a goddess."

"I'm hoping the doctor can give you some medication to make Danu go away."

"That's not how it works. At least not in the supernatural world that our family inhabits."

"You think the Fae need that substance for their magic?" Sophie asked from the back seat.

"Yes," I replied. "And something tells me the magic will not be benevolent. In fact, it probably—"

I went away again at the worst possible time for my family, regardless of how brief it would be.

This time, I wasn't in a primeval forest, but in total darkness. Danu's face appeared, illuminated like an overly large moon.

"Do not be concerned about what the medicine woman tells you," Danu said.

"You mean the doctor?"

"I chose you because you are healthy. And in due time, the health of your mortal body won't matter."

"That's not exactly reassuring."

"You must be pure in spirit. Your body does not matter as much."

"Wait, what do you mean? Are you implying—"

WHEN I RETURNED, SOPHIE WAS LEANING OVER THE SEAT, staring at me, her eyes welling with tears.

"You're freezing more and more lately," she said.

"But I was gone for only a little while, right?"

"More and more 'little whiles' add up. Mom, I don't want to lose you."

"Don't be silly. I'm not even sixty yet, and I'm in good health. We'll see what the neurologist says, but God willing, you won't lose me anytime soon."

"I had thought having the Goddess in you would make you immortal."

"I haven't found any new gray hairs in quite some time."

Sophie smiled, but only briefly. "Now I think that if you become immortal, it won't be as you, Darla Chesswick. You'll become Danu and go off to live wherever goddesses live. You'll leave Cory and me behind."

"With nothing but an empty husk who used to be me? Don't be silly."

"That's what happens when you go away. Eventually, you'll go away forever."

"What's the difference between doing that and simply dying like everyone does? No one lives forever."

"Mortal humans die when their bodies give out on them. You're going to be taken away from us when Danu wants to take you," Sophie said with anger.

"I'm sorry you resent her so much."

"No, it's that I owe you so much. Not just for bringing me into the world and raising me. Looking out for me after Dad left and not getting bitter about it. How many times have you saved me from myself? My money problems, boy problems. My substance-abuse disorder. Paying for an expensive rehabilitation center that I ran away from, then went to the scummy place that sold me to vampires."

"That's what mothers do."

Sophie barked a laugh. "You did much more than what mothers have to do. You couldn't afford to pay for my college, but you somehow did. And what did I do with my degree in fine arts? Nothing. Right? I sketched and painted and waited tables. I couldn't afford my own place, so I lived with Grammers before I moved in with you and Cory."

"We couldn't operate the inn without your help," Cory said. "Very few artists can support themselves. And you were never suited for the corporate world, which is okay because you discovered your true talent—magic."

"My magic doesn't pay the mortgage or add to your bottom line."

"It would be the same if you had continued to pursue being

an artist," I said. "When you have a gift, cultivate it, even if it doesn't make money."

"You're too kind to me, even after all the nasty fights we've had over the years. Even after I stole from you when I was on drugs."

I didn't reply. She wouldn't understand until she became a mother herself.

"Now I understand how vulnerable you are as Danu's human vessel," she continued. "Yes, I've seen you use her powers, but you're utterly defenseless when you go away. I want to protect you. It's the least I can do after all you've done for me."

"I'm not stopping you."

"You're not making it easy. Why do you need to involve yourself with the Fae and the Elves?"

"To protect the earth. Isn't that a good reason?"

"Let Danu protect the earth."

"That's what she's doing. By using me."

Sophie had a stricken expression as she realized I was right. She sighed in defeat.

"Who am I to claim I can protect you?" she asked. "I've got wraiths coming after me. And one day, the villagers will come after me with their pitchforks and torches because I'm a witch."

"When you need protection, too, that's fine. It's not a one-way street. We can protect each other, whoever needs it most at the time. It's like love—sometimes, you feel you give more than you receive. Other times, you receive almost more than you can contain. We'll work this out together as a family."

"Thanks, Mom," she said, wiping away a tear. "But I fear there are going to be a lot of times when we won't be able to help each other."

"We have our psychic connection, and our love, and they will give us strength when we're alone."

"I think we'll need plenty of magic, too."

THE THREE OF US SAT ACROSS FROM THE NEUROLOGIST IN HER office. It was nice to consult with a doctor without having to sit on an exam table covered with paper.

Dr. Alohabi pulled up two images of my brain on the large monitor behind her desk. She smiled. Her eyes were wise and kind.

"You have a healthy brain, Darla," she said. "No signs of dementia or stroke damage."

"What's that?" I asked, pointing to a roundish white mass on the right side of one image.

"That is a cyst. A benign cyst. It might cause minor seizures, but, and I stress this, it's not cancerous."

Cory made eye contact with me. I knew he thought that when I "froze" or "went away," it might be a simple seizure, not a visit to Danu. I also knew that he didn't really believe this hypothesis. Deep down, he knew Danu was real. The plant seedlings that popped up in areas at home that I'd touched, like bathroom grout, were only one proof point.

"I want you to get another MRI in sixth months to see if the cyst is growing," Dr. Alohabi said. "I suspect it is not."

"Another MRI?" I whined.

"It's okay, Mom," Sophie said. "We don't want to worry about you."

"If the cyst can cause seizures, can it also cause hallucinations?" Cory asked.

"Not likely with the kinds of seizures this cyst might cause," the doctor replied.

I caught Cory's eyes again. He nodded.

Perhaps the cyst had something to do with Danu's presence in my head. But I was certain, and I believed my family was, too, that Danu was real.

Science and the supernatural complement each other, I'd learned. Neither can rule the other out.

My worry was that the Fae would use the power of nature to warp the power of their magic. We all should worry about that.

CHAPTER 8

SOPHIE

"I 'm not doing assassinations anymore," I said. "If the Council has a problem with that, they can take it up with me."

The young, skinny woman, barely older than a teenager, seemed frightened by me. She handed me the piece of paper and looked like she wanted to run away.

"I don't know what your assignment is," the waif said. "I'm just an admin who keeps track of dues payments from the guild members. My boss gave me this note and told me to deliver it to you."

I glanced at the small piece of magic-imbued parchment. When I opened it, the lettering appeared. It read:

Evict the troll Smeldman from his residence beneath the Bridge of Memories. He must move to a bridge where he cannot prey on dogs being walked.

It was a reasonable request. I'd heard about the number of dogs plucked from their leashes, the abductions performed so quickly that the human pet owners never saw the troll.

But I didn't want to evict anyone. My empathy was turning me into a softie.

"I'll perform this task," I said to the messenger. "But tell your boss to send word to the Council that I want an audience before them so I can resign my post as an enforcer."

She nodded, nervous and not happy to be in the middle of this.

"Thank you," I added and jerked my head to indicate she should scram.

Scram she did, almost sprinting from the front door of the inn.

The note grew warm in my hand, so I placed it on the cobblestones at my feet seconds before it burst into flames. The fire, a magical failsafe feature, burned quickly and thoroughly. Nothing was left of the note, not even ashes.

Even though this assignment wasn't an assassination, the Council would want total secrecy and deniability. I understood fully, but it made getting paid a pain in the butt because I couldn't send them an invoice. I had to depend on their honor.

No wonder I hadn't been paid yet for destroying the vampire nest. If they were going to stiff me for not killing Diego, there was nothing I could do about it.

That evening, I told Mom and Cory that I had dinner plans and headed out for the bridge. My sword, Alfie, was in a large duffel bag so it wouldn't attract attention from civilians.

Crossing the Sangre River on the historic Bridge of Memories and heading toward downtown San Marcos was beautiful. With the ancient buildings, gas lamps, and horse carriages, you felt as if you were walking into another century.

I, however, was walking in the opposite direction, heading toward a seedier part of town near the beach. Here, you'd find the cheaper motels and restaurants. And a much safer environment for a troll who ate pets.

When I reached the other side of the bridge, I took a sharp right and descended an embankment toward the river. If anyone saw me climbing under the bridge, they'd assume I was homeless. Even though someone attempting to sleep under this end of the bridge would suffer the same fate as the unfortunate dogs.

I reached the seawall and turned to face the dense shadows beneath the bridge. Riprap, the chunks of concrete placed to prevent erosion from flooding, rose at an angle toward the underside of the bridge. The descending bridge and the rising ground formed a V, and in its point would be the lair of Smeldman.

At the moment, I saw no signs of him. Trolls had preternatural abilities to camouflage themselves. After all, they were ambush hunters.

Yikes, there were fresh bones nearby. I didn't want to guess what they had belonged to.

"Mr. Smeldman, I humbly request a word with you," I said, speaking loudly to be heard over the hum of car traffic above us. "My name is Sophie. I represent the Executive Council of the Guilds."

He didn't answer. But he was there—I could sense his supernatural presence.

"Mr. Smeldman, I'm afraid I must ask you to vacate this property. The Council, and your own guild, has issued this order. Your killing of dogs has created too much risk that you'll be discovered by humans. As you hopefully know, we're in the middle of the Great Unmasking. All supernaturals must err on the cautious side."

Was that a growl coming from the darkness? Too difficult to tell with the noise from the bridge traffic.

I summoned a simple illumination orb and sent it floating toward the point of the V beneath the bridge. The yellowish light showed no troll, only a large concrete structure that appeared to support the bridge.

But I knew otherwise.

The orb crashed into the structure. And two green eyes appeared in what had looked like concrete.

"Mr. Smeldman, I respectfully—"

The structure transformed into a troll of the same color who barreled down the slope of riprap toward me. And he meant business.

I cast a protection spell around myself while simultaneously pulling my sword from the duffel bag. The troll flung himself at me, and I danced aside at the last instant. His weight and momentum should have sent him into the river, but he stopped at the edge of the seawall with surprising agility.

Trolls are quite dexterous when in their habitats. And a troll was what he looked like now, his camouflage gone. Giant in stature, heavy brow, massive lower jaw, broad nose, pebbly skin.

And enormous teeth for crunching bones.

I sent energy into my sword, and it shot purple lightning at Smeldman. The troll staggered backward, smoke rising from the old canvas tarp he wore like a toga.

"There's no reason to get upset," I said. "All you need to do is make your home beneath a different bridge, like the one over the Intracoastal Waterway on Highway 207."

He roared. Maybe I had accidentally insulted him.

"Or the bridge on 302," I said. "That's a much nicer one."

He came at me again, but I held him off with another lightning burst.

This was what I hated about so many enforcer assignments. They turned into a contest of wills. My role was to use magic to knock some sense into my opponent, but sometimes their skulls were too thick for the sense to get inside.

The reason I was usually hired was that persuasion had already been tried and failed. So, nothing could be done other than use magic as brute force. In this role, I was less a witch than a thug.

It was at this most inopportune time that my unfamiliar powers as an empath kicked in.

Right after blasting Mr. Smeldman with lightning, I felt his pain and sorrow. His loneliness. The bewilderment of spending two centuries beneath this bridge, hearing the traffic above evolve from horse carriages to automobiles, watching the world change at a crazy pace, all because of the humans. More and more humans making his unmasking become more and more likely.

And those months last year they spent doing maintenance on the bridge? Unbearable!

But did he lash out and eat any humans? Nope. He only dined on an overfed dog now and then. Still, he was misunderstood, and this eviction was completely unfair.

The reason I knew this was how he was feeling was because I felt it myself.

Including his growing anger at the sharp pain of my lightning.

"I'm so sorry, Mr. Smeldman," I said in a tender voice. "I didn't mean to hurt you. Why don't you gather your stuff and move along now?"

Because he was too angry now. At me.

He lunged, and I wasn't quick enough. His cement-bag-sized palm struck my protection bubble, and the impact sent me flying from beneath the bridge, landing unhurt on the grass near the river's edge.

"Don't make me shoot you again," I said, pointing my sword at him.

"Why does that lady have a sword?" came the drunken voice of a man from the walkway of the bridge above me.

"Cause she's a witch!" said an equally drunk woman beside him.

"How do you know she's a witch?"

"Because she has a sword and all those pouches hanging from cords around her neck."

"I thought she was a hippie."

"Hippies don't carry swords!"

Jeez Louise, this was not good. I scurried into the shadows beside the bridge. Mr. Smeldman looked like he was going to charge again.

Meanwhile, the drunken tourists had reached the end of the bridge and were heading down the slope toward me. Along with other random tourists.

They were forming a mob. A common occurrence nowadays since the Great Unmasking.

"Mr. Smeldman, humans are coming! You need to hide. Better yet, jump into the water."

I sensed his fear of the humans, but also his stubbornness.

"They're probably carrying guns and will try to kill you." I pleaded, "Please escape."

The strangest thing happened. As I tried to convince him to fear for his life and flee, I was naturally increasing my own fear and urge to flee.

And though my words weren't convincing him, I pushed my emotions at him. I wanted him to feel what I was feeling.

The crowd was coming closer. Soon, they would be able to see the troll.

"I thought witches had broomsticks," the drunken man said.

"When they're traveling," said an unfamiliar voice. "Otherwise, they carry wands. Not swords."

You must flee. I willed the imperative into Mr. Smeldman.

Here, at the edge of the shadows, I saw panic fill the troll's face.

He turned, took three long, loping steps, and dove into the river. Thanks to the incoming tide, the current should take him right to the bridge on Route 302.

"What the heck was that huge splash?" the drunken woman asked. "It sounded like a whale."

"Or an elephant."

The crowd of six unruly tourists appeared at the water's edge, staring at me as I stood beneath the bridge.

"The witch!"

"Let's burn her!"

"Toss her into the river! Witches sink."

"I thought they floated."

Jumping into the river with Alfie (which I refused to abandon) was not a good idea in this strong current. That left fighting them with the sword, which would put me in jail. Or fighting them with magic, which would prove that I was a witch. Or—

A spotlight shone down on the mob from the road.

"Break it up and move along," said a male voice over a loudspeaker. It sounded like a cop.

"We ain't doing nothin' wrong," a man called back to the cop. "We're just gonna burn a witch."

The cop beeped his siren-horn and turned on his strobe lights. The car pulled into the adjacent parking lot of a motel and blasted his spotlight at the mob.

They finally got the message and moved briskly back to the sidewalk. The cop, a slender older man with a thick head of white hair, got out of his cruiser and watched them walk by toward the motels and restaurants.

"She's a witch, officer," a woman said.

After they had moved on, he approached and looked me over.

"Are you okay, ma'am?" he asked.

"Yeah. Thanks for chasing them off."

"Why do you have a sword?"

"I was heading home after dance practice. We were learning the Scottish Sword Dance. I was practicing here, under the bridge, because my apartment's so small."

I realized my mistake when he asked to see my driver's license, which had the Esperanza Inn's address—a street with no apartments.

"Do you know Detective Michael Samson?" I asked.

He returned my ID and inquired why I was asking.

"He's a friend of the family," I replied. "He can vouch for me."

He stared at me for an uncomfortably long time, then spoke into the radio mic attached to his shirt.

"Please relay a message to Detective Samson. I'm interviewing a suspect at the eastern foot of the Bridge of Memories. She requested him."

The dispatcher acknowledged the request. Then the cop's eyes bored into me.

"You can't blame them for thinking you're a witch, what with the sword and those amulets you're wearing. And your . . . outfit."

The outfit was my usual Goth look.

"I shouldn't be attacked because of the way I look."

"These days, you can be," he said. "I'm not saying it's right. But that's the way things are. People are afraid."

"The police should protect weirdos like me."

"That's what I did tonight. But you can't egg on the crowds. You need to look more. . . normal."

"I see."

"And this isn't a Renaissance festival. You can't bring weapons like that out in public."

"I'm sorry. I won't do it again."

An unmarked car pulled in beside the police cruiser. Samson got out.

Thank God.

He was a handsome man, with salt-and-pepper hair and a beard. He was also a werewolf.

And he was in love with Mom.

CHAPTER 9

SOPHIE

"You know, you really shouldn't bring that sword out in public," Samson said as he drove me back to the inn.

"I keep it hidden in my duffel bag," I replied. "Unless the sword is in use."

Samson glanced at me. "Do you like being an enforcer?"

"No. Not anymore. I used to have a lot . . . a lot of anger. Dark stuff in me. I guess it was from trauma when I was younger. I learned some good attack spells, and I just like blowing stuff up."

"I get it. That described me when I joined the Marines."

We were silent for a while. I guess we didn't want to share our traumas.

I liked Samson. He and Mom had worked together informally on some murder cases; Mom used her psychometry to gather memories from crime-scene evidence. It had looked like they were close to becoming an item while Cory was missing, and Mom had thought he had bailed out on her.

After Cory was rescued, things cooled down between Mom

and Samson. But he remained someone we could always count on.

"You can quit being an enforcer," he said.

"I know. That's what I plan to do."

"All of us supernaturals need to keep a low profile for a while. The unmasking could get a lot worse because politicians are getting involved. Things could turn real nasty. For witches, too. Like what happened tonight. You would think witches and psychics would be safer because you're human with no physical attributes revealing that you're supernatural. But it also means they can accuse anyone of being a witch, so witches are going to be their favorite targets."

"I know."

"If I hadn't come by tonight, Officer Lembke would probably have arrested you, or worse. The governor is putting pressure on law enforcement agencies to take a hard line on anyone suspected of being supernatural."

"How do we stop this?" I asked.

Samson pulled up to the curb in front of the inn.

"Either the haters kill all of us, or we stop the hating. We take the power away from the haters and change the subject."

"Who is 'we'? Are the guilds powerful enough to do this?"

"I don't know. I have my doubts about the Council."

I thanked Samson for rescuing me and went inside. Surprisingly, at this late hour, light from the kitchen poured into the hallway. I looked inside the open door to find Mom sitting on a barstool at the butcherblock island, sipping a glass of wine. She looked tired.

"Mom. Why are you still up?"

"Too many worries." She smiled, but it wasn't convincing.

"About the inn?"

"No, stuff I shouldn't have to deal with. The Fae are trying to complicate my life once again. I told you about Wilference's visit."

"Yeah, and they want you to help the Fae get a mysterious substance from the Elves."

"I didn't want to bother you about this," she said, "but you're family, and you should know if we're about to get pulled into a conflict between the Fae and the Elves."

"Why can't you just refuse to help them?"

"I plan to do that, with a little help from the Elves. But you should know the Fae might want to hurt me if I don't cooperate."

"Wilference threatened you?"

"No. I read his thoughts. He believes others of his people have bad intentions. It has always been that way after Danu came into me."

"I thought it was a rogue faction of the court who wanted to harm the Goddess. The Faerie Queene was grateful that you healed her, right?"

"So I believed. I think Danu's desire to protect the earth will always be a threat to the Fae's desire to exploit it. I'm stuck in the middle."

"I'll do everything I can to protect you," I said, reflexively touching Alfie in its duffel bag.

"We need to avoid being involved in any supernatural business during these calamitous times."

"I know. I'm going to resign as an enforcer. An assignment went sideways tonight, thanks to a mob of humans accusing me of being a witch."

I assured her I hadn't been hurt. But what I was too tired to mention was the odd way that my empathy helped convince the troll to do what I wanted. I was definitely going to pursue Mom's offer to get me empath training.

"The Council has failed to meet this challenge," Mom said.

Yes. Forcing me to destroy rogue vampires did nothing to address the cause of the problem.

"Goodnight," I said before kissing her cheek. "And take care of yourself."

Speaking of the Council, after I went up to my room, I got a text. It was from Orlena, the mage who served as the head of the Magic Guild.

The Council has agreed to meet with you, her text said. *Wednesday 7:00 pm.*

THE SUPERNATURAL GUILDS OF SAN MARCOS AND GREATER Northeast Florida are not like a branch of the government imbued with tradition and solemnity. They are merely practical organizations, like merchant guilds or trade unions, that bring safety and order to the supernatural community.

Members pay dues to their guilds, which help protect their members and enforce behavioral guidelines to prevent infighting and, most importantly, uphold the Equilibrium. If the Equilibrium were to be lost, chaos and killing would follow.

Which was exactly what we were seeing during the Great Unmasking.

Because of the humble nature of the guilds, the Executive Council did not meet in a marble hall filled with statues. They gathered in whatever facility was available at the time. On Wednesday, it was an oil-stained garage at Baldric's auto shop that specialized in European cars.

I arrived to find a group of bored-looking guild leaders who didn't look as panicked as they should have, given the situation after the Great Unmasking began.

Sitting on folding chairs in a half-circle on the concrete floor were Rufus, alpha of the Shifter Guild; Gaarg, chief of the Troll and Gnome Alliance; Sybil, queen of the Elven League; Timothy, president of the Union of Undead Flesh Eaters; Evelyn, priestess of the Psychic Guild; Orlena, arch mage of the Magic Guild; Dave, director of the Guild of Unclassifiable Monsters; the vampire, Lethia, duchess of the Clan of the Eternal Night; and Baldric, chief of the Guild of Fae and Wee People, who was currently the president of the Council.

"Why did you request this meeting?" Baldric asked, with no small talk or pleasantries. In his human form, he had a sexy Southern-European look, with dark hair and eyes, olive skin.

"I'm resigning as an enforcer."

"What? You can't do that."

"Watch me."

"In these times, we need an enforcer more than ever," Baldric said, leaning toward me in his chair, his hands gripping his knees.

"In these times, we need to do more than police supernaturals. We need to fight the humans who are exploiting this frenzy."

"Spoken by an enforcer who failed to complete her mission to eliminate rogue supernaturals," said Lethia with disdain.

The ancient vampire appeared to be only in her late twenties in body age. She had a large mane of red hair and a slim, toned body. I felt like a Goth dork compared to her.

"You're right," I replied. "I didn't kill Diego, a friend of our family."

"You can't allow your feelings to get in the way of your work."

"Who sent the wraith to our inn to punish me by killing a guest?" I demanded. "Was it you, Baldric? You once taught me magic. How could you have betrayed my family like that?"

"It was me," Lethia said. "Don't look so surprised. The

wraith was the spirit of a human I killed. An ancient vampire, such as I, has the power to enslave the spirit and force it to do as I wish."

"If you're so angry at Diego, why don't you attack him yourself?"

"That has nothing to do with it."

"Another reason I'm resigning is because the message the Council gave me with orders to destroy the nest had vague threats of harm coming to my mother."

"How so?" Baldric asked.

"It said something about a loved one being at risk."

"Bah," Lethia said, waving her hand in dismissal. "Those were my words. Anyone who doesn't follow my orders faces retribution."

"We wouldn't want anything to happen to Darla," Baldric said. "We expect great things from her."

"Like what?" I asked. His comment made me suspicious.

"To ensure peace."

"Between whom, exactly?"

"The Seelie and Unseelie Courts, for instance."

Between the Elves and the Fae.

"Why would that concern you?" I asked. "You're a local faerie who's not a subject of the Unseelie Court."

"Conflict between the two courts would destabilize everyone."

Warning vibes radiated through my body. Why did Baldric know about the Fae trying to get my mother involved in their scheme? Baldric was supposed to be on the side of humans and the local supernaturals. He should have nothing to do with the Fae. Right? He was of their species, but he had grown up among humans in San Marcos, not with the Fae of the Unseelie Court. Their imperialist population wasn't even from America. They came from the land of Faerie and had declared themselves to be enemies of humans. They'd even planned to invade San Marcos in the recent past.

"Back to the matter at hand," I said. "Sorry for any inconvenience, but I'm done with being your enforcer."

"Shall we accept her resignation?" Baldric asked Lethia.

Why was he asking her? He was the president of the Council.

"If she's gone soft, she's of no use to us," Lethia replied. She turned to me. "We accept your resignation with one condition: you make amends for your failure at the vampire nest. You will destroy Diego."

I shook my head. "I can't. You're the most powerful vampire. You can do it yourself."

"It's your defiance I can't accept. No one defies me. Destroy Diego or I will destroy him myself, along with your life—in ways you can't imagine. Instead of one vampire, many humans close to you will die. If he hasn't been assassinated by dawn, I will come for him and for you."

Baldric reached over and put his hand on hers. I assumed it was meant to calm her, but I couldn't help but notice the intimacy it implied.

The other guild leaders remained quiet but were visibly uncomfortable. I tried to catch the eyes of Orlena, my guild leader, but she looked away.

Diego had been right. The Council was corrupt and weak. The only two who appeared strong had their own agendas, which had nothing to do with making sure their members were safe and thriving.

"You'll find Diego in the Flagler Heights neighborhood," Lethia said. "Find him and kill him before I kill you both."

I stormed out of the garage, spewing dozens of curse words under my breath.

And I don't mean magical curses. I mean drunken-sailor curses.

The Council could go to hell. But then I remembered: they owed me back pay that I would now never see.

And the fear spread over me about what Lethia would do to me.

First, I must find Diego. Perhaps we could save each other.

FLAGLER HEIGHTS WAS A RESIDENTIAL NEIGHBORHOOD WITH large homes built in the late 1800s, in styles ranging from Victorian to Queen Anne. In its heyday, it had been the most desirable address, until it went into decline as the wealthy bought newer homes in the expanding suburbs.

Today, the neighborhood was rejuvenated and desirable again, the homes renovated and the landscaping lush and well-manicured. Diego would feel at home here if he hadn't been desperate and in exile.

How the heck was I supposed to find him?

The magic spells I knew for finding people required the use of one of their belongings. I didn't have anything of Diego's. All I had was my witch's sensitivity to supernatural beings and forces.

As I strolled down the well-lit sidewalks, I picked up on the presence of at least three supernatural creatures. Only one broadcast energy powerful enough to be from an elder vampire.

The energy was strongest outside a two-story brick home with a detached garage. Several of the home's lights were on, and

I was pretty sure humans were living there. I couldn't ring the bell and ask if a vampire was in there with them.

"Good evening. Are you looking for me?"

I jumped. Diego had shown up right behind me without my noticing. He wore a black sport coat, black trousers, and a dark-gray dress shirt. In short, he looked like a homeowner in this neighborhood.

"How did you know I was out here?" I asked.

"I scented you."

"Do I need to buy a better deodorant?"

He laughed. "I identified your unique Sophie scent. Vampire senses, remember?"

"Of course. I came looking for you to let you know that it's Lethia who wants you destroyed."

His face betrayed no emotion.

"And," I said, "she ordered me to do it tonight, or else she would kill us both."

"You don't have your crossbow or wooden stakes. How am I supposed to die?"

"I guess the choice is up to Lethia. I'm done with the Council. You're right—it's corrupt. I'm just not ready to be an insurgent like you."

"Well, I would appreciate the company." His white teeth gleamed in the illumination of the streetlamp. His fangs were retracted, thankfully.

"I know it's none of my business, but you deserve better than Lethia. You know, you're a really cool guy, and she doesn't appreciate you."

"Indeed. Ordering me to be destroyed is the very essence of unappreciation." His mouth quirked in irony.

"I don't know what to do to stay safe from Lethia. I'm

worried if I go home, I'll put Mom and Cory at risk. But she could go after them even if I'm not there."

"Darla needs your protection."

"You're right," I said. "Cory can't guard her alone, and Roderick is no match for Lethia, even though he's a vampire."

Diego's phone chimed, and he took it from his pocket. He frowned. "On second thought, it might be best for you to avoid your home," he said.

"Why? Who texted you?"

"It wasn't a text. It's an alert. There's this extremist group of humans, Mothers Against Monsters, who developed an app that publishes the names and addresses of people suspected to be supernatural—usually with no evidence. It's called the Monster Monitor." He rolled his eyes. "I check it to see if vampires I know are called out. This new listing was just published."

He handed me the phone. My face, name, and address filled the screen, with the notice: *Suspected witch. Armed and dangerous.*

Nausea spread through me.

"That's horrible," I said.

"I'm sorry."

"Why did they use my driver's license photo?"

"The group gets data from the state. The Great Unmasking is becoming more than internet hacks and mobs of misinformed people. I believe it's government-directed and systematic. A program to cleanse the state of supernaturals."

I had no words. His phone went to sleep, thankfully, so I didn't have to look at my pasty face anymore, and I returned it to him. How did I end up in the app? Did Officer Lembke report me?

"Where are you staying?" I asked.

"I'm holed up in the attic of the detached garage." He pointed toward the house. "I don't recommend you stay there with me. As a vampire, I'm much better than a human at keeping myself undetected. Also, there's no bathroom."

My face grew hot with embarrassment as I realized he thought I was trying to invite myself to his hiding place.

Diego pressed a key into my hand.

"Stay in my apartment above the restaurant. I haven't been able to return there because of Lethia's spies, but she won't be looking for you until after tonight, when she realizes you didn't destroy me. You'll be safe there from the humans."

I hesitated.

"Don't worry," he said. "The security system is off. And my restaurant has been closed since I've gone into hiding from Lethia."

"I feel like the world is spinning around me."

"Hole up at my place tonight and tomorrow. My refrigerator has nothing in it but pints of blood. However, there should be crackers in the pantry for guests. Meet me tomorrow after sundown at *La Fortaleza*."

He disappeared in an instant, leaving me alone on the sidewalk.

I knew I should go directly to Diego's place, but I feared I would have to avoid my home for a long time, and I needed my sword, some clothes, and personal items. I figured I had some time, because my listing had only just been published on the app.

I drove home, ran up to my room, and filled a backpack with a couple of outfits and some necessities—you know, the incidentals you don't want to forget, like your deodorant and your crossbow. I slipped on the backpack, slung the bag with my sword over my shoulder, and went downstairs to say goodbye.

Mom was in the cottage, reading a novel in her bathrobe, while Cory was snoring in the bedroom. She looked up at me with surprise.

"I don't have time to explain," I said, "but I'm going to lie low for a while. Lethia will be after me for not killing Diego, and some extremists unmasked me on their app as a witch."

"Goodness," she said in shock. "Where are you going?"

"I can't tell you for your safety. But I promise I'll keep in touch." I kissed her on the cheek.

"This makes no—"

Mom froze. Her eyes were open; she was clearly awake. But her eyes were focused on something far in the distance. She had gone away again on goddess business.

I shook my head in sorrow and turned to go.

"They say you're a witch," said a man standing in the cottage's open front door.

It was Mr. Humphrey from Ocala, staying in Room 203.

And he was aiming a gun at me.

CHAPTER 10

DARLA

The last time I involuntarily "went away" or "froze," as my family puts it, I visited the Goddess. In my other out-of-body excursions, I *was* the Goddess, doing her work, such as healing a mountainside after a wildfire.

This time, I was a squirrel.

I'm not joking. I perched atop a limb of the giant live oak tree across the street from the inn and made high-pitched squeaks about the indignity of it all. Clutching the bark with four claws, I used my wide-angle vision to take in my gray fur and a trove of ripening acorns on the branch below me.

A squirrel scampered along the limb toward me. She looked familiar to my squirrel eyes, though when in human form, I found all squirrels to look the same.

Wait a minute. It was night. Why were we squirrels out and about in the dark?

I realized the squirrel was Summer, the half-elf fellow member of the Memory Guild. She twitched her fluffy tail in greeting.

"Your presence is requested in Ehrendil," she chattered through her squirrel mouth, but I heard it in my head as if she was speaking normally.

"By whom?"

"Leighnel, a mage of the court."

"Am I in trouble?"

She chittered a laugh. "Follow me."

Summer ran along the limb toward the tree trunk. I followed, at first a little unsteadily, but I soon felt confident on my squirrel feet. She placed her front paws on a knothole just above the limb joint, and a round wooden door appeared. She opened it and I followed her inside.

With no physical sensation of transformation, I was instantly in human form again, as was Summer. Although we were obviously miniature sized, because the interior of the tree trunk felt like a large building.

We stood on a wide landing made of natural wood just inside the door. A spiraling staircase, carved from the wood of the hollow trunk, wrapped around its walls for seemingly hundreds of feet above and below us.

White, glowing orbs provided ample illumination. They were attached to the interior walls of the trunk, while others floated slowly upward and downward in the towering vertical space of the tree's interior.

We were in Ehrendil, which I had visited with Summer once before. Ehrendil is the Land of the Elves, and it could be anywhere and everywhere. Essentially, wherever elves dwelled was Ehrendil. Every hollow tree they inhabited was a hall of Ehrendil.

I followed Summer down the staircase, passing hallways extending out from the trunk that were the hollow interiors of tree limbs. They led to living quarters and various common areas.

Every so often, we passed landings for exterior doors. Whenever elves go outside, they are transformed into squirrels (or occasionally birds, chipmunks, or other critters) to allow them to go about their business unnoticed by humans. Should a predatory animal attempt to attack one of the illusionary creatures, the predator would suddenly face a full-sized elf, thrusting a spear at them. Most hawks, foxes, and other predators are smart enough to know the difference between a real squirrel and an elf manifestation.

We finally descended to the base of the oak tree, its widest section, which contained kitchens, a banquet hall, theater, gymnasium, and other public spaces.

I—or I should say, Danu—had once been the guest of the Elven King and Queen at a banquet in a tree like this.

We didn't stop here where the stairs ended. Instead, Summer led me past a kitchen to one of several doors. We entered a much more confined staircase, little more than a ladder, that twisted downward.

"We're inside the uppermost portion of the root system," Summer said. "We're almost there."

We carefully went down the narrow, steep stairs, deeper and deeper underground, a shadowy, claustrophobic passage with only occasional orbs providing light. At last, Summer stopped at a round metal door next to the stairs without its own landing. She used a metal door knocker shaped like an acorn. The deep clangs echoed in the narrow staircase.

The door opened and a slender male elf smiled at us. He was handsome and blond, like most elves, but with a wispy blond beard.

"Leighnel, meet Darla," Summer said in English. "She is the human incarnation of Danu."

Leighnel bowed. "Thank you for coming. Welcome to my lab. We elves spend little time underground, unlike the Fae, but my work requires my proximity to tree roots."

He led us into a cavern carved into the earth, with light orbs floating at the ceiling. The dirt walls were studded with rocks here and there, as well as the elbows of roots that poked in and out of the surfaces. Colorful, ornate tapestries hung as an antidote to the rawness of the walls.

The room was large, but crowded with tables covered with beakers, flasks, metallurgical tools, and vials of powders. One wall was covered entirely by a giant bookcase overflowing with ancient, leather-bound volumes.

"Please be seated," Leighnel said, gesturing to two austere wooden chairs. "I asked you here, Danu, out of a sense of alarm."

"You can call me Darla. I'm not really Danu quite yet."

"Um, I will try, Divine One, but the impression you give is more that of a goddess than a human."

"I'll take that as a compliment."

He smiled. In the better lighting of the room, compared to the stairs, I got a good look at him. His face had wise eyes with wrinkles around them that showed older age, though he still came across as young as all elves do.

He said, "I was alarmed at the mention of phytolucine, which Summer had brought to my attention."

I glanced at her, and she shrugged. "Sorry," she whispered with a naughty smile.

"It was right of you to tell me, Summer," Leighnel said. "The fate of the planet in these trying times rests upon phytolucine. And the fact that the Fae know of it and want it is very disturbing."

"I don't understand what phytolucine is or what it does," I said.

Leighnel chuckled. "You, along with all of us. Phytolucine is a substance made by trees and certain plants, those with the deepest roots. Its creation is aided by certain fungi and, frankly, a form of magic possessed by the forests that we have never fully understood. It is so hidden and manifests itself in ways that defy the way we look at the world."

I nodded, but I still didn't know what the stuff was.

"We know phytolucine works with the mycorrhizal network, the various fungi that live among the roots and allow trees to communicate with one another. And we know, but only indirectly, that phytolucine has effects beyond the concerns of the trees and forests. We believe it is, in a way, critical to the future survival of earth."

"Wow," I said.

"Do you know how the Fae plan to use it?"

"No. I wasn't told. Except that it would be used in magic making."

"Summer told me they wanted you to be the representative between our courts to help them procure it."

I nodded. "But I didn't agree."

"Far be it from me to make a request of a goddess, but I humbly beg that you do not help the Fae. In fact, we need you to stymie their attempts to find this substance."

"I don't know how I could stymie them."

"You will find a way. As you will with my last and greatest request. As the health of the forests has declined dangerously over the last century or two, the production of phytolucine has decreased. Only phytolucine will help the earth survive the changes it is undergoing, especially as humans and faeries continue to ravage our planet for material gain."

"What are you asking?"

"I'm asking—begging—for you to help our forests produce more phytolucine."

"How on earth can I do that?"

"Exactly. You are the earth mother. If anyone can do it, it's you."

"No offense," I said, "but you appear to have dedicated your life to studying phytolucine. Passing the buck to me is like abandoning your work and hoping providence will finish it for you."

"No offense taken. You speak frankly, as humans do, but you underestimate the powers of Danu."

"Or, you overestimate them. If Danu can help increase production of such an important substance, why hasn't she already?"

"Elves don't worship Danu directly, so we've never asked this of her before. Even a goddess can't be everywhere at once. This is like a situation in which a village is suffering from a drought, so they pray to the gods for rain. But in this case, it's on a world-wide scale."

"I can urge Danu to help," I said, "but I can't tell her how, because I don't know how."

"I am not simply handing off my work to providence," he said with a reassuring smile. "I will be involved every step of the way."

His words made me feel better. I couldn't speak as to how Danu felt, because my consciousness was fully my own, Darla's. And it was Elven magic, not hers, that enabled my transformation into a squirrel and then into a miniature, astral version of myself that could exist in this magical world inside a tree.

As if the Elven magic were responding to my thoughts, I suddenly found myself no longer in the underground lab, but sitting on the ground at the base of the live oak tree in the yard across the street from the inn.

I was normal-Darla, sitting on the damp grass of my neighbors.

No, scratch that. I wasn't normal; I was naked. If I was really here, and naked, that could create a scandal in my neighborhood or send me to jail. Fortunately, the lights were off in my neighbor's house, and the nearest streetlamp was too far away to penetrate the darkness beneath the tree.

Ever wonder why the people interviewed in articles about living in nudist colonies are always saggy and middle-aged or older? Well, that described me.

When a raccoon strolled by without noticing me, I thankfully realized I wasn't here in a physical sense. My body was still back at the inn. I relaxed enough to realize why I was here right now.

My hands were pressed to the ground on either side of my crossed legs so that I could commune with the tree via its roots. I'd done that before, using my psychometry enhanced by my goddess powers.

My psychic senses penetrated the soil and connected with the thick, ropy tap roots closest to the tree, the lateral roots spreading horizontally, and the sinker roots growing downward from them, branching out into countless, tiny capillary-like vessels.

With southern live oaks, the roots grow farther outward than downward. The lateral roots of this one extended beneath the entire front lawn of the house, contacting the roots of a magnolia and a palm tree. They were of different species, but were associates of a sort.

My senses probed more intently, and I somehow joined the energy surging along the network of roots. While they slowly soaked water from the soil and sent it upward toward the trunks, branches, and leaves, they also sent electrical impulses with the help of the mycorrhiza fungi.

I detected a humming sensation. Information traveling along the roots. The trees were not sentient in the way we humans understand the concept. Yet they could communicate with each other.

Would they speak to me?

I drifted into a trance-like state as my consciousness became one with the trees.

Mother.

Did I actually hear that word, or did I feel the emotion associated with it? I didn't know. But the trees knew who I was. Their earth mother, Danu, even though I was still Darla.

"Can you hear me?" I whispered aloud as I sent the question psychically through my fingertips, down through the soil and into the roots.

I sensed an affirmation from the trees.

"Can you tell me about phytolucine?"

No answer. I waited, but I felt no response.

"Can you make more of it, for the good of the earth?"

Again, no answer. Somehow, I sensed they had heard me, yet didn't want to answer.

Abruptly, my psychic connection shut off. Footsteps approached on the sidewalk from a human and a dog. And here I was, naked in the dark beneath a tree.

I take that back. Now I was back in my cottage, sitting in the same chair I had occupied before I "went away" to Ehrendil. I was wearing my robe again, by the way.

Most of the time when I "went away," it was only for a few seconds here in reality, even if it felt like much longer in the places where I went.

But this time, I was alone in the room. Hadn't Sophie been here speaking with me when my consciousness bailed out of my body? Yes, she was panicking that she had been unmasked on the internet.

Normally, she would still be here, glaring at me in frustration like she usually did when I "went away." I hoped she hadn't fled and gone into hiding already.

Cory had been asleep in the bedroom. I walked back there, my body feeling a little stiff. The bed and the room were empty.

How long had I been away?

With growing unease, I checked the bathroom and even the second bedroom, which we used as an office. No Cory. No Sophie.

It wasn't like them to leave me when I wasn't in my body. Even if I was essentially only an empty husk, you don't leave a person in that condition, whether she was catatonic, suffering a seizure, lost in dementia, or off visiting the Elves.

I left the cottage and crossed the courtyard to look for my family in the main building.

That's when the gunshot broke the stillness of the night.

CHAPTER 11

SOPHIE

"I 'm not a witch," I said as calmly as possible to the man pointing a gun at me.

"It says you are on the app." He pulled out his phone and turned the screen to face me. My profile page filled it. "Same address. This is your picture. It's a bad one."

"Driver's license photo," I said. "My eyes don't normally bug out like that."

"It says you're armed and dangerous. Drop those bags."

I complied, slipping off my backpack and placing the bag with Alfie gently on the floor so it wouldn't clang. Mr. Humphrey, stocky, in his early sixties with short white hair, was nervous. I cringed as he waved the gun carelessly.

"Why did you bring your gun with you on vacation?" I asked, trying to buy time while I conjured a spell to disable him.

"I always have a gun on me. I got two on me now, since I'm here in the big city."

Good to know he had a second gun.

"San Marcos isn't a big city," I said.

"Yeah, it is. And they say an old city like this has more monsters in it." He frowned. "Stop trying to distract me. I'm taking you to the police station right now."

"Why don't you just call them?" I hoped an officer who knew us would come and vouch for me.

"The police get too many calls about vampires and witches and the like. So they don't always respond. If I want to get paid, I've got to take you in myself."

"Get paid?"

"The bounty. Mothers Against Monsters is paying a bounty for every monster captured. Come on, let's go."

He pointed the gun at my head. With no choice, I complied, trying to keep his attention on me and not on Mom sitting behind me, frozen, her mouth slightly open and her eyes staring blankly.

The spell I had been casting would have heated the metal of his gun until it was too hot to hold, but I had released the spell before it was complete. I didn't want the dropped gun to go off accidentally and shoot Mom. Also, he had said he had a backup gun.

A sleep spell would be better, though a bit harder to cast. Most of my spells were dramatic, offensive weapons. I wasn't as experienced with defensive spells like that.

He gave me a not-so-gentle push out the door and into the courtyard. The screen door slammed shut behind us, hopefully waking up Cory.

"My family is hosting you in our home," I said. "Why do you want to harm us?"

I tried to sense his emotions. He felt anxiety, hatred, and a bit of guilt. Perhaps my untrained empath powers could influence him, like they had with the troll beneath the bridge.

"Why do you want to ruin my life?" I continued. "Just because of some app created by extremists who know nothing."

"Come on," he said, anger rising in him. "My car is parked nearby. Can we get through this gate to the street?"

"I don't have the key. We need to go through the inn."

I didn't know how to use my empath powers on this tough case. I vowed that if I survived, I would get training. In the meantime, my sleep spell would have to do.

As Mr. Humphrey pushed me across the courtyard, I conjured the spell.

"Stop resisting," he ordered. "I don't want to shoot you."

I cast the spell.

He gave me a rough shove.

The spell wasn't working.

"Are you trying to use magic on me, witch?" he growled. "I can sense it. I'm a faith healer with powers of my own. Your evil magic won't work on me."

"You have the supernatural in you, too!" I said. "You're one of us."

"I use the powers of the Lord. Not the powers of evil, like you."

"Black magic is evil. I practice elemental magic using the powers of the world around us. The world created by God."

"You're evil!" he shouted, pushing me toward the door to the inn.

"Cory!" I screamed. "Help me!"

Where was Cory? And would a guest hearing my screams call 911? Of course, if the police arrived, I might go from the frying pan into the fire.

Mr. Humphrey pushed the gun's muzzle against my head and wrenched open the door. I fell inside, landing on the floor of the hallway.

He grabbed me by the hair and lifted me to my feet.

"Get moving, you spawn of Satan!"

I stumbled down the hallway, past the living room and the kitchen. The foyer was just ahead.

That's when the door to the courtyard burst open and Cory came running in, bearing my sword.

Why he had the sword, I didn't know, since he and Mom kept a gun in a shoebox on the top shelf of their closet. But anything to change the odds made me grateful.

My captor swung around to face the skinny guy in his underwear, charging with a sword pointing ahead like a rhinoceros horn. Mr. Humphrey aimed at Cory.

I jumped on his back, grabbing his arm, and he stumbled sideways.

Cory lunged forward, the sword missing its target as he flew right past us.

Mr. Humphrey tried to throw me off his back. I'm in decent shape, but I'm not big, and there was no way I'd win a contest of strength with this country boy from Ocala.

He flung himself backward, smashing me into the wall. These were sturdy stone walls, not drywall. I wheezed as the breath was knocked out of me and slid to the floor.

Cory had recovered from his momentum and swung the sword at Humphrey just as he squeezed the trigger.

The shot rang out, echoing in the hallway. Both men missed their marks.

"Take cover, Cory!" I shouted.

Cory ducked into the supply closet before Humphrey could get him in his sights again. Then the gun swiveled toward me.

I scrambled into the kitchen. Man, I wished I had my sword. I quickly cast the metal-heating spell I had originally considered using.

Humphrey filled the doorway and found me crouching behind the butcherblock island. I smelled steel and gun oil heating, but he raised the weapon and aimed ... and suddenly got yanked into the air.

Archibald was attached to the wall above the doorway, clutching Humphrey by the collar.

The man gasped with surprise, immediately followed by a painful yelp. He dropped the gun, and I caught a whiff of burned flesh.

Dangling three feet in the air, Humphrey tried to reach for his rear waistband, where his other handgun must have been.

Cory appeared behind him and plucked the gun from Humphrey's trousers.

"Should I impale him with your sword?" Cory asked me.

"It's not good business to kill our own guest. Let me take care of him temporarily."

My sleep spell hadn't worked on him, so I wracked my brain to think of a disabling spell that his rudimentary supernatural powers couldn't block.

The smaller of the two refrigerators moved away from the wall, and out came Roderick in his dusty old suit.

"Evening, Roderick," I said.

"What on earth is creating all this commotion? I nearly drained a cow tonight and wanted to retire early," he complained, before noticing Humphrey dangling from Archibald's clawed hands. "Good gracious, who is this gentleman?"

"Lord Almighty, is that a vampire?" Humphrey asked.

"This is a guest who used a deadly weapon in order to abduct me, claiming that I'm a witch, so he could earn a bounty," I explained to Roderick.

"This inn is full of monsters!" blustered Humphrey. "Who, or what, is holding me in the air?"

"Never you mind," said Mom, appearing in the hallway behind Humphrey.

"Everyone's here now," I said. "I might as well make coffee."

I recounted to Mom what had happened after she "went away."

"All of that went down in the few seconds I was gone?"

"It was more than a few seconds, Mom."

"I demand to be freed this instant!" Humphrey thundered.

"He's going to have Sophie arrested, Roderick staked, and the inn shut down," Cory said. "I say we kill him."

"No!" Humphrey shouted.

"We can't let him go after all he's seen," Cory said.

"Right," Mom said. "He'll give the inn a horrible internet review."

"I would use a spell to cleanse his memory, but he has rudimentary supernatural powers himself," I said. "He blocked a sleep spell I tried. Can the Goddess do anything to him?"

"Alas," Roderick said, "if only I didn't lack the ability to mesmerize prey into forgetfulness."

"A witch, a goddess, a vampire—you're all blasphemers! You're all minions of Satan!"

"Shut your bloody mouth," Archibald said as he continued to hold Humphrey.

"Who is that, and how is he holding me up?"

"I should just bash his head on the ceiling, and perhaps the blow will give him amnesia," Archibald said.

"Sophie, do you think your memory-cleansing spell would work if you had a burst of extra energy?" Cory asked.

"You mean from the ley lines? Yeah, I believe it would work."

"Do you really want to put yourself through that, dear?"

Mom asked him. It had been a long time since he'd gone through the exhausting experience of drawing energy from a ley line and transferring it to someone else.

"I can do it," he replied.

"What are you blasphemers talking about?" a frightened Humphrey asked, his arms and legs flailing.

"Never you mind," Mom said, stepping carefully around him into the kitchen. "Calm down and relax."

She caught his hand and held it still while she sang to him—an ancient Celtic song I couldn't understand, but which had a relaxing effect on me, too.

The man stopped moving and hung limply from Archibald's claws. He cooed and gurgled like a baby.

"Mom, you infantilized him," I said.

"The mother goddess in me did."

Cory put Humphrey on the hand truck we kept in the closet, and he and I wheeled him out to Cory's SUV. Mom joined us, and we drove to the tiny waterfront park just north of the ancient fortress. The park was where a major and minor ley line intersected underground.

To explain in the simplest terms, ley lines are natural features that transmit elemental energy. Some historians have claimed that ley lines formed to connect important religious and mystical centers around the world. Others contend the lines connected geological features and the human structures came later.

Any witch, such as me, could get a boost of energy for their magic by drawing upon ley lines. But Cory had the ability to connect directly to the lines—like grabbing hold of a high-tension power line—and absorbing the energy.

The wizard who had taught Cory magic used to exploit this gift. He would force Cory to harvest the energy and then would drain it from him. The trauma had been one of the reasons Cory had avoided practicing magic over the years since then.

Once Cory transferred the ley-line energy to me, it would increase the power of my spell a hundredfold. It would be impossible for Humphrey to block.

It was late enough that there was no traffic along the waterfront. We parked nearby, leaving Humphrey in the vehicle, and walked to the tiny park. Mom and I stood out of the way while Cory walked in circles, sensing the actual location where the major and minor lines intersected.

He dropped to his knees and bent over with his hands and head touching the grass. I sensed his own energy probing the ground, trying to connect with the lines.

It was almost as if he'd been electrocuted. His body jerked, and he lifted his head from the ground, remaining on all fours.

His hair stood up straight. An ecstatic smile filled his face.

"Nothing else in the world can make you feel like this," he murmured.

Soon, he struggled to his feet and staggered away from the spot. I rushed over and grabbed his arms to steady him. His body hummed with energy.

"Ready?" he whispered.

I nodded.

He put a hand on either side of my face and turned on the switch.

He was correct: the euphoria was more than any drug, or any emotion, could give you.

"Let's do this now," I said. My tongue tingled along with every inch of me.

Leaving Cory to rest, Mom led me to the SUV. I climbed into the back seat where Humphrey was sprawled languidly.

I constructed the spell to wash away all his memories from

tonight and as many of the supernatural conspiracy theories as I could locate in his mind. Everything about the Great Unmasking would go. I even held up his phone to his face to unlock it, then deleted the Mothers Against Monsters app from the device.

When I sent the spell into him, and all the energy flowed from me with it, he twitched. And I almost fell out of the vehicle from exhaustion. I was completely depleted.

With Cory and me so enervated, we had to let Mom drive us home. We'd been trying to prevent her from driving, ever since her moments of freezing increased in frequency. Tonight, though, we had no choice.

We arrived safely and got Humphrey upstairs to his room. After I initially objected, we agreed to return his firearms to his room after we put him on his bed.

When he awoke in the morning, he would have no memories of this. I hoped that between then and when he checked out, he wouldn't catch the witch-hunt fever again.

I had to repeat my explanation of why I needed to stay away from the inn for everyone's safety—both because of Lethia's retribution and the risk of other people recognizing me from the app. Cory and Mom did not want me to leave.

"At the soonest possible time, please get me an appointment with Arch Mage Bob," I asked Mom. "I want to optimize my empath abilities. I think things are going to get hairy around here really quickly, and I'm going to need all the power I can get."

CHAPTER 12

SOPHIE

I'd never been in a vampire's home as an invited guest before, as opposed to a nest raider.

Well, except for the sober home owned by the vampires who kept me captive back when I was in recovery. And the one time I peeked into Roderick's crawlspace. Most vampires would never live in the cramped, musty room Roderick had been sealed inside as punishment. For some reason, probably stubbornness, he had never abandoned it, even after Mom freed him.

As I crossed the empty parking lot behind "14 Granada Street," Diego's restaurant, I was full of anticipation—and dread —at what I might find in his apartment upstairs.

Diego's vintage Aston Martin was still parked behind the building. After Diego and Lethia had their falling out and he fled from her, the restaurant had remained temporarily closed, much to the chagrin of its many devotees and the restaurant critics.

Diego has been a big deal in the San Marcos restaurant scene for years. Almost 500 years, to be exact. Sure, he had to use alibis and fake documents to keep people from figuring out the dude had been in this town since shortly after it was founded by the Spaniards in the 1500s.

Years of success with his various eateries, and centuries of compounded interest, had made Diego crazy rich.

I unlocked the back door that led directly to the stairs. This building was at least a couple hundred years old, but it was still younger than its owner. It seemed odd that Diego lived in a modest apartment above his restaurant when he could afford a mansion on the beach, but I guessed keeping a low profile was smart for a vampire.

The wooden stairs creaked, and I paused. Was some whacked-out human lurking here hoping to destroy a vampire? You never knew nowadays.

Along the wall of the stairwell were pen-and-ink drawings of San Marcos street scenes over the centuries. All of which Diego would have seen in real life with his own eyes.

At the top of the stairs was another locked door. I used the key and entered the vampire's lair.

Hmm, I guess a better label would be the vampire's designer show home.

Sumptuous living and dining room areas filled the large open space, with an eclectic mix of antiques and contemporary furnishings. To my left was a small room that served as a library. Beyond the dining area was an open kitchen. Because of Diego's culinary prowess, this was the best-equipped private kitchen I had ever seen, with two sinks and three ovens, plus a giant six-burner gas range with copper pots hanging above it.

I walked through the kitchen and down a hallway, past a laundry room and an en-suite guest bedroom. At the end of the hall was the master suite with its own bath and sitting room.

The master suite was unlike the rest of the condo. In here, where only Diego and his lovers went, it looked like one of the

San Marcos historical museums. No sleek modern furniture or delicate antiques—this was heavy, crude wooden furniture like the earliest colonists built.

The four-poster bed was low to the floor, and I half expected to see a straw mattress, but, no. I peeked under a luxurious duvet to confirm that Diego had a comfortable modern one. Aside from the electric lights, all the chests, table, and chairs in here looked like they were from the sixteenth and seventeenth centuries.

Were they originals? They appeared to be. If not, then Diego was so nostalgic he had them built to remind him of his early days in San Marcos.

When he had been turned.

He'd never told us who the vampire was who turned him and how the creature had gotten to the New World. Maybe the indigenous people had vampires, too.

I shouldn't be poking around in Diego's private space, but my curiosity overwhelmed me.

As I stood beside his bed, I picked up the scent of his unique cologne. There was also a man-smell lingering above the sheets, which hadn't been laundered in a while. But there was something different about his scent than that of boyfriends I'd had.

It was the fact that Diego was undead. His body probably functioned like a living body, but I guessed some functions weren't the same. Vampires didn't sweat as much as living humans and didn't produce as much skin and hair oil. Who knows, maybe their skin cells didn't shed as often as ours. And, of course, their digestive system worked differently.

His bathroom was luxurious and completely modern, which relieved me, because if it had been true to the sixteenth century, then it would have meant Diego was one weird dude.

There were no stray hairs in the sink or on the counter. I

noticed things like that, because witches often use hair to tie our spells to people. But it got me thinking: when vampires lose a hair, does it instantly disintegrate like their bodies do when they're killed?

On the bath counter, I spotted a small silver picture frame. In it was a daguerreotype of an unfamiliar young woman. I couldn't tear my eyes away from her.

Was she his lover? The image was obviously taken long after Diego had been turned. But was she a human then, or a vampire? Did she still exist as a vampire today somewhere, or did she pass from the earth centuries ago? Did he still feel love for her?

Diego must have had so many memories, and so many secrets, after all his years of existence. Could he remember them all, or were there too many? Did he still savor them, or did any haunt him?

It bothered me a little that I was thinking this intently about Diego's personal life. Was being in his intimate personal quarters influencing my thoughts? If I truly was an empath, I supposed I would be hypersensitive to his emotions, even if he wasn't here with me.

It definitely wasn't because I was interested in him. Nope. No way. I would never be interested in a vampire.

I went to bed in his guest bedroom, which was tidy and sterile and didn't trigger any thoughts of Diego's romantic history. And I vowed to stay out of his master suite for the rest of my time here, however long that might be.

I SLEPT LONG AND HARD. WHEN I GOT UP IN THE LATE morning, I found the crackers and some instant coffee he kept for human guests. A coffee maker sat on the counter, but there was no real coffee to be found.

I realized Diego, a true gourmet, would only drink coffee made from the freshest, most recently roasted and ground beans. He wouldn't leave any lying around to grow stale, especially if he knew he would be absent from his apartment for a long time.

I was watching cable news when Mom called my cell phone.

"Are you safe?" she asked.

"I wouldn't have answered the phone if I wasn't."

"What's Diego's place like?"

"Impeccably tasteful." I decided not to mention his nostalgic sixteenth-century bedroom furniture.

"I figured as much. Look, dear, I convinced Gloria to make a house call to Diego's place, so you didn't have to go out in public to travel to her shop. She'll be there in an hour, okay?"

"I'm not going anywhere."

"And Bob graciously agreed to stop by tonight after sunset, although he's not sure his magic can help you."

"I'm not sure either, but it's worth a try."

I thanked her and promised to let her know if I would be staying anywhere else.

After watching another hour of cable news, hoping to not hear anything about the Great Unmasking in Florida, I was relieved when the doorbell rang, and I could end my torture.

I went downstairs to greet the petite elderly woman with straight silver hair.

"Thank you so much for coming here," I said, hugging her.

"I wouldn't want you to be attacked by the rabble rousers. It's only a matter of time before they come after us psychics, too. My shop makes it all too obvious what I am."

Gloria offered "Psychic Consultations" in a storefront near

the tourist district. It was much classier than the kind of fortune tellers you find next to pawnshops and tattoo parlors. Despite this, she offered the services you would expect, such as tarot card readings, crystal-ball consultations, palm reading, and contacting your departed loved ones.

I led her upstairs.

"Can I offer you anything? All we've got is bottled water and instant coffee. And some stale crackers."

"Nothing for me, thank you." She sat on the sofa and looked around, shivering. "I've never been in a vampire's home before. It makes me uncomfortable."

"Really?"

"Yes. The psychic in me senses that people have been preyed upon here."

"I didn't sense that. I guess I'm not much of an empath after all."

"We'll see, Sweetie. Pull that ottoman over here and sit on it, facing me, so I can do a reading of you."

After I complied, she leaned forward and placed her palms on each side of my head. I didn't move, and she didn't speak for what seemed like an eternity.

"Oh, yes," she finally said. "You have psychic abilities. They bloomed in you after you reached adulthood, just like your mother. And, yes, you're an empath. I'm just trying to isolate what kind you are. Certainly, an emotional empath, not a physical empath, or a geomantic empath. You're not a psychometrist, like your mother, but I sense just a bit of telepathy like she has. There are many types of empaths, and they can blend in different ways."

Something caught my eye. Behind Gloria, leaning against a sofa table, was Sage. She smiled at me and gave a silly wave.

Sage was a ghost, though also a member of the Memory Guild along with Gloria and Mom.

"Hi, Sage," I said.

"Sage is here?" Gloria asked, surprised. Never taking her hands from my head, she looked behind me. "I don't see her."

"She's close enough for you to touch. You're the medium. You're connected with her more than anyone else is."

"Ah, now I see her."

"Sophie spotted me before I fully manifested," Sage said with amusement. "I believe she's a medium, too."

"Let me see." Gloria resumed her focus on me. "Well, wouldn't you know it? Yes, you're a medium empath, too, Sophie."

I wasn't sure if this was a useful ability or not.

"What's the difference between that and what you are?" I asked.

"Very little. It's more a matter of semantics, how our abilities came to us, and how we developed them. You're clearly sensitive to spirits. If they're near you, you should be able to sense them, how they feel, and what they want to say. We'll see if you learn how to track them down in the afterlife and summon them for a conversation."

This explained why I had experienced the wraith's emotions. But I didn't see how this ability to connect with spirits would be helpful to me, unless I wanted to charge clients to speak with their Great-Grandma Mildred.

"You've got some power in you, girl," Sage said. "We ghosts are attracted to that. That's why I hang out with Gloria all the time."

"I thought it was because we're friends, Sweetie."

"Um, yeah. That too."

"So," I said to Gloria, "I'm an emotional empath *and* a medium empath?"

"Yes, but it's not as if they're job titles. You're basically a psychic, like me and your mother. You're especially sensitive to the unseen elements of the world that aren't picked up by the five senses. That includes being able to sense supernatural stuff. Psychics have specific strengths, and yours involve emotions. Does that make sense?"

"As much sense as anything that is completely new to me."

"With time, you'll learn more about your abilities and how to control them."

And that's why I wanted to see Bob. Being a witch, I knew there were innumerable ways that magic could enhance one's normal human abilities. I wanted to be powerful at something other than killing.

"Thank you, ladies, for coming by," I said. "This has been very enlightening."

"CAN I OFFER YOU ANYTHING?" I ASKED BOB AS HE STOOD IN Diego's living room, his nostrils flaring like a dog sniffing for squirrels. "I only have bottled water and pints of blood."

"Is the blood past its expiration date?"

I checked the fridge. There were four pint-sized bags of blood on the top shelf, the IV-style, clear-plastic receptacles you find in hospitals and blood mobiles. I studied each of them.

"They're good until the end of the month," I said. "There's an O-positive and the rest are AB negatives."

"Awesome, I'll take the O, dude."

I put the bag in the microwave for just under a minute and

handed it to him. A box of sippy straws with pointed ends sat on the counter nearby. Bob took a straw and punctured the top of the bag. I turned away when he began to slurp the crimson liquid.

"So, have you been affected by the Great Unmasking?" I asked, awkwardly trying to make conversation.

"I, like, keep a low profile at my surf shop. There was one holy roller who came into the store and saw me walk by on my way to my office. You know, I'm not as tan as I used to be when I surfed during the day."

Not as tan? He was as pale as death. But I didn't say that. Otherwise, he was the same tall, barrel-chested guy with shaggy blond-going-to-gray hair. His beer gut was greatly reduced, but he had never had the physique you'd associate with a lifelong surfer like him.

"So, this troublemaker, he, like, started talking really loudly that I was a vampire, trying to get the other customers to leave my shop. That didn't sit good with me."

He consumed the last of his blood bag, his straw making disgusting bubbling noises.

"We took care of him," Bob continued.

"You killed him?"

"That would have gotten the police involved. No, we, like, made him change teams."

"You turned him?"

Bob laughed a deep but quiet laugh.

"Yeah, he's moving here from Iowa to work for me."

I shuddered, but part of me was glad there was one less witch-hunter to worry about, even though there was one more vampire.

"Did Mom tell you why I needed to see you?"

"Something about making your empath abilities stronger. Do

you, like, really need to weaponize *all* your supernatural abilities? Are you that angry?"

"What are you talking about?"

"Dude, you know you've got a righteous temper."

I tried not to let said temper get inflamed.

"I've heard that some empaths don't just experience other people's emotions, but can influence them, too." I explained how I influenced the troll to leave the bridge. "In today's environment of fear and hatred, maybe I can cool people down. I'm not trying to weaponize anything."

Bob looked skeptical. "I don't think it's as easy as that. Emotions are gnarly things. You try to get ahold of them, and they slip out of your hands like a fish. And once you've got them in your grip, they're often not what you thought they were."

Okay, enough of the surfer philosophy. "Are you ready to start?" I asked.

"Me? Sure. But you're the one who's gonna do all the work. I'm just here as your coach. Let's start with a magic circle. Are these real hardwood floors?"

"I think so."

"So they are. Well, this chalk shouldn't damage them."

He crouched down in an open space between the living and dining rooms and drew a giant circle with white chalk. It was a remarkably accurate circle, though two feet of the circumference were left incomplete.

"Let's get in there," he said, entering the circle through the opening.

I followed. We kneeled on the floor, facing each other, and Bob handed me a cork-stoppered vial from the satchel he wore slung diagonally over his shoulder.

"Sea water," he said. "For your elemental energy."

As a water witch, all water gives me power, but sea water provides the most.

Bob completed the last segment of the circle and said, "Gather your energies."

This was the usual routine prior to casting a spell. Focusing inwardly, I envisioned my natural psychic energy and gathered it together. Everyone possesses such energy, but those of us with the witch gene grow more of it and can amplify it. Which was what I did.

Next, I drew the elemental energy from the seawater. The vial grew warm in my hand as the energy flowed into me and joined my internal energies in my solar plexus.

I nodded to Bob.

"Now, you're gonna direct the energy into your brain and your heart," he said softly. "Pretend a spotlight is examining you—who you are, what makes you tick. Ya gotta be honest with yourself."

This seemed like a silly exercise, but I followed the instructions.

And I saw a deeply flawed woman. I saw my scars from emotional traumas, my petty resentments, my insecurities. And I saw the anger like a dark blotch on an MRI image.

Did the anger come from those traumas and resentments, or had I been born with it?

"You're struggling," Bob said. "Look at yourself with eyes wide open. You can't understand others' emotions if you can't deal with your own."

I realized that, in the past, my anger had caused me to be cruel and to do bad things. It blocked acceptance of others and ruined my happiness. Yeah, it also made me a vicious fighter and effective killer, but I wanted to put those days behind me.

More of my commonly experienced emotions became

obvious to me. We feel various emotions every day but don't always acknowledge them. Bob's magic enabled me to see them in a harsh light. For instance, there were my love of family and my loyalty, of which I was proud.

I identified feelings that I didn't know I had and wished I didn't. Jealousy. Yep, I was jealous of Lethia for having such a sweet and accomplished lover wrapped around her finger.

But I had no interest in Diego, I swear. It would be nice to meet a human just like him, though.

"I see things I want to change about myself but don't know how." My voice sounded so sad.

"I can't tell you how. I'm not a life coach. But just like you do when you build a spell, ya gotta focus on those bad things, isolate them, and work around them. Like when you've got a pulled muscle, your other muscles compensate for it."

I nodded.

"Now, forget about yourself and how you feel. Cleanse your emotions. Picture yourself as an empty vessel and wait for it to fill."

This was not at all like my usual magic-making, but I did as he said.

After several minutes, I achieved a Zen-like state of emptiness.

And then, emotions poured in, at first in a trickle, and then a flood.

I sensed Bob's affection for me, his concern about my welfare during this time of witch hunts. I also felt his regret for no longer being human, and how his immortality made him more mellow as well as more nihilistic.

"It's working," I whispered.

"Awesome. Now, try to send your own emotions outward. It's

simple. Focus on an emotion, pour all your magical energies into it, then send it out toward a target. Try me, at first."

I did as he'd instructed. It was like casting a spell, except I didn't recite magic words, and what I sent from me wasn't a spell but emotions.

"Good, dude," Bob said. "I'm wowed with curiosity and an eagerness to learn. I'm glad that's the way you feel."

Unexpectedly, new emotions from someone else came into me. They weren't from Bob. They were feelings of anguish and a frenzied need to escape.

They were coming from a ghost trapped in Diego's condo. From someone who had died well over a century ago, before Diego owned the place.

From a person murdered nearby.

"Feel sorrow no more," I whispered aloud to the spirit. "You are free to go from here. Seek the bright light and go to heaven."

A rumbling came from below, and the floor vibrated, snapping me out of my meditative state.

Gale-force winds pummeled the room, though no windows were open. An unearthly howl filled my ears.

"What did you do?" Bob asked, frightened.

I had released the anguished spirit from its confinement. But instead of seeking happiness, it sought bloody revenge.

CHAPTER 13

SOPHIE

The floor trembled like in an earthquake. Diego's bric-a-brac danced upon the tables, and the dinnerware clattered in the kitchen. Wind blew through the apartment, buffeting the curtains, but didn't touch Bob and me inside the magic circle.

I worried about causing damage to Diego's flat, before I realized I really needed to worry about receiving damage to myself.

"Don't break the circle," Bob said. "And stay inside it."

"We'll be safe in here?"

"Depends on how powerful the spirit is."

A window blew out.

"I think it's pretty powerful," I said.

Being a vampire, Diego kept heavy drapes over the windows, so the glass didn't go flying. But my muscles tensed even tighter, waiting for the next act of destruction.

"Do something!" Bob shouted over the wind's howling.

"What am I supposed to do? You're an arch mage. You have way more power than me."

"You're an empath. Your powers woke the spirit! Communicate with it and tell it to chill out."

"Hey, ghost!" I yelled. "Chill out."

The tumult continued. Bob glowered at me and shook his head in disappointment.

Okay, I had to get my crap together. The magic session had clearly optimized my empath abilities, especially those of a medium empath, but I had yet to learn how to control them. I mean, look what I did—I awakened a dormant spirit without even trying.

I had a feeling that simplicity was the key ingredient. Pretending that the spirit was merely another person, I shut down my thoughts, ignored the chaotic conditions, and opened my heart. I was feeling for what the spirit was feeling.

Out of all the supernatural energy around us, I isolated the presence of the entity and focused on it. Gradually, emotions poured into me.

Anger. Betrayal. Frustration. Despair. A thirst for revenge.

Um, not good. It was unlikely I could convince the ghost to knock it off with the negative emotions.

No, I was an empath. I had to be empathetic. Even while under attack.

Instead of merely receiving emotions, I sent some outward to the entity, enhanced by my magic.

Warmth. Friendliness. Sympathy. Concern.

The emotions coming from the ghost intensified as it focused its attention entirely on me.

Most important, the supernatural activity in the apartment dropped off, so I didn't have to worry if Diego had ample homeowner's insurance.

"Bob," I whispered. "Can you cast a spell on me to enhance

my Spanish-speaking skills? They're pretty basic, and this ghost feels ancient. It probably knows archaic Spanish."

"No prob. Easy peasy."

He muttered a quick incantation and touched my lips with his fingertip.

"I am here for you," I said in fluent old-fashioned Spanish. I wished I could go back and retake my final exam in Spanish class. "My name is Sophie. What is your name?"

Acora, responded a thickly accented voice in my head.

It wasn't a Spanish name and sounded totally unfamiliar. Maybe she was an indigenous person.

"Are you Timucuan, by any chance?" I asked.

Yes, my people are the Timucua. This is our land, even as the Spaniards come here in droves.

"What happened to you? Why are you lingering in this place, so unhappy?"

The floor began trembling again, but it quickly receded. My questions were forcing her to face unpleasant memories. But it seemed to be the only way to free her from being bound to this place.

My home was here, built by the Spaniard I married. He was a black-smith for the soldiers of the fort. I cooked the dishes of my people and sold them to the soldiers and the people of the town that grew here.

This spirit was much older than I had thought. Her home had been on this site long before Diego's building was constructed in the 1800s.

She sent vibes that strongly suggested she had come to a terrible end. After all, why would she be haunting this place if she had died peacefully in her bed? But I didn't want to ask her what had happened. I mean, how rude is that?

I was tempted to text Diego and ask him if he knew his place was haunted by this ghost, but I didn't want to break my connection with her.

"Acora," I said, "you don't have to stay here. You can go to the land where your ancestors dwell."

She didn't respond. No supernatural activity was going on in the apartment, but I sensed her spirit was still near me.

"Acora, why are you so sad?" I risked asking.

I jumped as a loud *thwack* came from the kitchen. From my angle, I saw a long carving knife impaled on a cutting board, still quivering.

"Dude, that's some dangerous poltergeist action," Bob said in a low voice.

"She's just a little touchy, okay? I think I should—"

We both were knocked from our kneeling positions as an invisible force hit the protective shield created by the magic circle. It felt like a bus smashed into us. Bob and I had barely managed to stay within the circle.

"Maybe she doesn't want a therapy session right now," Bob said.

"I don't want to be stuck hiding in this magic circle forever."

Why was she still lingering among us?

"Acora, what happened to you? Why are you haunting this place?" I asked, figuring I would go for broke.

I braced myself for her next attack.

Instead, an ethereal face appeared only inches from mine, just outside the magic circle. The image of a beautiful young woman in her early twenties was semi-transparent, but I could see her long black hair, almond-shaped eyes, and olive skin. Her expression was miserable.

My husband, Eduardo, and I were happy, she said. Her emotional pain spread through my heart. *Life was hard in this town, even with the help of my people. But we were happy. Until the Inquisitor arrived.*

"Inquisitor? You mean like the Spanish Inquisition?"

Yes, in a ship from Cuba that wrecked here on its way to Spain. Eduardo and I were arrested because he was a Spaniard, and I was Timucuan. I had not been baptized in Eduardo's faith, though I went with him to church. I promised I would get baptized.

The face disappeared, and sobbing filled my head.

The Inquisitor said I was a witch. His men tortured me to make me confess, but I refused. I refused.

"They killed you?"

I curse his black heart, she said through her sobs. *Just as I cursed him when the flames rose to my feet. And up my legs. And my death came to me as a grace.*

"I'm so sorry." I sent her my sympathy and care.

So, now what should I do? My medium empath ability had made me find her and inadvertently rouse her. Was there a way I could bring her peace and help her move on to the next world?

"Acora, are you still there?"

The apartment was silent. Nothing rattled, and no wind blew.

"I think she bailed," Bob said. "Hopefully for good."

"No, I sense her lingering nearby. I hope I helped her, at least a little. I wouldn't want to have gone through all this drama for nothing."

"She's a ghost, dude. They're totally unpredictable. Sometimes, they act like the people they once were, but most of the time, they're unintelligent manifestations of spiritual energy, that's all. If she keeps haunting this place, you might need to do an exorcism."

"With a priest?"

"It sounded like she wouldn't take too kindly to a priest. You could hire a necromancer or learn how to do it yourself."

Frankly, I had other priorities at the moment. I thanked Bob for his help, and after he left, I rushed to the fortress to meet Diego. I was an hour late.

THE MASSIVE STONE FORTRESS SQUATTED ABOVE THE DARK BAY with its cannons facing the ocean inlet a few miles to the east. It was devoid of tourists at this hour, and the parking lot was empty. I wandered around the periphery, hoping Diego would find me and not be angry that I was late.

Although I was there only to discuss strategy with Diego, I was armed with my crossbow hidden in my backpack and my sword in my duffel bag. I was well prepared to fight vampires and other monsters. But if a common criminal tried to rob me? Sometimes, I wondered why I didn't carry a handgun.

After about ten minutes, my senses prickled as they alerted me of a supernatural presence.

I unzipped my backpack and duffel bag in case the presence was malevolent.

Thankfully, it was just Diego emerging from the shadows of the fortress's towering coquina-rock walls. That area was closed off from visitors, but he casually leaped over the moat like he was stepping over a crack in the sidewalk, then effortlessly climbed the security fence.

"You're late," he said, though he was grinning.

He drank in the sight of me with pleasure, so much so that I wondered if he was developing an affection for me. Or wanted to feed on me.

"Sorry. I had a visitor who delayed me."

I explained the visits by Gloria, Bob, and the ghost.

"Fascinating," Diego said. "I'm not surprised the place is haunted, but I've never encountered this ghost before."

"She broke a window. Sorry."

He laughed. "Ah, so she's not just a flittering specter. You're the reason she made her debut?"

"Yeah." I told him about what I'd learned so far about my empath abilities. "I didn't realize I'd cause spirits to come out of the woodwork."

"It's an interesting ability, if not very useful."

"I'll make it useful. My regular emotional empath abilities should help me influence people emotionally. I wonder if they work with vampires."

"Try them on me."

I cleared my mind and opened my senses to see if I could feel what Diego was feeling. More than a minute passed, and I felt absolutely nothing—no anxiety about our situation, no cocky arrogance. And certainly, no emotions regarding me.

Was he disciplined enough to keep his emotions in check and hide them from me? Or did he have none?

I tried sending emotions in the other direction. My strongest one at the moment was anger at the people who had whipped up the anti-supernatural frenzy that put me and my family at risk. I broadcast anger at Diego.

"What emotions are you feeling?" I asked him.

"Boredom. You see, I can block your probing. You were trying to send anger to me."

"You can do that because you're a vampire?"

"Perhaps. And I knew what you were trying to do."

"I wonder if it will work on these guys."

I pointed to three male vampires who had suddenly appeared behind Diego.

He had sensed them before my words were fully out of my mouth and had swung around, bracing for their charge. But instead of absorbing their attack, he leaped upward just as the vampires reached him.

I quickly retreated to a safer distance.

Diego's mid-air kicks from both legs knocked two of the attackers backward before he dropped onto the third vampire.

Diego and his opponents moved at vampire speed, which meant they were a blur to me. Diego wrestled the third vampire to the ground and a furious fight ended in only a few seconds.

One vampire, minus his head, was destroyed for eternity, leaving Diego embroiled with the remaining two in a slashing melee that moved from street level to midair.

I removed my weapons. I didn't dare fire my crossbow at the quickly moving targets, but I held my sword with two hands, pointed in their direction in case one of them came at me.

A wooden stake, produced by one of the attackers, flew at me, landing just inches away on the asphalt of the parking lot. It had been broken in half.

A mangled vampire landed hard beside the broken stake. He deteriorated into dust, which blew away in the wind sweeping in off the bay.

The flurry of blurred motion ceased, revealing Diego standing, holding the final vampire aloft, both hands around his neck. The vampire moved only slightly, barely conscious.

Both Diego and his defeated foe were covered with blood. In the light of the security lamps above the parking lot, I watched Diego's wounds heal. The other vampire appeared too weak to use his preternatural healing abilities.

"Lethia sent you here because you're a young vampire," Diego told him. "You're dispensable to her. She sent you to your destruction just to make me fear her. Well, I've spared you so that you can return to her and tell her I do *not* fear her. And if she has an issue with me, she can tell me to my face. Do you understand?"

The other vampire whimpered. I'd never heard a vampire whimper before.

Diego tossed his foe so forcefully that he flew out of the lighted area, and I didn't see him land.

"We must go," Diego said to me. "I would wager that Lethia will come after me tonight."

"Should I go back to your apartment?"

"That vampire will tell her you were with me tonight. She will track you down too, no matter where you hide. You'll be safer if you're with me."

"And you'll be safer too," I said, returning my sword to its bag.

Diego laughed. "I'm not so sure about that."

CHAPTER 14

SOPHIE

"You don't think Lethia can find us here?" I asked Diego as we sat on folding chairs on the rear porch of a vacant waterfront house.

"Oh, she'll find us before the night is done. Since I'm under her thrall, she can locate me anywhere. But I chose this place because her power will be diminished here."

"Why?"

"This house was built on ancient burial middens created by the Timucua. They had a fishing camp here until the Spaniards took over. This is holy ground, which will weaken Lethia."

"Won't it weaken you, too?"

His fangs flashed in the moonlight as he smiled. "As silly as it sounds, no. When I was human, I was a Christian. My beliefs were deeply ingrained in me—even to this day, hundreds of years after I became a vampire. The beliefs of other religions simply don't have power over me."

"The Timucuans' beliefs will affect Lethia?"

"Lethia was human in a pre-Christian place and time. She

didn't worship the same gods as the Timucua, but my guess is she'll be affected by their style of religion. If I'm wrong, we'll find out quickly."

We sat in the darkness and listened to the tree frogs chirp like loud crickets. The house was dilapidated, but the property had to be worth a lot, being on the Intracoastal Waterway.

"When you told me the ghost in my condo is Timucuan, it got me thinking," Diego said. "I came across the middens beneath this house about a hundred years ago, long before the house was built. I immediately sensed the psychic energy here, though it didn't affect me."

"I see."

Diego was in a talkative mood, and it seemed like his strategy was simply to wait until Lethia found us. What would happen then, I didn't know. Just in case, my crossbow sat loaded in my lap, and my sword was propped up against the side of my chair.

"Do you remember what happened to me a few years ago, not long before the Fae contagion drove nearly all the vampires in town insane?"

"Mom had mentioned something about you being possessed."

"Yes, I was. By a supernatural entity derived from the spirit of an inquisitor from the Spanish Inquisition."

"Yikes. Acora said she was killed by the Inquisition."

"Most likely by the same inquisitor. Before I turned him."

"You turned him into a vampire?"

"I should have just killed him, but I was spiteful. You won't find this mentioned explicitly in history books, but the Inquisition hunted and staked many vampires over the years. This particular inquisitor did the same thing here in San Marcos. Until I put an end to it. He was a hypocrite, an impious man who abused his power and caused countless innocent humans and vampires to suffer."

"I understand why you did it."

"He himself was staked a few hundred years later. How ironic that he should get a last opportunity to torment me by possessing me. But enough about me. I only wanted you to know about this connection I have with the ghost."

"She said she lived where your building is now," I said. "But maybe she's haunting your place because of you—of what you did to the inquisitor."

"I believe you're correct. I only wonder why she never appeared to me."

"I guess we'll see what happens, now that I've stirred her up."

Diego's need to talk seemed to have dried up, but I had questions.

"Sorry to mention this," I said, "but since we're waiting for Lethia to come here and kill us, I'd like to know how you went from lovers to enemies."

"Typical relationship problems."

"*Typical?*"

"For vampires, I mean. She's more powerful than I am because of her longevity. She claims to be the oldest vampire on earth, after all. I'm fine with being less powerful. But she runs the Clan of the Eternal Night like all its members are her slaves, and I disagreed a lot with her style. She's ruthless and drunk on power and uses the guild to increase her riches. She also appeared to be corrupting the leaders of the other guilds. So, we disagreed often."

"Yeah, that's a problem."

"She also began treating me like an inferior, which stung a lot. I told her I wanted a little time apart. She didn't take it well and banished me from her home. Then, she decided I must be destroyed. Why, I don't know."

"Do you think something is going on between her and Baldric?" I asked, nervous about how he would take that.

Diego's eyes fixed on me. "I do. And never underestimate the treachery and guile a faerie is capable of."

"I'd always thought he was one of the good ones. But the way the Executive Council has turned out, I'm not so sure anymore. And I'm sorry about him and Lethia."

Diego looked away, out toward the water and the streak of moonlight on its surface that seemed to point toward us.

"No apologies necessary for Lethia," he said. "When you've been on this earth as long as I have, you learn to allow your heart to dry up and grow hard. It's the only way to carry on."

I guess he did truly love her and still might.

We remained quiet for a long time. Occasionally, fish would splash in the river. For a short while, came the putter of a catamaran motoring slowly past, its sails furled. I caught myself falling asleep.

Suddenly, the hairs on my arms and scalp prickled.

Diego jerked his head around toward something behind me.

I was yanked upward by my hair until I was dangling in the air. My crossbow clattered to the porch floor, and my sword was agonizingly out of reach.

I wished I had kept my hair short instead of letting it grow for my "professional" look. Stylish and great for gripping.

"Why is she with you, Diego?" Lethia asked from immediately behind me.

Diego had already leaped to his feet.

"Like me, she is being hunted," he said. "She needs protection."

"It's too late for that," Lethia said in a menacing tone. "She's your human toy no longer."

"She's not my toy. I'm friends with her mother. And after she wisely refused the Council's order to destroy me, she needs protection from the likes of you."

"No one can be protected from me. I will decide if she lives or dies."

"I lobby for letting me live," I said.

"I will kill her right now in front of you," Lethia said to Diego, "unless you renounce your love for her."

Diego laughed. "I don't love her."

Lethia reached from behind and wrapped her other hand around my throat. That meant she'd been holding me up all this time with only one hand. Impressive.

"You're not convincing me," she replied. "Shall I pop her head off and present it to you as a memento?"

"Let her go. She's nothing to me. I'm not interested in humans, anyway."

"You're saying you found your entertainment from vampires in the various nests you've been living in?"

"There has been no one since you," Diego said in a low, calm voice. "You're the one I loved, but you drove me away."

"You ran away like a spoiled child."

"I was continuously humiliated by you. I didn't mind that you're more powerful than me or that you were the vampires' leader. But you treated me like a slave."

"You would return to me?"

"If we could start over. No more abuse. And no more ordering vampires to kill me. Let's be mature, respectful partners —not like a pair of praying mantises where the male gets devoured."

Lethia laughed. "Sometimes, insects have more common sense than people."

"Let Sophie go," Diego said. "And I'll return with you tonight."

"What if I say her death is the price to be paid for us to start over?"

"That's entirely unnecessary." He feigned indifference to my fate. At least, I hoped he was feigning.

"Kiss me," she said, as if the kiss would be a test.

He came over to us, and Lethia tossed me behind her. I landed on the painted wood and slid until I hit the rear of the house. While being flung like a rag doll, I didn't see them kiss, so I couldn't give him points as to how convincing he'd been. He now held her in his arms, tight against his body.

"Come," Diego said to her. "Let us return to your house."

I wished my empathy could tell me their true thoughts. But no, Diego was blocking me, and Lethia seemed impenetrable. Still, reading body language was enough for me to understand that Diego still had feelings for her. Why did that bother me?

As for Lethia, she was a psycho. Her body language showed a passion for Diego, but it was of all the extremes of the passion spectrum, from love to hatred.

She pushed him away, hard enough to send him staggering backward across the porch, almost losing his balance.

She strode to him and slapped him hard in the face. Even with Diego's vampire fortitude, that must have stung.

"I don't trust you!" Lethia shouted.

Diego touched his face in disbelief. "I've never been unfaithful to you."

She slapped him again. "You left me."

"We've already been through this." He was angry now. "I left you because you treat me like excrement. Like you just did. It's wrong to abuse your partner."

"You made me do it with your dishonesty."

"I never made you do anything. I've been nothing but loving and respectful to you, bending over backward to make you happy. And I've treated Yena like she's my own daughter, even when she bites me."

Lethia had a daughter who'd been turned into a vampire by the same demon who turned Lethia. Yena was permanently two years old and had some behavioral issues, to say the least.

"Don't bring Yena into this!" Lethia slapped Diego again.

Witnessing this was getting extremely awkward. Rage at Lethia was threatening to overwhelm me. I couldn't flee from the porch without passing the vampires, so I inched my butt across the floor toward my abandoned weapons.

"You want me to strike you?" Diego said. "I won't."

"Because you're weak. You spent centuries in this backward town, running your silly little restaurants, content for Pedro to be your leader and never challenging him. When he was destroyed, you let me take over the clan without a challenge."

"Because I respected your power."

"You cringed before my power. You became my lover to insinuate yourself into my inner circle and protect yourself from my wrath."

"You don't have an inner circle. You've alienated all the vampires you lead. Fear is the only thing compelling them to serve you."

"Is that so? I must keep the fear strong, then. I must stoke it by making an example. By putting you in your place."

I was now behind the chair I had been yanked from. My weapons were within reach. I remained still, watching to see if I would need them.

OF ENVY AND EMPATHS

Diego stepped away from Lethia, studying her warily. She pointed her arm toward him, then clenched her fist, face frowning with concentration.

Nothing happened.

She shook her head and tried again with the same lack of result. She must have been trying to use some sort of telekinetic attack on him.

"You're a powerful vampire, my love," Diego said with tenderness. "But there are other forces in the world beyond your control. We're on the site of an ancient burial ground."

Lethia growled with frustration as she attempted to use the same power with both arms. Nothing happened.

"So be it," she said, her voice low. "You mock me, so I must destroy you."

In the blink of an eye, she darted to him and slammed him against a wooden post supporting the porch's roof, smashing the wood to pieces. A portion of the roof lurched downward. Diego looked stunned and unsteady on his feet.

Lethia picked up a shard of wood and pressed its point against his chest.

"Submit to me," she commanded.

"I love you," Diego said. "But I am not your slave."

She pushed the makeshift stake, and blood ran along it, dripping to the floor.

"Submit, or you will be destroyed."

"I don't care anymore."

Anger surged through me, the kind of blind fury that used to get me in trouble before I mellowed out with age. Before my empathy supposedly took over. I had to intervene. Especially since Lethia would kill me as soon as Diego was destroyed.

Grabbing my sword while I crouched behind the chair, I conjured my attack magic.

The purple lightning shot from the end of my sword and struck Lethia's upper back. She stumbled, dropping the stake, and turned toward me with a stare full of contempt.

"You? You puny little mosquito? As if you could stop me."

She stepped toward me, and Diego dropped to his knees and wrapped his arms around her legs.

"Get off me!" she shouted with a backward punch to his face. Blood poured from his nose and mouth as he crumpled to the floor.

A larger blast of lightning left my sword and struck her head. Her hair caught fire, and she was momentarily stunned, but she tamped out the flame and resumed her march toward me.

"I'm going to torture you, then drain you to the last drop," she said.

She crouched before leaping at me, and just as her legs were springing her forward, Diego's right hand grabbed her ankle.

Her leap was cut short, and she stood teetering on one leg.

Before she could free her leg from Diego's grip, I cast a spell to weaken her, drawing elemental energy from the nearby waterway. I was counting on her already being disadvantaged by the spiritual effects of the burial ground.

Sure enough, my spell seemed to work. She couldn't break Diego's grip on her ankle. In fact, she became completely enervated. Vampires, especially powerful ones like Lethia, can resist some magic spells. But not on this sacred ground tonight.

Carrying my sword just in case, I walked over to Lethia and pushed her with my free hand. She collapsed onto the floor beside Diego, completely devoid of strength.

Except for the hatred in her eyes that blazed at me. That hadn't weakened one bit.

Diego's vampire healing powers were fast at work, erasing

the wound on his chest and the other damage caused by Lethia. I offered a hand to help him up, but he stood on his own.

"Let's go," he said. We left the porch and circled around the house. "We'll leave her here. How long will your spell last?"

"A couple more hours."

"Good. She'll have time afterward to return home before the sun comes out."

"You realize she'll track us down again."

"Perhaps not. She thoroughly humiliated me tonight. Perhaps that will be enough for her."

"You know it won't be enough," I said. "She's determined to kill us, especially me. And she's going to try to finish the job soon."

CHAPTER 15

SOPHIE

It had been a couple of nights since our confrontation with Lethia, and I'd been staying at cheap hotels because I wasn't safe from her at Diego's place. I was homesick and wanted to return to the inn.

"I believe we don't need to worry about Lethia," Diego told me over the phone. "For the immediate future, at least, you'll be safer at your inn."

When I returned to the inn the next morning, Mom greeted me with a hug and said, "You need to alter your appearance and keep a low profile." She patted my cheek and added, "There are too many crazies out there who could recognize you from that app."

"I know. I'm going to investigate getting myself removed from the app. Even if I have to hire a lawyer."

"Excellent idea. But first, help me with breakfast. It's been a disaster trying to run this place while you've been away."

It felt good to be needed. I supposed. Yeah, I thought as I

filled the coffee urn in the dining room, manual labor was my true calling.

After breakfast, and all the work of cleaning up, I went upstairs to my room, fired up my laptop, and began looking into Mothers Against Monsters, the organization behind the Monster Monitor app and other efforts of the Great Unmasking.

It wasn't long before I realized MAM was a shifty bunch. There were plenty of mentions of them in the news, as well as interviews with their founder and spokesperson, Marge Moosebacher. Her recurring message was that supernaturals were responsible for all the ills of our society. But I couldn't find any meat about the organization itself.

They had a website filled with stock photos of cute kids and cliché illustrations of scary Halloween monsters that allegedly were preying upon the cute kids. Just so you know, the guilds strictly regulated creatures that preyed upon humans, and in no circumstances were kids to be targeted.

The website had buttons encouraging you to donate and a form where you could anonymously report suspicious neighbors, but there was no address or phone number for the organization.

I downloaded the Monster Monitor app for $3.99 to see if it had any contact info. Nope, just the donate buttons and the accusation form. The developer was a third-party company with no way to contact it.

With sick fascination, I scrolled through the app, through all the unfortunate citizens anonymously accused of being monsters. My profile was still there, of course, giving me chills. There was one for Diego and a few members I recognized from the various guilds.

The owner of a nearby pastry shop was in there. I'd passed her shop on the way home recently and found it boarded up. Now I knew why. I also came across the profile of a former college professor accused of being a werewolf. And, no surprise, a local political adversary of the governor had a profile. She was accused of being a witch, like me.

I was concerned that the app had gotten addresses and driver's license photos for the accused. One could find addresses on the internet, accurate or not. But getting the license photos required cooperation from the state.

My call to the Motor Vehicles Bureau resulted in repeated transfers until the line went dead. I called a local journalist who had published a story about MAM. She told me that the state had stonewalled her too when she inquired about the photos.

After all my research, the only valuable thing I'd learned was that Marge Moosebacher was from San Marcos, and I guessed MAM might be based here as well. It wasn't surprising, because as the nation's oldest city, we probably had the highest population of actual monsters.

Not that Marge would know that. She was only interested in accusing people of being monsters, whether they truly were or not.

As I browsed through various news articles that came up from my internet search, I learned Marge was a prolific public speaker. Going out there to get the yokels all riled up was important if your goal was creating mass hysteria.

And what was mass hysteria supposed to do for her? That was the big question I needed to answer if I was going to battle this campaign.

First of all, the Great Unmasking gave Marge Moosebacher a certain amount of fame and notoriety. Perhaps she wanted to go into politics. Which was the second goal of creating mass hysteria: helping politicians allied with her find electoral success and the power to exploit people.

Third, she might simply be a fanatic who did this because voices in her head told her to.

I continued scrolling, and aha! That very evening, Marge Moosebacher was to be the featured speaker at the Florida Skunk Ape Society's monthly meeting in San Marcos. The skunk ape was Florida's version of Bigfoot, allegedly seen—and smelled—in the swamps and forests of the state.

Just for the record, I have never met a skunk ape, and there was no guild representing them in San Marcos. But the members of the Skunk Ape Society would surely enjoy hearing Marge talk about all the monsters in their midst.

When I arrived at the meeting room of the Sleep Cheap Motel near the interstate, I had no strategy about how to confront Marge. I simply paid my non-member entry fee and sat in a chair near the back of the room.

I watched the true believers troop in and sit down around me. They looked like everyday people. Sure, many of them were wearing skunk ape T-shirts in various designs, but no one was dressed in a skunk ape costume. There were only three women and twenty-five men, most of them wearing wild beards desperately in need of trimming. I guessed that was as close to a skunk ape costume as they could muster.

I picked up an array of emotions from the attendees. The strongest ones were curiosity and anticipation. By far, the most powerful emotion was skepticism.

Sure, the skunk ape was real, but the supernatural wasn't?

Marge Moosebacher entered the room and walked directly to the podium in front of a large video monitor. Her skin was paler and her hair redder than in her photos on the internet.

"Welcome, concerned citizens," she said with too much enthusiasm into the microphone, though none was needed for this small crowd. "I'm Marge Moosebacher, president and cofounder of Moms Against Monsters. Our mission is to educate folks about threats against them and their children from creatures that get written off as superstition. I'm super thrilled to speak to a group like yours with the courage to believe in things others do not."

A smattering of applause. Lots of heads nodding and beards wagging.

"Did you know that in these United States, more than six thousand of the people reported missing each year are never found? And over fifty percent of murders are never solved? What if I told you that many of those cases were not solved because the perpetrators were not human?"

A few gasps of astonishment and many grunts of approval. She clicked through several slides with photos and illustrations of supernatural creatures on the monitor above her.

"Humankind has believed in witches and werewolves, vampires and ghouls, ogres and trolls—plus many, many others—since the beginning of our existence. And then the Age of Reason came along, and a bunch of smarty pants said that believing in supernatural creatures was stupid and backward. Only the uneducated peasants, they said, believed in stuff like that."

I sensed anger rising in the crowd.

"The smarty pants said that science was the true religion and the religions we grew up with were nothing but superstition."

Anger was growing more intense, but some attendees grew suspicious when she denigrated science.

"Nowadays, they say the same about the passionate people who believe in the skunk ape."

Okay, now she had them hook, line, and sinker.

"I'm here to tell you that people wouldn't have believed in supernatural creatures since the beginning of humankind if these creatures didn't exist. They hide here among us and attack our children and families. It's time to drag them from under their rocks and get rid of them like cockroaches and bedbugs."

She didn't specify how she wanted to get rid of them, but it was easy to guess that she didn't mean simply running them out of town.

The audience was scared and angry—the perfect emotions for being whipped up and controlled by demagogues. I wondered if my empathetic abilities, coupled with my magic, could soften the emotions in the room.

I didn't yet have the skill to do it to so many people at once. But I would endeavor to learn how, because the mass manipulation of emotions was exactly what I needed to do to end the Great Unmasking.

Marge Moosebacher clicked to a slide showing the home screen of the Monster Monitor app.

"You can make a difference in keeping your family and neighbors safe," she said. "Just download this inexpensive app, and you can see which dangerous creatures have been spotted in your area. You can also upload photos if you see a suspicious individual. We use artificial intelligence to assess if the creature is supernatural, then we match the individual to government records to make a positive identification."

Marge was making money off the app. Could the app be the whole reason she was pushing this campaign?

No, she seemed like a true believer with an agenda. The most dangerous kind of human.

Marge demonstrated the app by clicking through several listings of alleged monsters, with driver's license photos or snapshots taken by witnesses. My heart lurched as she clicked through my listing, but she passed over it so quickly, I doubted anyone recognized me. So I hoped, as I sank lower in my chair.

"I want to make it clear," Marge said. "Merely reporting a monster on the app doesn't take care of the problem. It warns us to keep our children away from the beast, and it alerts the police, but the police won't pursue every subject. If you have reasons to believe the suspect committed a crime, you still need to call the police. Mothers Against Monsters will pay you a cash bounty for every monster you deliver to the police."

After the app demonstration, Marge opened the floor for questions, and called on an obese man with a gigantic, unkept beard.

"How much is the cash bounty?"

"It varies on the species of monster and their danger level," she replied. "The bounties can be as high as five thousand dollars."

"What should we do if we think someone is a monster, but we're not sure?" asked a middle-aged woman who seemed sincere.

"Better to accuse someone falsely than to allow them to get away with murdering our children," Marge said ardently. "It's not yet illegal to be a monster."

Not *yet*?

"But if there's a possibility the suspect has committed crimes, the police will investigate. If they're innocent, then it all works out."

"Doesn't the app encourage vigilantes to take the law into their own hands?" an older, bearded man asked.

"Exactly!" Marge beamed. "In our cities, with crime going through the roof and not enough police to protect us, we must take the law into our own hands. If you have an organized neighborhood watch or not, the Monster Monitor is the perfect tool to keep your neighborhood safe. If you recognize someone from the app, call the police, and attack the monster."

"Are we allowed to shoot monsters?" asked a scruffy man.

"I'm not an attorney. I can only advise you to do what's necessary to ensure your safety."

"I got a neighbor," the same man asked. "He only goes out at night, and I never see him during the day. I can't tell if he's a vampire or if he just works the night shift."

"What kind of car does he drive? American or an import?"

"One of those fancy European cars."

"Sounds like a vampire to me. You should follow him one night when he leaves his house and see what he's up to."

A young woman in a skunk ape trucker cap raised her hand. "I have a coworker who's into all that New Age crap. You know, she's got crystals on her desk and burns incense, even though that's against the office rules. She also eats a lot of granola. One time, she had a book about Wiccan magic. Is she a witch?"

"It certainly sounds like it."

"Do I need to report her? I mean, she's kinda weird, but she's just a person, not a vampire or werewolf or anything. Is it really so wrong if she makes magic spells at home in her free time?"

"Yes! Witches are allies of Satan. They drink the blood of babies and cavort naked in the forest with Satan during their sabbaths. Her magic could give you cancer if you make her mad at you. Witches are worse than many monsters, because they have God-like powers given to them by Satan—powers they have no right to have."

Okay, then. I was Public Enemy Number One. When exactly did we return to the Middle Ages when it came to magic and mysticism?

I was too angry to listen closely to the other questions. Before long, the presentation was over, and as everyone filed out of the Sleep Cheap meeting room, Marge handed out bumper stickers and T-shirts promoting the Monster Monitor App and Mothers Against Monsters.

When everyone had left, and Marge was packing up her laptop, I approached her, trying to quell my anger and open my empath sensitivities.

"Why are you doing all of this?" I asked.

"Why, to keep our children safe, of course," she said without thinking.

"Is this a business opportunity for you?"

Her eyes narrowed as she realized I was a critic. "Our organization needs funding to survive. What are you insinuating?"

"Nothing," I said, trying to calm the interaction and allow my empathy to go to work. "I'm just curious about what motivates you."

Suspicion of me came off her in waves. Defensiveness, too.

In response, I sent her feelings of goodwill and trust. To fundamentally change her from being a hater and make her lose her drive to persecute the "others" of our society would require more than my empath powers alone. I would need to use magic, too. This was why I had my session with Bob: to prime my abilities so that, combined with magic, I could truly change people's hearts and minds.

I sent feelings of love and benevolence toward Marge and pumped them up with some elemental energy.

But instead of her face softening with warm feelings, her body language closed up, and she frowned at me.

"You're a witch, aren't you?" she said in a threatening voice. "I sense magic coming from you."

"How can you—"

Then it struck me. Why hadn't I sensed it until now?

Marge was a faerie.

"And you're Fae," I said. "What is your real agenda?"

Were the Fae intentionally stoking the fires of hatred and fear among humans? Was this part of a plot to weaken and harm us?

"Nice try," she sneered. "I call you a witch, so you accuse me of being a supernatural, with no proof. If you really believe it, report me to the app."

"Good idea," I said before snapping a photo of her with my phone as she stormed out of the room.

THE NEXT MORNING, I OVERSLEPT BY NEARLY AN HOUR. I would have expected Mom to rouse me from bed, but I guess I wasn't late enough to cross that threshold. I skipped showering, washed my face, threw on clothes, and rushed downstairs.

A tantalizing aroma of brewing coffee wafted from the kitchen, and I went straight for it to satisfy my caffeine craving. The oven was heating, but the ingredients for the scones were sitting on the counter. The giant cast-iron skillet sat on the stove, but no eggs had been cracked yet.

It appeared Mom was running late, too.

I looked for her in the dining room. One table had been covered with a tablecloth, but the rest of the linens lay dropped on the floor.

Something was wrong. Had Mom "gone away" again? But her physical body had to be somewhere.

I searched the entire first floor of the inn, including the bathroom and closets, without finding her. Strangely, I came across puddles of water on the floor of the hallway to the courtyard.

Her car was sitting in its usual space on the street. I texted her and called her without a reply. My blood chilled when I heard ringing in the kitchen. Her phone was on a counter beside an unopened carton of eggs.

This was not good.

Finally, I checked the cottage. Cory was coming out of the front door, ready to get to work on some project or another.

"Morning," I said, trying to keep the fear from my voice. "Have you seen Mom?"

"She went in to make breakfast about an hour ago. She's not in the kitchen?"

"No. She's missing."

"You mean, like abducted?" Cory asked with growing panic.

"Wait, let me check one last place."

He followed me as I raced through the inn to the utility room, which housed the laundry, workshop, and storage. I exited the back door into the alley.

Her motor scooter was missing.

"When was the last time Mom used her scooter?" I asked.

"She gave it up when she stopped driving her car."

"It looks like she took it."

"To escape from someone?"

I turned and headed for the parlor. "Roderick would have been asleep when Mom left, but maybe Archibald heard something."

Even in his inert stone form, the gargoyle was a busybody, knowing most of the goings-on in the inn. I called his name and waited impatiently for him to animate beneath the fireplace mantel.

"Did they return?" he asked.

"Who?" Cory and I replied simultaneously.

"The hoodlums. They were creating an ungodly racket shortly after dawn."

"I heard nothing," I said.

"You wouldn't have heard them from the third floor. They sounded like humans, but I sensed they were supernaturals. Darla started up her motor scooter, and the place quieted down. I believe they were trying to abduct her."

I tried to tamp down my anger. "Jeez Louise, why didn't you tell us?"

"I just did. This happened only moments ago. And moments for you are a fraction of a second for me."

"We have to find her," I said. "She's in great danger."

CHAPTER 16

DARLA

I f Sophie hadn't overslept—and I hadn't been spreading tablecloths like she should have been doing—I wouldn't have seen the creatures drop out of the chimney into the dining room fireplace.

The soot-covered winged creatures were faeries in their natural forms. There were two of them. One hovered above me, wings buzzing like a bee's, while he drew his bow, aiming an arrow at me like a hideous Cupid. The other flew from the room, and I heard the click of the main door unlocking.

Heavy footsteps thudded in the foyer, coming my way from whomever the faerie had let inside.

I tossed a folded tablecloth at the faerie above me, messing up his shot, while I bolted toward the kitchen where I'd left my phone. There, I could arm myself with butcher knives.

However, I was met by two faeries in human form charging down the hall toward me. One carried a hood and ropes, the other an assault rifle. They both wore black T-shirts and trousers. The faerie who had let them in was behind them, shifting into his human form, also wearing black.

It goes without saying that the three faeries were gorgeous in their human guise, as they usually were. But I should mention these guys were big, muscular brutes.

They were obviously not here to sample my scones.

I turned on my heel and hurried away from the kitchen, toward the door to the courtyard and my cottage. I didn't want to endanger Cory, but I could use all the help I could get. Along with the gun in our closet.

But the faerie with the bow and arrows had transformed into human form and stepped out of the dining room to block my path. His bow hadn't become larger, but he had more than enough muscle to stop me.

It was times like this I wished I were a witch like my daughter and mother. A psychometrist couldn't do diddly when it came to battling bad guys. And the goddess powers in me wouldn't harm anything other than unnatural mutations that posed a threat to their species and the planet.

The Fae were just another species that had the same right to be on this planet that humans had.

But they had no right to be in my inn.

I was desperate now. And, thankfully, the Goddess woke up inside me. Danu, the mother of all the earth's living creatures and its waters.

Waters.

The oven was on in the always-hot, poorly-air-conditioned kitchen. A room plagued by humidity.

Water molecules in the form of vapor simply love to rejoin their other water molecule buddies.

Taking on the Goddess's persona, I gathered the humidity from the kitchen and turned it into a dark cloud floating in the hallway. I pushed it in front of me toward the faerie blocking my path.

The sight of it confused him. Especially as it floated into him and began raining.

When I slammed my body into his, taking him off guard, he slipped on the wet centuries-old floor tile and went down hard. I tumbled over him, slid across the floor, and crashed against the French door to the courtyard.

The faerie crawled toward me, but I reached up and opened the door latch, squirming outside and pulling the door closed behind me before the faerie reached it.

I rolled down the three steps and got to my feet but didn't go into the cottage. Instead, I unlocked the wooden door in the stone wall separating the courtyard from the street. And rather than escape down the sidewalk where I would be caught, I turned right into my neighbor's property and ran to the alley on the other side of our inn.

That's where I kept my motor scooter, with its key hidden in a cranny between the limestone and wood of the utility-room window. I had been ordered by my family not to drive my car anymore because of my "going away." Sometimes, though, I snuck off on my scooter. I never had a blackout on it, and if I did, I would hopefully hurt only myself and not someone else.

My scooter and I shot out of the alley onto Hidalgo Avenue. I couldn't go too fast over the cobblestones, but I hoped to make it into downtown, where I could hide among the tourists and locals.

I had only traveled two blocks before a black SUV, engine roaring, came up behind me, inches from my rear wheel.

The vehicle gently nudged me to force me to lose control, but I maneuvered my scooter like a pro.

Few people know Old Town San Marcos as well as I, and certainly no faeries did.

Up ahead, to my right, was a walled compound containing small historical homes and an ongoing archeological dig. I'd visited there many times before, though it had been years ago. I made a quick turn off the street at a small wooden pedestrian gate and leaned forward over the handlebars to unlatch it. Thank God it was unlocked. I goosed the throttle and shot inside.

The SUV stopped at the gate, unable to fit through. Two faeries jumped out and followed me inside on foot as the vehicle burned rubber and took off around the block to find the vehicle entrance to the compound.

I bumped along a cobblestone path shaded by trees, past a fountain and an antique well. When I heard the pounding of running feet behind me, I turned and threaded my way through the narrow space between two low stone buildings in the Spanish Colonial style and jolted down a few steps.

I came across a plot of earth being excavated, covered by wooden stakes with multi-colored markers. A tarp stretched over a large pit in the center. Seeing a shovel planted in a pile of recently dug earth, I had an idea.

I dismounted and quickly tossed shovels full of earth atop the tarp. It was reasonably covered with a thin layer of soil by the time the two faeries caught sight of me. Crouched on the opposite side of the pit, I pretended to fiddle with my scooter as if it had broken down.

The sight of me so vulnerable was too irresistible to the faeries. They sprinted straight toward me, evidently not noticing the tarp beneath the thin layer of soil.

They yelped as the tarp gave way beneath their weight and

they disappeared into the pit. A flurry of curse words in Faerie echoed behind me.

I fired up the scooter and took off, knowing that the two faeries were only temporarily delayed.

Adjacent to the excavation was an office trailer and a parking lot. The black SUV barreled toward me, as if it intended to run me over.

I simply retraced my route up the steps, heading toward the gate I had originally entered. But I took a sudden detour when I saw a group of the first tourists of the day entering the grounds from the historic home that served as the museum's welcome center.

Pounding footsteps approached. The faerie with the assault rifle was nearing me.

A female tourist screamed.

If the faerie's goal was to capture me, I didn't know what the assault weapon was for. Blowing away bystanders would not help their cause. The only time faeries used firearms was when in human form, and I wasn't confident they practiced proper gun safety.

The double doors in the rear of the welcome center opened, and an elderly couple came out and headed into the compound, the wife using a walker. They froze in fear as my scooter roared past them into the building.

The faerie was close behind me. Until the woman pushed her walker into his path and he tumbled to the ground, legs tangled in the walker.

As with most tourist attractions, the only way to exit was through the gift shop. The eyes of the cashier behind the counter widened as he watched me navigate my scooter through the books and T-shirts and bags of saltwater taffy.

"There's a guy with an AR-15 just outside. Have a nice day," I said as I motored past him and out the door to the street.

My original plan to flee to a crowded place was obviously not going to be sufficient. If I wanted to escape abduction—or death —I needed to make it to the police station.

Man, I sure regretted leaving my phone in the inn's kitchen.

Sophie, are you awake? I sent the thought to her telepathically. *I need you to call the police for me.*

I was mildly telepathic, a gift I'd had all my life that was tied to my psychometry. Sophie was not telepathic, per se, but we often could communicate this way. It was partly a mother-daughter spiritual connection, but it was also because of Sophie's burgeoning psychic skills as an empath.

Sophie! Can you hear me?

No answer. She must be sound asleep. Story of my life.

Samson, I need help. I tried to reach him as I turned down a side street. *I'm being chased by a big black SUV filled with faeries trying to kidnap me. I'm heading downtown.*

Samson was not telepathic. I've found, though, that sometimes my telepathic messages get through to those who don't have the gift. It was worth a shot with Samson, though I doubted it would work.

You might wonder why the Goddess wasn't rescuing me. Because if she took me away, my body would be left behind to be snatched up by the faeries, even if I wasn't present mentally.

Criss-crossing on side streets, and avoiding the busier ones, I made my way northward toward downtown. So far, the SUV hadn't found me. So far.

Finally, I reached the historic main plaza, a park that stretched from the cathedral toward the bay and the Bridge of Memories. I had to get past it to reach Old Town and the commercial district, with the police station.

The plaza contained monuments, an amphitheater, and grassy sections with palm trees.

And today, it hosted the weekly farmers' market, packed with booths and people.

Of course, now the SUV caught up with me.

Without thinking, I gunned the scooter and entered the plaza as the shoppers looked at me with horror. If the faeries caught me here, they'd have to haul me away in front of hundreds of witnesses.

Or I'd get arrested. That seemed appealing to me right now.

I drove into the plaza and straight toward the market with one faerie on foot behind me. The SUV was dropping the others off at points around the plaza so they could converge on me.

Accidentally—I swear it was by accident—my scooter clipped a folding table at a produce booth, and an avalanche of peppers and zucchini tumbled off and rolled across the grass. The faerie behind me took a spill and landed with his face rammed into a watermelon.

With the other faeries fanning out through the plaza and the rows of market booths, I turned the scooter around. Now was the time to hit the streets again.

But the produce vendor, screaming at me in Spanish, grabbed my handlebars. I abandoned my scooter and took off running. It was probably for the best, because the scooter was too easy for the faeries to spot.

I had to blend in. So, I plucked a wide-brimmed straw hat from the head of a man dozing on a park bench, and ran into the nearest booth, slipping behind the counter.

"I'll have two beefs," a customer told me.

Two beef what? I looked inside the case. *Oh, we're selling empanadas.*

"Coming right up," I said, not sure which of the deep-fried

pastries contained beef, because the little identifying placards faced the other way.

"With a side of chimichurri sauce," the customer added.

"Of course," I replied. Where the heck was the chimichurri sauce kept?

"What are you doing?" asked a stern young woman in an apron who appeared beside me.

"I'm your new intern," I replied. "Which of these is beef, and where's the chimichurri sauce?"

"Will you please get out of my booth before I call the police?"

"Actually, I wouldn't mind if you called them. I would have myself, but I don't have my phone. I'm being chased by bad guys in a black SUV."

She whipped out her phone and dialed 911 in a panic.

And I looked up at the crowd and locked eyes with a faerie, the one who'd been defeated by my indoor cloud.

I dashed behind the booth's backdrop to where the makeshift kitchen was located. Back here, behind the booths, was a narrow no-man's-land of coolers, portable generators, crates of vegetables, and plastic boxes between two parallel rows of booths.

I ran across to the opposite row and ended up at a barbecue stand. I stood near the grill, hoping the smoke would obscure me.

Help me, Samson, I repeated in my mind. *I'm at the farmers' market. A black SUV and four faeries are after me.*

I heard someone running behind the booth, and I took off out into the crowd with a faerie close behind. Up ahead, I saw a thick throng in front of a French bakery's booth, drooling as the owners pulled a fresh batch of bread from the oven. I pushed myself into the crowd.

Then, I dropped to the ground and crawled on all fours through the forest of legs.

I ignored the squeals of surprise and angry words, squeezing through the customers and beneath the service table. When I was clear, I got back on my feet, sprinted through the rear of the booth, and headed toward the nearest street outside the plaza.

But there was the black SUV double parked on the street.

I was behind the amphitheater now, and a 1960s cover band was playing a favorite song of mine by the Mamas & the Papas.

I climbed up the rear steps to the stage, found a tambourine sitting atop an amplifier, and joined the band. Not that they had any say in it.

I hit the tambourine in perfect rhythm and even harmonized with the singers. One of them looked over her shoulder at me but smiled instead of kicking me off the stage.

Before the song ended, flashing lights caught my eye. A police car pulled up behind the black SUV.

Was this because of the SUV's double parking? Nope, a second police car pulled up.

Did my telepathic calls to Samson work, or was this because of the empanada lady calling 911?

The scene beside the SUV was difficult to make out because of a tree in the way and lots of people walking on the sidewalk at the edge of the park.

But then I saw him—Samson. He was interrogating the faerie driver.

The cover band ended their song to much applause, and I was tempted to see what they would play next. But my desperation made me bolt from the rear of the stage and rush toward Samson to save me from the faeries.

Halfway there, two faeries appeared on either side of me. They hooked their arms in mine, as if we were three friends on a stroll through the park. And they led me through the crowded plaza toward the waterfront where the crowd was absent.

We were near the busy street that curved from the base of the Bridge of Memories to the promenade along the river. The faeries stopped abruptly.

"We need to take alternate transportation," one of them said to me.

The other one wrested a sewer grate open. And there, before my eyes, he shifted into his natural faerie size and appearance, along with his black outfit. His partner did the same, then pointed both hands at me. I felt a weird sensation and realized I was looking at them eye to eye, as if we were the same height. We were. Their magic had shrunk me.

I waved my arms, trying to get the attention of a passing car. Was that Sophie's VW a block away?

With a swift kick to my butt, the faeries sent me falling into the sewer.

Into the underground world of the Fae.

CHAPTER 17

DARLA

By car, it's about a five-hour drive south down the east coast of Florida from San Marcos to Palm Beach. Via Fae magic, it was darn near instantaneous.

The Faerie Queene's Winter Palace was one of the many oceanfront mansions along the section named Billionaire's Row. From what I'd heard, the monarch of North American Fae had her main palace on a craggy mountain somewhere in Faerie. The palace supposedly looked like the Disney World castle, which is what you'd expect from the Faerie Queene.

You would not expect her "vacation home" to be plopped between a hedge-fund manager's manse and an estate owned by the heir of a toothpaste fortune, not far from a club belonging to an American president. Nowadays, even supernatural species needed to rub elbows with the most powerful humans if they wanted to get anywhere in this world.

Especially if your goal was to rule this world—something the Fae had been trying to do since humans first climbed out of the trees. The results have been mixed.

Which was why they dragged me into their affairs. After constant failures to conquer humans and all supernatural creatures, they needed a goddess to bail them out.

When my captors and I appeared inside the palace, they were in human form again and I was back to my normal size. The Queene and her court were in human form, too, when I was led into the throne room. I didn't believe this was a courtesy to me. It was simply how they lived their human-adjacent lives in Palm Beach.

The Queene looked resplendent upon her throne in her jewel-encrusted gown and ermine-lined robes, just like a sixteenth-century European monarch. The throne was on a dais at the far end of the room with a broad expanse of shiny marble floor that I had to traverse while bowing every third step, as the royal protocol demanded.

Her court gathered on either side of the throne, her courtiers wearing modern human business attire, the generals in uniform, the ladies-in-waiting dressed in chic Palm Beach resort wear, various advisors in drab suits, and the priests, including Wilference, in their monk-like robes.

I was tempted to think I was at Versailles attending Louis the Fourteenth, except for the views of the ocean through the floor-to-ceiling windows on my left. And the roar of a pack of motorcycles cruising up A1A.

"Your Majesty, Queene Ookee the Thirtieth," boomed the court herald, "I present you with Darla Chesswick, human vessel of the Goddess Danu. And proprietor of the Esperanza Inn."

I curtsied as low as I could get to the floor, which wasn't very low at my age.

"We're running a promotion now," I said to the courtiers. "Stay three nights, get a fourth night free."

The Queene frowned. "It is my understanding that we

enlisted your help in procuring a rare substance from the Elves. Why have you not done so?"

"The Elves can't procure it either, Your Majesty," I replied. "The forests have successfully kept their secret away from all intelligent creatures."

I didn't mention that the Goddess wanted nothing to do with helping the Fae get ahold of any phytolucine.

"That is unacceptable. Where is my Chief Sorcerer?"

"I am here, Your Highness." A tubby guy with a white beard, wearing a red robe and a turban, emerged from the crowds beside the throne.

"Is this human telling the truth?" the Queene asked him.

The sorcerer approached me in his ridiculous getup, a hostile expression on his face. "I wish you'd cooperate," he said to me in a voice too low to be heard by the others. "You're making my life miserable."

He placed his palm atop my head, and a tingle went down my scalp.

"No, Your Highness," he announced. "She's obfuscating. I sense insincerity in her agreement to help us."

"I did as I was told and contacted the Elves," I said. "They don't have any phytolucine and don't know how to harvest it."

"The Goddess doesn't need help from the Elves," said the Faerie Queene. "Danu could locate the substance on her own. In fact, she could coax the forests into producing more of it."

"Let me make one thing clear," I said. "I am *not* Danu. At least, not yet. I am only her human vessel and can't tell her what to do. Last time I heard from her, she did not want your people to get your hands on phytolucine and cause harm to the earth."

"Nonsense!" the sorcerer said. "We wish no harm to the earth."

"Oh, knock it off, Magor," said the Queene. "We want to

OF ENVY AND EMPATHS

harm humans and the Seelie Court. If there's collateral damage to the planet, I really don't give a hoot."

"Sorry, but Danu doesn't want me to help you."

The Queene's face flushed with anger. She turned to the group of priests standing off to the side.

"Are any of your prayers and sacrifices helping with Danu?"

"No, Your Highness," said Wilference. "They have gone unheeded."

The Queene returned her blazing eyes to me.

"You, 'I'm Just a Human Vessel,' will remain here until you convince the Goddess to help us."

"Can't do it. I need to get back to the inn to prepare for afternoon tea," I said, my voice lacking the confidence of my words.

The faeries who had captured me at the plaza appeared and seized me by each arm. They carried tasers, now that I was no longer a guest but a prisoner.

"Be forewarned," the Queene called out as the guards led me from the throne room. "I have no patience for you whatsoever."

The guards led me through the main hall, toward the rear of the palace. "Palace" was what the Fae called it. It had been built in the 1920s by a wealthy human family. The Queene purchased it, her servants hung a bunch of Fae tapestries on the walls, and they named it the Winter Palace.

It goes to show that while the Fae claimed to be the superior species, humans dominated the world. Which is why the Fae have been hellbent for centuries to topple the humans.

Their quest to get phytolucine probably had something to do with that. I assumed it would give them incredible power so they could finally put us humans in our subservient place.

We exited the hallway through a barely noticeable door into

a narrower, unadorned passageway. It must have been for servants.

Suddenly, we stopped in front of a closet. My guards opened the door and pushed me inside. I thought they were going to lock me in, but they stepped into the closet with me.

"This is a bit too intimate for me, fellas."

My skin tingled as a wave of magic swept over me. And then, the closet was no longer claustrophobic. Because the two faeries had shrunk to their natural, diminutive size—and transformed me along with them.

The guard on my right opened a panel in the rear wall at floor level and dragged me through the opening into a narrow corridor of limestone blocks. The other guard was just behind. They both produced glowing orbs they held in their palms, illuminating our way along the downward-sloping passageway.

The natural habitat of the Fae was underground, the same as Dwarves, with whom they had frequently fought throughout the centuries and often enslaved.

We passed various corridors that branched off from this one, but continued to descend until there were no longer any limestone blocks along the walls, but only natural limestone, dripping with water. I couldn't tell how deep underground we'd gone.

Finally, the guards stopped at a heavy wooden door reinforced with strips of iron. The guard in front unlocked it with a large key and pulled it open with the creaking of rusted hinges. He pushed me through, and thanks to faint illumination from a single orb on the ceiling, I could see it was a small cavern. The guard slammed the door closed behind me. The lock clicked.

That's when I saw the elf, Leighnel, lying on a mat on the floor, in chains.

"Oh, no, Leighnel! How did they capture you?" I asked, squatting beside him, tenderly stroking his arm. "Are you okay?"

"My team and I were tunneling to explore the forest root system, close to where you visited me before. It turned out the Fae were tunneling in the same area. Not to examine the roots, because they are ignorant of the secret lives of trees. Their tunnel broke into ours. The faeries were there to attack us, hoping that we'd found some phytolucine. We hadn't. But they took me to get information."

"They're interrogating you?"

"Torturing is a more accurate word."

"I'm so sorry."

"I'm sorry that you're now trapped here, too."

His elegant face was pale and strained. He had no visible bruises, but the Fae had methods of torture more sinister than physical blows.

"Are you in pain?"

He nodded. His wispy beard was patchy, as if it were shedding hairs.

"I can use the power of Danu to heal you. Sit tight."

As Danu's human vessel, I could access her basic powers, such as healing and creating fertility, without fully becoming her. I simply went into a meditative state and reached inside myself until I felt the power brewing in my solar plexus.

The few times I'd had to destroy evil creatures, the power manifested itself as a burning sensation. When healing, the feeling was of a natural spring of pristine water bubbling up inside of me. Cool, refreshing, soothing, rejuvenating.

I placed my hands on Leighnel's shoulders as soft notes of song escaped my lips and the rush of energy flowed through me, along my arms, and into the elf.

His eyes closed, and a half smile curved his lips. His complexion grew healthier as vigor filled his body.

Then, beyond my control, the flow of energy simply stopped, and I felt like my normal self again. I removed my hands.

"Feeling better?" I asked.

He nodded. "Thank you. There's something I wish to tell you now that I feel like I'm in your debt."

"You don't owe me anything."

"In my research, I've discovered something important, but I don't want the Fae to know about it."

"Don't speak aloud. I'll connect with you telepathically."

I cleared my mind and focused all my concentration on these simple words:

Can you hear me? Respond to me with your mind.

Yes, I can hear you. Can the Fae intercept our conversation with their magic?

I don't think so. But, just in case, tell me quickly.

We used to believe that the forests had always produced phytolucine, that it was a basic biological process that we simply didn't understand. But I discovered evidence that the forests only began production of it a couple of centuries ago. And that it isn't a natural process, but something the forests decided to do.

Decided to do?

Yes. We don't know if forests have consciousness or intentionality, but we've suspected they do in a very primitive but effective way. The evidence suggests that for some reason, they developed a need for phytolucine and went through mutations that allowed them to produce it.

But why? To what end?

That is still the biggest mystery. As is the question of how the Fae learned about phytolucine and decided it could help them. We Elves are so intimately connected to forests that we have known vaguely about the substance, which is why it is in our legends. It was almost as if the forests didn't mind if we knew. But they certainly wouldn't want the Fae, who are like predators, to know.

So, the forests began producing phytolucine for a purpose we don't know, I said. *Recently, though, the production has decreased. Why? Because the substance isn't needed anymore?*

I don't believe that is why. I think it is because the forests are ailing. Or they don't want the phytolucine to fall into the wrong hands, somehow sensing that the Fae are seeking it.

Wow. But why do the Elves want the forests to resume their production?

Though we do not understand the true purpose of phytolucine, we know that it is critical for the health of the forests. And, in turn, for the health of the earth. That is why we need Danu's help.

I'm doing my best to get her to do so, I said, right before my concentration was shattered.

The heavy wooden door creaked open. My two faerie guards entered, followed by a faerie wearing a crimson robe like the Queene's chief sorcerer. This faerie's head was shaved, and his ears were more pointed than other faeries'. His eyes burned with sadistic excitement.

I recognized him as one of the faeries who abducted me and took me into the sewer after shrinking me.

"Darla Chesswick," he said. "I must have a word with you. The Queene is extremely upset that you won't enlist the Goddess Danu's help in our cause. I'm here to encourage you to persuade her."

Two different species wanted Danu's help with the phytolucine, for two different ends.

The guards dragged me across the rough floor of stone and dirt and enclosed my neck in a metal band attached to a chain bolted to the wall.

The faerie in the crimson robe stood above me, looking down at me and licking his lips.

Of the two species seeking Danu's assistance, one appeared willing to torture me to influence her.

"This will hurt a bit, my dear," the faerie said.

CHAPTER 18

SOPHIE

Complaints about my culinary skills came quickly and savagely.

"How could you *burn* scrambled eggs?" asked the old crone from 304 with maximal superciliousness. "And the scones are underdone. It's like eating dough. I want to speak to Darla about this."

The old crone—I couldn't remember her name without checking the computer—was a regular guest at the Esperanza Inn. She apparently believed that gave her the right to be snotty to me.

"Darla is not here this morning," I said.

"Aha! That explains the subpar scones. You know, Darla's scones have gotten quite a reputation. Just look at the online reviews."

I didn't care. My mother was missing, and my life was in danger. At any moment, Lethia could come after me again, and if any guest happened to browse through the Monster Monitor app, I could be killed or arrested. I refused to go into hiding because I couldn't abandon the family business during its own crisis.

"Will Darla be here tomorrow morning?" the old crone asked. "It will be my last breakfast before I check out."

She was a serious antique enthusiast who lived in a city without the great prices you find in San Marcos, where practically everything was an antique.

"I hope she will be here," I replied before I could think of a good lie.

"You *hope?* Is she okay?"

"She had to leave for a family emergency, which I hope will be resolved soon."

"I'm sorry to hear that. My thoughts and prayers. And I plan to have breakfast elsewhere tomorrow."

Good. One less person to complain.

The inn was only half filled, which was bad for our bottom line, but good for my chances of surviving this breakfast. After the dining room cleared out, I endured the colossal task of cleaning up. I couldn't imagine how Mom had bought food, cooked, and cleaned every morning on her own before I moved in and helped.

It made her even more of a hero in my eyes—eyes that were welling with tears at the thought of her safety.

Cory was more of a mess than I was. I found him at the front desk checking a guest out, then resting his face in his hands.

"We need to hire a temp," he said. "If I hear one more complaint about the scones, I'm going to explode."

"Let's get Grammers to bake for us."

"I don't want your grandmother mixing love potions into the batter. Besides, that's too much to ask of her every day. We need a temp."

"How do you find a temp who's a great scone baker?" I asked.

"I don't know. The job-listing websites don't have that as a category. Nor do they filter for people who don't mind working in a hotel that's as haunted as ours, where they might run into a vampire and a gargoyle. We can't expect every normal human to be as open-minded as Bella is. We need a supernatural employment agency."

"Indeed, we do. Maybe we can get a referral from one of the guilds."

"I thought they were all corrupt now."

"Just the Executive Council," I said. "I'll contact the individual guild leaders and ask if any of their members need work."

"The temp we hire should be more than a decent cook."

"Who bakes awesome scones."

"Yes. But he or she also needs to be outgoing and charismatic, like Darla. I want the temp to host the Afternoon Tea and the Wine Hour, too."

"Shouldn't you host the Wine Hour, Cory? The family who owns the inn should do it. Right?"

"What about you?"

"I'm not outgoing and charismatic. I have a temper, you know."

"Even now that you're an empath?"

"Yes," I said wearily. "I still have a temper, but if I lash out, I regret it even more now. I have to endure the person's feelings I'm hurting."

"Neither of us has time to host anything. We need to find Darla. I've asked Detective Samson to help us, but there's only so much he can do because her abductors are supernatural, so he can't treat this like a normal missing-person case."

On the morning Mom disappeared, Samson had told us he sensed she was in trouble, and was trying to reach him telepathically, but he didn't know what was wrong. We called him shortly afterward to report Mom was missing and that Archibald had told us supernaturals in human form had broken into the inn.

After Samson heard on the police radio that a 911 caller had reported a woman being pursued by a black SUV, the police stopped one, and Samson spoke to the driver. Mom wasn't in the vehicle. He sensed the driver was a supernatural but couldn't tell which species and didn't have probable cause to arrest him.

At the same time, I was driving randomly around town, looking for Mom. I had no idea she had been at the farmers' market.

"Is it safe to assume the Fae took her?" Cory asked.

"Yeah," I replied. "They're the only supernatural species who want something from her that she can't deliver."

"What if supernatural rapist-murderers took her?" Cory's face blanched as he voiced the nightmare scenario. I felt the panic surge inside him.

"Highly unlikely. That sounds like propaganda from Mothers Against Monsters. My guess is the Fae took her under orders from the Faerie Queen. Let me look for clues that the Fae took her." I added, "If we're not confident about that, we'll file a missing-person report."

"How are you going to look for clues?"

"With magic, of course."

I BEGAN IN THE HALLWAY THAT RUNS PAST THE KITCHEN, living room, and dining room on its way to the door to the courtyard. I hadn't been able to stop wondering about the strange puddle of water I'd found here the morning Mom disappeared.

Being born with the magic gene naturally enabled me to

sense supernatural creatures and magical activity in the here and now. But not whatever messes they left behind. I needed a magic spell to enhance my limited human sensitivity.

Standing in the hall where the puddle had been, I cast the simple spell which enhanced my five senses plus my sixth. If Fae magic had anything to do with the puddle, I would sense it.

I didn't.

The magic made my vision so acute I could see individual specks of dust on the centuries-old tile. I could hear the blood move through my veins and the buzzing of a fly on the second floor. My nose scented a few drops of wine that had been spilled in the foyer during a previous Wine Hour.

You get the point. The spell worked, but I didn't find Fae magic. The puddle must have appeared naturally, like from a spilled glass.

No, wait. I sensed something odd about the evaporated puddles. And it was my sense of smell, not my sixth sense, that informed me.

The tiles where the water had been smelled of rain. You know, the fresh scent of recent precipitation. But why would it have rained inside?

The Goddess. Mom must have used her divine powers to help her evade the faeries in some fashion. What exactly she did, I wouldn't know without asking her.

And I prayed I would get the chance to ask her in person very soon.

My spell was still active, and I fed more energy into it so I could continue to look for signs of Fae magic.

I felt compelled to enter the dining room and was drawn toward the fireplace.

When I was about eight feet from it, my entire body suddenly tingled. Yep, magical activity of some sort had occurred here. My previous studies of magic under Baldric's tutelage had taught me enough about the structures of Fae magic to suggest that was what I was sensing.

It wasn't magic directed toward an object or creature. It was magic a faerie had used inwardly, the same way I was using my magical energies to enhance my senses.

If I had to guess, I would say the faerie had used the magic to shift one way or another between his human and natural forms.

So, that settled it. Faeries *had* been inside the inn, which must have been why Mom had escaped on her motor scooter.

But all I'd done was confirm what we had already suspected. What I needed to find out was where they had taken her. It could be anywhere.

Mom had had previous entanglements with the Fae. Indigenous faeries, such as Baldric, lived mainly in human form, blending into our communities. But the primary habitats of the species, especially those of the Unseelie Court from the land of Faerie, were underground complexes of tunnels and, when in Florida, the natural limestone caverns that were common beneath our state.

Mom had said the monarch of the Fae, the Faerie Queene, mingled with the billionaires down in Palm Beach. In my mind, this would be the most obvious, but least likely, place they would have taken her.

I had no way of narrowing down where Mom could be. No way other than magic, that is.

I'd never tried to locate anyone with my magic before. That wasn't the kind of spell I'd been interested in. I had preferred attack magic, like the purple lightning that I shot from Alfie. I didn't care about creating spells to look for someone's lost wallet or pet.

Or someone's mother.

Things sure had changed in my life. Right?

Well, it was time to learn a spell to find someone. And since Mom and I were of the same blood, I knew what the spell's main ingredient would be.

I went up to my room where I kept a few ancient grimoires in a bookcase. These contained directions for a wide variety of spells, most of which I had no interest in.

Ridding your herd of cowpox. Making your hens lay more eggs. Causing your rival's hair to fall out. Turning iron ingots into gold . . .

Hmm, that last one was rather interesting.

Anyway, back to the matter at hand. I had leafed through two leather-bound tomes, that made me sneeze from all the dust that rose from the pages, when I saw the small chapbook.

Blood Magic, by Josiah Engel, Wizard of the Twelfth Arcane.

The book was the size of a pocket diary, about 100 unnumbered pages, with a hard-stock cover wrapped with what appeared to be thin animal skin. I hoped the skin was animal and not human.

A former magic teacher had given me this book as a gift, not long before he met an untimely end. As a result, I didn't want to discard the book, but never wanted to read it, either. Today, necessity overruled any sad memories.

The book was a compendium of spells that used blood as an ingredient or spells that affected blood, such as thinning it, coagulating it, boiling it inside someone's blood vessels—you get the idea.

One spell that claimed to enable levitation required the blood of an aardvark. Yeah, like I'll ever cast this spell. Even over the internet, it's next to impossible to find aardvark blood unless you buy an aardvark. And I've heard they don't make good pets.

Flipping through the pages, I was nearly at the book's end,

and despairing of finding the spell I needed, when I came across one with a ridiculously long name:

"For the Purposes of Reuniting with One's Kin, a Spell that Uses the Familial Nature of Blood to Locate First- and Second-Generation Relatives. (Not recommended for beginners)."

Okay. Game on. I scanned the ingredients list and the directions, which were written like a dinner recipe.

One-quarter teaspoon of fresh familial blood. (I was already prepared to spill my blood.)

Fresh tears from the relative who is searching. (No problem. Got plenty of these.)

One magic circle.

Five red candles. (Need to make a run to the store.)

Incense made of sandalwood and myrrh. (Believe it or not, I had some in a drawer in my bedside table.)

One hair, fingernail, or similar such object from the relative you are seeking. (I would get the hair from Mom's hairbrush.)

The casting of the spell seemed straightforward enough, though there was an incantation in Latin that would be tricky for me to pronounce correctly.

I spent the afternoon before Teatime gathering the ingredients and rehearsing the incantation. Teatime felt like it lasted an eternity. Wine Hour seemed to take 180 minutes. After a quick meal of frozen dinners with Cory in the cottage, I went to my room to wait for the inn to settle down for the night.

My room didn't have enough floor space for a decent magic circle. So, just before midnight, I went down to the kitchen. Cory was asleep and all the guests were in their rooms, so I drew a large circle on the kitchen floor tiles and ringed it with lighted candles, their warm glow providing the only light in the room.

Kneeling inside the circle, I lit the incense and sliced open my thumb. In a small pewter dish, I squeezed out the required amount of blood atop a hair from Mom. I shed some tears into the dish that came with little prodding. Then, I gathered my energies and bound them to the dish of blood, hair, and tears.

It wasn't in the spell book, but I had a bowl of seawater beside me, from which I drew extra power to add to the spell.

I recited the incantation once, twice, three times, uncertain of how or if the spell would work.

The flames of each candle erupted several feet into the air like from flamethrowers, and their illumination blinded me.

Finally, an image filled my eyes. A seagull's-eye view looking down upon a mansion facing the ocean, with a two-lane road between the two.

The image faded to black until I saw a grimacing face streaked with tears.

Mom's face.

The image disappeared, and I was once again staring at a candle in the kitchen. The spell had released itself, so I broke the magic circle to allow my energies to return to normal.

Two pairs of hands clapped behind me.

"Bravo!"

"Well played."

Roderick stepped forward into the candlelight, smiling. I stepped to the wall and flicked the light switch. Archibald was perched on the wall above the counter.

"I came in here to be alone," I snapped. "I didn't realize you guys were spying on me. After you did absolutely nothing to protect Mom."

"Ahem," Roderick said, clearing his throat. "The unfortunate event happened after sunrise, and I was asleep."

"I've already explained myself, love," said Archibald. "Tell us where you found Darla."

I described my vision.

"Ah, she is in Palm Beach at the Faerie Queene's Winter Palace," Archibald said. "I told you so, Roderick."

"Mom has been there before, right?"

"Indeed," the gargoyle replied.

"How will you rescue her?" Roderick asked me. "The palace must be heavily guarded."

"You mean, how are *we* going to rescue her. It won't be only Cory and me."

"I suggest you enlist Diego's assistance," Archibald said. "He was with Darla when she visited the place. Or, I should say, raided the place."

"If they raided the Queene's palace before, won't that mean she will be extra certain not to be raided again?" Roderick asked.

"I would think so," I said. "Raiding that place would be a suicide mission."

Yet, it was a mission I felt I had no choice but to perform.

CHAPTER 19

SOPHIE

C ory and I began planning a rescue mission, debating who we could recruit and who we could trust to even hear our plans. I first reached out to Diego because of his knowledge of the Palm Beach location, but he didn't respond to my texts or calls.

In fact, we hadn't talked since I moved back to the inn. I hoped he wasn't avoiding me because he was embarrassed by Lethia's treatment of him.

Contacting guild members to help us was risky. Ever since the Great Unmasking, and the non-transparent way the Executive Council was acting, all the members had been consumed by paranoia.

That didn't stop us, though, from asking for referrals for a good cook. When you own a small business like ours, you can't simply abandon it when you face a crisis. As much as we feared for Mom's safety, we still had to interview prospective employees one by one in the empty dining room.

"What do you mean, you want me to wear makeup?" asked Trock, our first candidate.

He presented an extremely delicate legal situation. I wished we had a human-resources manager.

"To mask your green complexion," Cory said, stumbling straight into the minefield.

"This is my natural look," Trock said defensively. "I'm an ogre."

"I know," Cory replied. "But we don't want our guests to know."

"It sounds like you're discriminating against me. And I refuse to wear makeup for anyone. That's a threat to my masculinity."

"Mr. Trock," I said, stepping in. "You do understand how dangerous the climate is now, with supernaturals getting unmasked and reported? Your current position is a line cook at the school for the blind. There's no danger of anyone reporting you, except for your coworkers."

"Nope. They're all supernaturals, too."

"We're just a little bed-and-breakfast. Guests can easily look inside the kitchen and see you."

"Aside from your complexion, you could pass for a large, tremendously strong human with no visible neck," Cory said. "Would it trouble you so much to wear makeup in a color that matches human skin?"

"You're so afraid of someone reporting me?" Trock asked mockingly. "See how you'll feel when I report you to the Equal Employment Opportunity Commission."

"Now, now," Cory said. "No reason to get upset."

"I *am* upset!"

Trock pounded the table, which splintered in half, before storming out.

"Ogres have too much of a temper," Cory said. "It's okay that this didn't work out."

We had decided to hire a supernatural in the hope it would protect our privacy as witches with other supernaturals in residence. Vampires had been eliminated because we needed a breakfast cook. Zombies, ghouls, and the like wouldn't be suitable either, of course. I personally hoped to find a fellow witch to hire, but a shifter would suffice, too, as long as they didn't shift on the job.

We carefully kept track of which guild referred each candidate. For instance, if an interviewee came from the Magic Guild, we would know they were obviously a witch of some sort. Legally, we couldn't simply ask them what they were.

Our next candidates were a psychic, a witch, and a local faerie. They were all nice enough and had adequate cooking experience (although the faerie's favorite breakfast meats included lizards, which wouldn't fly with our guests). However, none were quite right for us. Especially because their scones didn't hit the mark.

Finally, Priscilla from the Shifters' Guild arrived one day at dawn, with the promise of cooking that morning's breakfast as an audition. She was tall and thin, about my age, in her late twenties or early thirties, with long black hair. Her perfume was a little too heavy, but I could overlook that.

Even though we knew she was a shifter, we couldn't ask her what kind. Most shifters I knew were wolves, except for one who was a black bear and another who was a Florida panther.

I showed Priscilla around the kitchen, culminating with Mom's variations on her scone recipes, handwritten on index cards.

"We specified that candidates should be good at baking,

particularly scones," I said. "I can't overstate how important the scones are to our guests, Priscilla."

"Don't you worry," she replied with a smile. "Scones are my favorites—banana muffins, too. I'll bake a batch using your mom's recipe. And you can call me Pinky. All my friends do."

Pinky? It sounded like something from the 1950s, but that was okay with me.

I left Pinky to her audition and went upstairs to call Diego again. I would feel more confident pulling off a raid of the Queene's palace with him because of his prior experience.

Yet, once again, Diego didn't answer. I left him a voicemail begging him to call me back. Had I sounded too desperate?

I returned downstairs shortly before breakfast time to help serve the food. Cory had already set the tables in the dining room and put out the fruits and juices on the buffet table. Store-bought sliced bread was stacked near the toaster. I went into the kitchen to get the coffee going.

And I was overcome by the most delicious scents. Banana muffins, fresh from the oven. Smoked bacon. Grilled tomatoes. Scrambled eggs laced with cheddar cheese.

And, most important, a blast of aromas as cranberry scones were pulled from the oven, intoxicating me with their buttery, nutty scent with hints of the cranberries.

I sampled a scone. Cory appeared beside me and did the same.

The slightest crunch on the outside, soft yet sturdy texture in the center, laced with just the right amount of cranberries.

I moaned in ecstasy. Cory appeared to be holding back tears of joy.

"You're hired," we both said at the same time.

"Awesome!" Pinky said, grinning. "Let's get the food out to your guests."

I placed the scones and muffins in baskets and covered them with linen napkins to keep in the warmth. Pinky scooped the eggs from the cast-iron skillet and placed them in a chafing dish. The three of us carried them, along with the side dishes, into the dining room and put the hot foods on the butane burners.

Guests began filing into the room, looking like they'd been hypnotized by the food scents.

"Oh, my lord, these scones are marvelous," said Mrs. Peters, a regular guest. "Darla must have returned."

"Not yet," Cory said. "We have a new employee to help us."

Pinky waved from the doorway.

"An undeniable success," Cory said as we cleaned up after breakfast was over.

"Great job, Pinky," I said. "If you don't mind my asking, how did you get that nickname? You're not wearing any pink?"

"Pinky rhymes with stinky," she replied.

"Oh." I didn't know how to answer.

"You know I'm a shifter, don't you?"

"Yes."

"I'm a skunk shifter."

"I didn't know there were skunk shifters," Cory said.

"There aren't many of us around here. You see, we're kind of territorial."

"Um, can you control your shifting?" I asked.

"You mean, am I influenced by the full moon like were-wolves? Nope. I shift whenever I want, but it's mostly at night."

"Do you, ah, spray?" Cory asked uncomfortably.

"Only if I need to. When dogs come after me. Or humans who are total jerks."

Good to know. I resolved to always control my temper with Pinky.

"Since I'm supernatural, my spray is much more potent than

normal skunk spray. I put an attempted mugger in the hospital once."

"Wow," I said.

"Wow," Cory echoed.

After an awkward silence as we scraped pans and loaded dishes in the dishwasher, Pinky spoke up.

"Other than my occasional nights rummaging around garbage cans, I'm perfectly normal. And that's a good thing now that everyone's on a witch hunt for supernaturals."

"I know," I said. I was tempted to confide that I was in the Monster Monitor app but stopped myself. You simply couldn't trust anyone these days.

My phone rang. It was Diego, finally. I went outside so I could speak to him in privacy.

"I thought you were blowing me off," I said like a sullen teenager.

"Sorry. I've had issues. I need to reopen my restaurant before I go bankrupt, but there are so many hurdles. There's Lethia, but after our confrontation, I'm more confident she won't destroy me. Then there's one of my suppliers. Somehow, he found out I'm a vampire, and he's threatening to report me if I don't continue ordering from him—but at twice the price."

"I haven't exactly had a peaceful time lately," I said.

I told him about Mom's abduction by faeries and where my blood spell located her.

"They took her to Palm Beach?" he asked, with dread in his voice.

"Yeah. Since you went on a raid there, I was hoping you could help us rescue her."

Diego was silent. I tried unsuccessfully to read his emotions.

"You don't have to take part if you don't want to, but we need you to give us intel on the Queene's palace and what to expect," I pleaded.

"It's hardly a palace. Just a big gaudy mansion. And there's something you haven't considered. The Fae would never keep a valuable prisoner like Darla above ground. She's probably underground somewhere, reduced in size magically so she could fit in the faerie tunnels. You or I could not physically reach her and bring her out."

I hadn't thought of that.

"Maybe I can learn the magic and shift myself," I said.

"The faeries shift naturally. It's an ability that's inherent to them, like with any shifter."

"Like a skunk shifter?"

"What are you talking about?"

"Never mind. Look, Mom doesn't have the ability to shift. If the Fae can shrink her, they're using magic externally."

"Fae magic that they're born with."

"What if I can learn the magic that does it? Even though I'm not Fae, maybe I can create magic that produces the same effect."

"I wouldn't know."

"Baldric taught me many spells based on Fae magic. I'm going to see if he can help me."

"Good luck with that."

He clicked off before I could ask him again to accompany us to Palm Beach.

I DIDN'T EXPECT BALDRIC TO ANSWER MY CALL OR RETURN IT. And I wasn't disappointed. So, I drove to his auto shop and walked directly into the work bay without any employees stopping me.

I recognized his legs poking out from beneath a red Maserati by his fancy shoes. Only someone like Baldric would wear them in the shop. He must have protected them with magic.

"Excuse me, Baldric," I said in my cheeriest voice. "I have a quick question for you."

He rolled his creeper out from beneath the car. "Ah, Sophie. What do you need?" He wasn't exactly unfriendly, but there was a wariness about him.

I explained what had happened to Mom, believing I could trust him since he was not allied with the Queene's court.

"Could you teach me the magic I'd need to shrink myself to fit into faerie tunnels?"

His face darkened. "No."

"You've taught me a lot of basic Fae magic. Why not this?"

"It's beyond the skills of a human magician. Beyond those of most faeries. We can all transform ourselves, but only our sorcerers can transform other species. If Darla is being held in the tunnel system, a sorcerer had to have shrunk her."

"You're a sorcerer. You can teach me how to do it."

"No, I cannot," he said, angry. "End of conversation."

I stood there for a moment, stung. When he rolled back beneath the car, I walked away.

Baldric used to be so sweet and eager to teach me. I wished I knew what had soured our relationship.

I walked past the office and through the waiting room. Only one customer was sitting there, and he caught my eye because he looked familiar. I couldn't place him. Was he a local TV news reporter? Or a personal-injury attorney who starred in his own commercials?

Anyway, I drove home fretting about how we could rescue

Mom if she was in a tunnel and we couldn't get to her. I wondered if Bob could help me. He was the most advanced magic-maker I knew.

I'd already asked too many favors from Bob dating back from before he was turned. But he was my only hope.

When I drove past the local community center that I'd visited only when it served as an election polling station, my memory kicked in. The man I had seen in Baldric's waiting room was a state senator.

I recognized him only because he'd been on television a lot lately. He was one of the loudest politicians in raising the alarm about supernaturals.

It was odd that he would be a customer of a faerie, especially the head of the Executive Council of the Supernatural Guilds of San Marcos. It was probably just a coincidence, though.

But what if it wasn't?

"DUDE, YOU CAN'T BE SERIOUS," BOB SAID AS HE SANDED A surfboard in the workshop at the rear of his store.

"Of course I'm serious," I replied. "Why else would I drive out here at night?"

"Maybe to buy something?"

"Sorry, but you're my magic mentor now. Baldric won't help me."

"It's best that you stay away from that faerie. He's supposed to be on our side, but I wouldn't trust any faeries nowadays. You can't trust anyone, really."

"You can trust me, Bob. And I trust you. Can you help me?"

"Changing your size is, like, way beyond standard magic. It's the kind of thing a medieval peasant would believe a witch could do, like changing someone into a newt. Or like you'd see in a 1960s sitcom—*Bewitched* or *I Dream of Jeannie*—where you twitch your nose and turn your neighbor into a cat."

"Fae sorcery can do it."

"Yeah, and that's serious magic that few witches could ever do. Their magic is built on a different system from ours. Faeries have their innate magic, but they also have a special gland that does the biological work. Using magic alone to change someone's size is a heavy lift. Only Fae sorcerers can do it."

"Could you do it?"

"Uh, yeah, I guess."

"You guess?"

"I'm an arch mage. I can do it. I think."

"Could I do it if I had extra energy from ley lines?"

"No. You don't have the training to do it."

I explained the very rough outline of a plan that Cory and I discussed. It was a bit nutty. We'd have to get into the palace somehow, distract the guards, shrink me and my sword to faerie size, and find the entrance to the tunnel system.

"And I would have to go with you so I could shrink you and then make you and Darla human-sized again when you got out of the tunnels? I don't think so. I've been to the palace before. Way too many guards."

"You've been there?"

"Dude, your plan has, like, a million things that could go wrong."

"It's just a rough plan."

"I could get captured or staked. Sorry. No can do."

"What if you didn't go to Palm Beach and shrank us here?"

"I don't know about the Fae sorcerers, but if I shrank you, I'd have to keep refreshing my magic to make sure you stayed small.

You wouldn't want to return to full size when you're in a tiny tunnel."

"Heck, no."

"Well, I can't refresh the magic from this far away. I'd have to go to the palace with you, and, like, no way."

I grudgingly admitted it would be asking too much of him. Cory and I would gladly risk our lives to save Mom, but we were family.

"I'll help you in any other magical way," Bob said when I was leaving.

I drove home trying to think of alternative plans.

The solution was obvious.

If Cory and I couldn't fit into faerie tunnels, I would simply have to enlist creatures who could. A local faerie I knew and her gnome allies.

CHAPTER 20

DARLA

I felt guilty complaining that cleaning the bathroom was torture, now that I'd experienced the real thing. And I'd learned there are forms of torture that can be more unbearable than abuse to your body.

The Fae are masters at the art of torture. They use magic, combined with an arrogant indifference to the suffering of other species, like mine, whom they deem inferior to theirs. Which would include all species other than theirs. If you couldn't tell already, I'm not fond of the Fae. Now more so than ever.

My torturer, the sorcerer, never told me his name. He didn't lay a hand on me. His magic did all the dirty work while he was elsewhere.

He began with attacks on my five senses. Ear-piercing whistles that jolted me out of my stupor and filled my head with pain. Or sounds so faint I wasn't sure I heard them, persisting until I was close to going crazy.

My eyes were blinded by light and then by darkness. Or they

deceived me with hallucinations of seeing rot on my flesh or rats creeping toward me in the dim light of our cavern.

I felt stifling heat and freezing cold, plus the sensation of snakes crawling beneath my clothes. Sometimes, I was tortured the old-fashioned way, with pain—burning, throbbing, stabbing, you name the variety.

When my torturer felt exceptionally cruel, he made me itch like I had poison-ivy rashes, or his magic tickled me. Talk about cruelty.

As to my senses of taste and smell, you're probably guessing he bombarded me with noxious odors and revolting flavors. But you could never imagine how truly awful this was, beyond the nausea and retching. It sent me to the brink of despair.

After each torture session that seemed to last for hours or days, my torturer would appear and demand that I convince Danu to help the Fae obtain phytolucine.

"I've begged her," I would truthfully say. "She never answers me."

"Perhaps when her human vessel is near death, she'll respond," he would say.

Aside from denying me enough food and water, they hadn't brought me near death. Yet. Who knew what further torture they had lined up for me?

Psychological torture, that's what.

My torturer didn't need to deprive me of sleep, threaten me, or tell me lies. His magic achieved all that and more, filling me with anxiety, depression, self-loathing, and fear.

Much of these were genuine feelings I had suppressed, just as we all do to make it through life. Such as my feelings of guilt for not remaining close to Sophie after I divorced her father before she went to college. That was when she fell into bad company and had her troubles with drugs. Even the undeserved guilt I felt for slowly falling for Samson when I believed Cory had left me, not knowing he had inadvertently gone to the In Between, where he was captured by an evil wizard.

Yet fear was the strongest emotion in the Fae sorcerer's arsenal. Not just fear that I would die, but that my family would, too. As well as all my fellow humans.

Leighnel had tried to comfort me with his words while I was screaming in agony or throwing up during my previous tortures. Now he had to play amateur psychologist while I sobbed or muttered that I didn't deserve to live.

"It doesn't matter what you think," he told me. "You *must* live because the fate of humans and Elves depends upon you and Danu."

He seemed to believe what he said, and he repeated it many times while my psyche was battered. His words helped a bit, I think.

In the rare moments when I was left alone and could think, I reached out with every fiber of my being, away from this underground dungeon. I tried to summon a gateway to allow me to escape.

Gateways are portals to the In Between or to other places on earth, even other eras in history. They used to pop up randomly, such as the door to an attic in the inn that didn't exist. Later, when the Goddess appeared in me, I could summon gateways.

That was when I learned gateways were actually intelligent beings—namely, angels.

Though I called, none would come to my prison.

I tried to communicate telepathically with Sophie, but I couldn't sense her. I even tried to feel for the thoughts of my torturer, but I couldn't.

Finally, I realized his magic must be blocking my psychic probes. I wasn't surprised.

The monster was a coward. He was too afraid to be in my presence when he tortured me. Less chance of him feeling sympathy for his victim.

Until one day, he did come in and face me.

I was resting during a lull between torture attacks. I lay on the dirty foam mattress. The bolt slid open in the heavy round door of the cavern, and the sorcerer came inside. Leighnel stood at attention. My steel neck collar, attached to a chain bolted in the wall, had enough slack to allow me to stand, but I remained sitting on my mattress, feigning disinterest.

The sorcerer stood beside me, towering above me. He was in his natural, diminutive faerie state, with a disproportionately big head and a face that looked like an evil doll-come-to-life in some horror movie. In my shrunken state, I was smaller than he was. Even full sized, I was a small woman.

"You will contact the Goddess now," he said.

"I will?"

He grabbed the chain attached to my collar and yanked me to my feet.

"You will. Now."

"I can't do it unless you take down the magic barrier around this place," I said. "It's blocking my psychic energy. I need to use it to connect with the Goddess."

He waved a hand. "It's down."

"Okay, thanks. Please be patient. She often takes a while to respond to me."

I closed my eyes and did everything except contact the Goddess. I telepathically called to Sophie and asked her to rescue me as quickly as possible. I begged a gateway to appear. Only after all that did I reach out for the Goddess.

I must have "gone away," because just as my consciousness slipped out of my body, I felt my torturer yank my chain.

But I didn't care, because I was on a cliff overlooking a dark, white-capped sea that stretched to the horizon beneath cloudy skies. The cliff was on a promontory jutting out from a coastline that curved inward to a green landscape devoid of trees. Far below me, waves crashed against rocks.

The rock on which I crouched was covered in moss, and wind whipped my hair. I wondered if I'd landed in the wrong place because I'd never been in this setting before to meet with Danu.

A hand touched my shoulder, and elation swept through me. I was in the presence of divinity, but I didn't turn around to look at her. She stood too close to me.

Not everything the earth provides is meant to be harvested by humans or Fae or any creature, she said in my mind in a voice as strong as oak and as silky as honey.

"I'm being tortured to force me to request the forests to produce more phytolucine and to allow the Fae to find it."

The forests have already begun to produce more phytolucine again, and they might grant the Fae their wish to take it. This is not a matter for me to decide. But if the forests grant this wish, the Fae and humans and Elves—and all others who exploit the forests—should be careful. Phytolucine is dangerous for you creatures and is much more powerful than you could know.

"Thank you, Goddess, for telling me."

Do not thank me. I have much that I will require from you soon.

"In that case, can you rescue me from captivity?"

Suddenly, I was back atop my dirty mattress in the cavern that was my prison.

"I guess that was a no," I muttered.

"What happened to you?" the sorcerer asked.

"I visited the Goddess. She said the forests are now

producing more phytolucine, but you should be careful because it's dangerous and more powerful than you imagine."

"Splendid."

"So, can I go free now?"

"I think not," he said before abruptly walking out of the cavern.

"Jerk," I muttered under my breath.

"Are you all right?" Leighnel asked me. "You appeared to go into a catatonic state."

"Aside from having been tortured and chained by the neck in an underground cavern, I'm just great. I was visiting Danu. You heard what I reported."

"I know. I was worried about you."

It wasn't bad to have a handsome elf, who looked much younger than me, worry about my well-being. When I moved to lean against the limestone wall in a pose of nonchalance, the chain to my collar rattled.

And I got an idea.

The sorcerer had handled the chain when he yanked me around. That interested me, because I'm a psychometrist, after all.

"Excuse me for a moment," I said to Leighnel. "I might go into a trance."

I traced my fingers along the chain until I sensed a concentration of my captor's psychic energy. At that specific point, I grasped the chain in my right hand and I—

—*am tired of this insolent, ignorant human. Why would Danu choose such a flawed vessel for her return to the world? If we get enough phytolucine, and it works with our magic like the seers say it will, then we'll be rid of all humans for good. Oh, she's snapping out of her trance—*

I guess I wasn't surprised by the memory I'd just read. What an evil jerk! The Fae were developing magic that would wipe out humans, and they expected me to help them get the substance that would enable them to do it? No way.

"You did go into another fugue state," Leighnel said.

"I have an ability called psychometry that enables me to read people's thoughts and emotions from objects they touched when they experienced them. I read what the sorcerer was thinking when he held my chain. And it wasn't good."

"Pray tell."

"The Fae believe the phytolucine will give their magic the ability to destroy the human race."

"The data I've collected suggests phytolucine is important for the health of the forests. It's just like the Fae to take something beneficial and turn it into a tool of evil. We must prevent them from obtaining it."

"As of now, they don't know how to harvest it," I said. "You're the one who's researching how to do it. Shouldn't you end your research?"

"Even if we did, the Fae could still discover how. Certainly, they're trying to do so."

"They're not as attuned to the forests as you Elves are."

"As you well know, the Fae will torture to get what they want. If their attempts fail, don't be surprised if they try to force you to get Danu to help them."

"She would never help them. And, honestly, I don't think she knows or cares how to harvest phytolucine. She's an earth-mother goddess. Deities don't worry about technical details."

A shimmering vertical disc appeared, hovering above the cavern floor near me. It was an angel serving as a gateway!

"Speaking of divine entities," I said, "my ride is here. And I'll take you with me, Leighnel."

You summoned me, but I cannot help you, said the angel's voice in my head.

"Why not?" I asked aloud.

Because you are chained to the wall.

"What do you mean? When I walk into a gateway, I'm teleported out of my environment. I would leave the chain behind."

Haven't you noticed that when we transport you, you arrive at the destination with all your clothing on, including objects on your person? The collar you are wearing would come with you. But it is chained to the wall.

"You're an angel. Can't you break the dang chain?"

The shimmering disc disappeared. The gateway had gone.

"This is embarrassing," I said to Leighnel. "Sorry to get your hopes up."

"The laws of physics must be respected."

I couldn't disagree more. But here I was, stuck underground. My only hopes for escape lay with the Goddess. Or with my daughter.

I prayed that Sophie had heard my telepathic calls to her.

CHAPTER 21

SOPHIE

Sophie, can you hear me? This is your mother. Please, please help me. The Fae are holding me prisoner beneath the Faerie Queene's Winter Palace. They're forcing me to get Danu to help them.

Mom's words came into my head as I lay in my bed, sleepless, at 3:30 a.m. At first, they were as clear as if she were whispering in my ear. But after the part about Danu, I heard only fragments of words before her voice faded entirely.

We could no longer wait for the rescue mission to begin.

GORKEE WAS WHAT MOM WOULD CALL A GOOD FAERIE. SHE was a local, not a subject of the hostile Unseelie Court. She was even dissatisfied with Baldric, the leader of her guild.

"I think he's taking money from the Faerie Queene and bribing human politicians," Gorkee said to me when we met in a coffee shop in the tourist district of San Marcos. She was in human form, of course.

That might explain why I saw a state senator in Baldric's auto repair shop.

"I'm glad you're willing to talk to me about what happened to my mother," I said. "Baldric doesn't want to help me."

"I would do anything for your mother after she helped us thwart the court's attempt to invade San Marcos two years ago."

"Mom told me about how you led a raiding party of gnomes into faerie tunnels outside of town."

Gorkee beamed. "A very successful raid. I'd wanted to get revenge against the Unseelie Court ever since they killed my cousin when I was young. I recruited the gnomes because they're excellent tunnel fighters, and they hate the Faerie Queene because she seized much of their territory. We wouldn't hesitate to fight her again."

"Good. Because you're my only hope for rescuing Mom from the Queene."

Gorkee's smile faded. "Oh. You want us to raid the tunnels beneath the Queene's Winter Palace? They're much different from the tunnel network we raided. The tunnels beneath the palace have tons of security, I'm sure."

"Yeah, but this time, you'll have magic backing you up. And we plan to distract the guards with some kind of attack above ground."

"I don't know. The raid I led before was just against common foot soldiers. I'm sure the Queene has her best-trained soldiers stationed at the palace and plenty of magic wards guarding the tunnels. I don't see how we can penetrate the defenses."

I, too, worried that my magic would be ineffective if I remained above ground during the raid. I could cause a lot of damage up there, but I probably couldn't disarm whatever wards Gorkee and the gnomes encountered inside the tunnels.

"I need to go down there with you, to make my magic the

point of the spear," I said. "Baldric says only a sorcerer of the Fae can transform me to faerie size."

"That's correct."

"Do you know where I can find one?"

"I don't know of any faerie sorcerers who aren't subjects of the court. Aside from Baldric, of course."

"He already said he wouldn't help me."

"We have no choice, then. I will lead the gnomes through the tunnels, and you'll help as best you can," she said with a fatalistic tone.

I struggled to think of other options, until an overlooked one popped into my head.

"Of course!" I exclaimed. "The Elves can help me!"

"How?"

"Mom told me they turned her into a squirrel. They could do the same to me!"

"Er, squirrels don't go underground. Perhaps the Elves could transform you into a mole or something."

"No, moles don't have gripping paws like squirrels do. I'll need to hold my miniature sword."

"A squirrel brandishing a sword."

"Yes."

"Perhaps you should re-think this."

Meanwhile, Mom was still being held captive, and time was running out.

"I'll work some more on planning," I said, "if you can put together a company of gnomes. Let's talk again very soon."

"DARLA IS *MISSING*?" MY MATERNAL GRANDMOTHER, SADIE,

asked after Cory blurted out the news when we were barely through the front door.

"Yes," Cory said, swallowing hard. "We thought you should know."

He had insisted we tell Grammers about Darla. I didn't want to tell her, especially not in person. Why freak her out when we hadn't even tried to rescue her daughter yet? But Cory prevailed.

"Did she leave you for another man?" Grammers asked him. "Or did she go to that alternate plane of existence that you guys disappear to?"

"The In Between? No," he said. "And no, she didn't leave me for another man."

"The Fae took her," I said. "Sort of like a hostage, I think. We're organizing a mission to rescue her, but it will be danger-ous. We wanted to keep you updated."

"Well, come in and sit down."

I would rather have cut the visit short, but I followed as she led us through the crowded Victorian home to the kitchen, the only room on the first floor where you could hang out. This home, where Mom had grown up, had been turned into an antique store after my grandfather passed away. Grammer's hoarding instincts had flowered, and she filled the structure with a crazy mixture of kitsch and quality.

Grammers named the business Elegant Eras. Mom called it the Junk Emporium. I found it charming, if a little overcrowded with stuff.

"Are you attacking the Fae with your magic?" Grammers asked me dubiously.

She, too, was a witch. In fact, I had no doubt I inherited the magic gene from her after it skipped a generation with Mom. But Grammers was a kitchen witch who dabbled in minor, harm-less spells, such as love potions for lonely neighbors.

"Yes," I replied. "I'll use my attack magic, but we have gnomes on our side to storm the faerie tunnels."

"There are gnomes in Florida?"

"Yes, and they're fearsome fighters. They're not like those adorable garden ornaments."

"I have some of those for sale."

"Of course you do."

"I'll give you a family discount."

"We have no need for gnomes," Cory said. "Fake ones, that is."

"Will your real gnomes be able to rescue Darla?"

"Yes," I said, though I was only mildly confident.

"Is her life in danger?"

"No," I lied. "The Fae need her because of her connection to Danu."

Honestly, I feared the Fae would kill Mom once she was no longer useful to them. I hung my hopes on the loyalty of Wilference, whom she had once helped, and the Queene, whom she—with the power of Danu—had healed.

Still, loyalty only got you so far when you were dealing with the Fae.

"Is there any way I can help?" Grammers asked.

"As a matter of fact, yes," I said, leaning toward her across the kitchen table, desperate to change the subject. "Scones. We need help with scones."

"Darla's recipe is based on mine. Don't you have it written down?"

"Pinky's scones are perfectly fine," Cory said.

"Pinky?"

"Our temporary cook," I said. "The guests seem to like her scones, but if she doesn't work out, I'll need help. I'm horrible at baking."

"Why won't she work out?" Cory asked.

"You can't depend on a temp to stick around. Also, she wears too much perfume. It drives me crazy."

"Pinky is a were-skunk," Cory explained to Grammers.

"There's such a thing as were-skunks?"

"Skunk shifter is her preferred classification. Anyway, I was wondering if you could bake scones for us if we need you."

"Of course," Grammers said. "But I want you to get Darla back."

WHILE I WAS FOCUSED ON RESCUING MOM, THE WORLD WAS continuing to descend into madness. That was clear the moment I saw the news on TV.

"Today in Tallahassee, three days after they were called here for a special session," the news anchor breathlessly announced, "the Florida House and Senate have both passed a sweeping bill that outlaws all supernatural and paranormal activities in the state. It also makes it illegal for any supernatural creature to live in the state. The bill is headed for the governor's desk, and she vows to sign it immediately."

"Jeez Louise," I murmured aloud. I couldn't believe it. This was insane.

A panel of so-called experts discussed the ramifications of the new law, but the buzzing sound in my head was so loud I could barely hear the commentary. I picked up snippets about the police now having the power to arrest supernatural offenders and the state attorneys having the power to prosecute them. People were encouraged to make citizens' arrests if necessary.

After the Great Unmasking began, journalists and government officials were careful not to talk about vampires, witches, and the like. They spoke in the vaguest of language about "supernatural offenders."

On social media, though, there was plenty of talk about us, especially from groups like Mothers Against Monsters.

But now, on cable news, I was looking at my screen filled with bullet-pointed lists of the offenders subject to arrest, including "witches, warlocks, wizards, psychics, lycanthropes, vampires, trolls, ogres," and dozens more.

It was a nightmare—for the creatures that are the stuff of nightmares.

I wasn't sure how much legal impact the new laws themselves would have, but I expected they would throw tanks of gasoline on the already inflamed public hysteria.

I left my room and went downstairs to share the news with Cory if he hadn't already heard. Low male voices came from the kitchen.

Samson and Cory were standing across from each other at the butcherblock island. They looked up nervously when I came in.

"I take it you two have heard the news?" I asked. "How bad is it going to be?"

Samson said, "The state attorney general has spread the word to all law-enforcement agencies to make this a priority. The governor said she wants to see arrests and prosecutions."

"How much of this is political theater?" Cory asked.

Samson snickered. "All of it. But it's theater with real-world consequences." He turned to me. "I was telling Cory that the Esperanza Inn is very vulnerable. Being so historic, with a reputation for hauntings, will make it a prime target of vigilantes. And no one even knows yet that you have a vampire and a gargoyle here, or that the owners are psychics and witches."

"We have a skunk shifter working here now, too," I said.

"Wonderful. Anyway, I'm going to open a case against the inn based on anonymous allegations of supernatural activity."

I gasped.

"Let me finish. It's a shell case, with no actual evidence. But I will own it. Any reports or allegations that anyone makes will have to go through me, and I'll bury them. For as long as I can."

"Thank you. I guess."

"Detective, how are you going to protect yourself?" Cory asked.

Samson shrugged. "I am what I am, a werewolf. I keep my personal life private, and I've earned a lot of seniority and respect on the force. All I can do is hope for the best."

"Why haven't I gotten any warnings or advice from the Magic Guild?" I asked.

"Maybe it's too early. The police were tipped off in advance that this was coming, but most people are only finding out now. And I'm not sure if we can trust the guilds."

"They're supposed to protect us, but they have lists of all of us," Cory said.

"The Executive Council has been acting suspiciously lately," I said. "Especially Baldric. I saw Senator Poxton getting his car repaired at Baldric's shop the other day."

"He was a co-sponsor of the bill," said Samson.

"And I heard Baldric has been bribing state legislators."

"It seems clear enough to me," Cory said. "We can't trust the guilds."

The three of us eyed each other warily. Waves of anxiety and distrust came from the men. And me, too.

"Let's resist the temptation to succumb to paranoia," Samson said. "Or we won't be able to trust anyone at all."

"Maybe we shouldn't trust anyone," I muttered.

"I wish Darla were here," Cory said. "She's the heart and soul of our family and this inn. She would give us the strength to get through these trying times."

"Working on it," I said. "The Fae picked a bad time to abduct her, that's for sure."

What Cory said was true, and it gave me a realization. Amid the love and gratitude I'd felt for Mom, I'd also been a bit envious. She was strong and brave, single-minded in her drive to be a successful innkeeper. Compared to her, I was a mess.

I had no real career. I had gone from making money waiting tables to making money serving breakfast and staking vampires. My powers of magic and empathy ought to be put to better use.

A pop and a scraping of wood came from the kitchen wall, and the older and smaller of the two refrigerators rolled on squeaky wheels away from the wall.

Roderick stepped out, adjusting his faded black-silk cravat.

"Good evening, everyone," he said. "Oh, hello, Detective. I thought I heard your voice. I also heard words claiming that Darla is the heart and soul of this establishment." He smiled at Cory and me, but his eyes were serious. "That is actually *my* role."

I snorted in derision. Cory frowned. It sounded like Roderick had his own issues with envy and insecurity.

"Indeed," Roderick continued. "Need I remind you that I am a previous owner?"

"You never cease to remind us," Cory said. "You went bankrupt, and the bank foreclosed on the inn. There have been four owners since then, not counting Darla and me."

"But I have been residing here, as a human and a vampire, ever since I purchased the inn in 1887."

"They weren't talking about whose physical presence has been here the longest," Archibald said. The gargoyle had suddenly appeared attached to the subway-tile backsplash above the sink. The kitchen was now Supernatural Central. "If that were the case, it would be me. Mr. Longstreet installed my fireplace mantel in 1866, after he purchased it from an English abbey."

"He's got you there, Roddy," I said. "Maybe I should clarify. Cory meant Mom is the boss around here."

"I meant she's our inspiration."

This was getting silly. Fortunately, my phone rang, giving me a distraction. The caller ID said it was Arch Mage Bob. That's how I had him listed in my contacts. I should delete "Arch Mage" in case someone stole my phone.

"Dude, can you believe this craziness?" he said, clearly very agitated. "Our own government is out to get us! Supernaturals have been living alongside humans for, like, thousands of years. We're total peaceniks, man."

I didn't contradict him, but our coexistence with normal humans had not always been peaceful. Monsters did, after all, prey upon humans before hunting was regulated by guilds. Villagers with their torches and pitchforks killed monsters in return. The Spanish Inquisition went after witches, and so did the Puritans in New England. The list goes on.

"People are afraid of those who aren't like them," I said. "And politicians take advantage of that to gain more power. Governor Witlessin is telling people she'll save them from 'the others,' and they'll gladly reelect her to stay safe."

"Well, it's not right. We supernaturals need to stick together against these hateful humans. And against the Fae. I changed my mind about what we talked about before. I'm gonna go with you down to Palm Beach and use my magic to shrink you so that you can fit inside the tunnels and rescue Darla."

"Bob, that's fantastic! Thank you so much!"

I relayed to Cory what Bob had said.

"Thank goodness!" Cory beamed. "Finally, we can get Darla back."

"Um, I don't want to overpromise," I said. "We need to find the tunnels before we can enter them. And just because we can enter them doesn't mean we'll exit them alive."

The front door chimed, meaning someone had entered. It was past sunset, but not yet late enough that all exterior doors would be locked and leaving access only to guests with key cards.

I gave Roderick a stern look, and he disappeared into his crawlspace behind the fridge. Archibald ossified into solid stone, making him appear to be a decorative feature, though who would put a gargoyle above their sink?

I went out into the foyer to find Officer Fernandez. The inn was part of her beat, and she's come here frequently over the years, thanks to all the weirdness that has ensued.

"How can I help you, officer?"

"We received a report about supernatural activity here," she replied, reading from a notebook. "Something about witches."

"What? Who reported it?"

"I can't divulge that. I'll just say it was a guest."

Could it have been Mr. Humphrey? He clearly had an agenda against us, but I had wiped away his memories of this place.

"When was it filed?" I asked.

"A few weeks ago. I didn't prioritize it because, you know, this place is like a freak show. But now, the attorney general wants us to fast-track these things."

"I'll take care of it," Samson said, entering the foyer with Cory.

"Oh, Detective. I didn't know you were here."

"I agree, this place is a freak show. I'm in charge of any investigation relating to the inn so we can weed out the frivolous complaints."

"Oh, no problem. I'd rather not deal with this, anyway. We've been getting dozens of reports of witches and monsters and all sorts of things tonight."

"It's only going to get worse. And most of the reports are probably nonsense. People imagining things or trying to get revenge against neighbors for petty feuds. Let's get out of here and let this family run their business."

He said goodnight to Cory and me. The two cops went out into the night, and I activated the lockdown half an hour early.

But would the lockdown save us, I wondered an hour later when the deep, repeated booms came from the side of the inn facing the alley.

"That sounds like it's coming from the utility room," Cory said, his face ashen.

We rushed down the hall and entered the laundry-workshop-storage room. The exterior door to the alley, where we received deliveries and took out the garbage, shook from heavy, rhythmic blows.

Cory put his eye to the peephole in the door.

"There's a mob out there with a battering ram!"

"Yikes! Let me look," I said, taking his place.

He was correct. About two dozen people were gathered outside, two of them swinging a battering ram like SWAT teams use. Their faces looked demonic and twisted with hate in the glow of the security light above the door. And it was not simply an effect of the peephole's fisheye lens.

The villagers, with torches and pitchforks, were here for us.

One person stood out as their obvious leader, barking orders and pushing individuals toward the door. It was Marge Moose-bacher, from Moms Against Monsters.

CHAPTER 22

SOPHIE

"I'm getting my sword," I said to Cory, shouting to be heard above the din of the crowd outside the door.

"You can't shoot them with your lightning! You'll give yourself away as a witch."

"Why else would they be here?"

"If you insist on getting your sword, fine," Cory said, rolling up his sleeves. "But I'm going to cast a spell to fortify the door. And I'm going to call 911."

"But we're the bad guys."

"Breaking into someone's house is still against the law. So is rioting."

He dialed 911 and put the phone on speaker.

"Emergency services," said a female voice. "What is the nature of your emergency?"

"There's a mob of people trying to break into our home and harm us. They have a battering ram. We're at three-thirty-one Hidalgo Avenue."

The operator paused. "Did you say *three-thirty-one* Hidalgo Avenue?"

"Yes. Please send the police here now."

Another pause. "Yes. Officers will come. Is anyone injured?"

"Not yet. But there could be at any moment now."

The operator paused again.

"When is someone coming?" Cory demanded.

"Officers are en route."

The call ended.

"She did not inspire me with confidence," I said.

"Better get your sword."

"You should get your gun."

"I don't want to kill anyone," Cory said.

"Then scare them instead. They probably have guns, too."

I ran upstairs, avoiding the elevator in case our power would be cut. The pounding against the door could be heard even on the third floor, and I passed some guests who stood in their open doors, looking concerned.

"Nothing to be alarmed about," I said as I ran. "Police are on their way."

Samson had given me his number, and when I reached my room, I quickly texted him that we were in trouble. After I retrieved my weapons, I ran back downstairs, sprinting past the wide-eyed guests with my broadsword strapped to my back and a crossbow in one hand.

"Nothing to be alarmed about," I told them again.

Something told me that most of our guests would cut their stays short. And we would never achieve full occupancy again.

When I arrived in the utility room, Cory stood near the exterior door with his arms straight out, palms facing the door. His face was strained.

My scalp tingled from the energy of Cory's spell, but I sensed another kind of magic coming from outside.

"A witch of some sort is out there," Cory said, "throwing magic at my spell. Weakening it. I don't know how long the door will hold."

"It's Fae magic," I said.

My weapons were meant for the worst-case scenario. I planned to use other tactics first.

Since the attack began, I'd been consumed with my fear and the adrenaline-driven urge to fight back. But now, the empath in me was kicking in, and I sensed the emotions coming from the mob.

They were feeling what you'd expect: fear and hatred. And I believed their emotions had been enflamed by Marge Moose-bacher's magic.

I tried to counter them by sending out feelings of calm, happiness, love, and understanding, enhanced by magic.

The steel fire door bulged inward. The mob was too far gone in their frenzy to be influenced by my emotions.

"I'm going to cast a sleep spell," I said.

After the next blow of the battering ram, the door buckled inward further. The hinges looked like they were about to fail.

Despite the danger of being crushed by a falling door, I put my eye up to the peephole. The sleep spell was supposed to work better if I had visual contact with the subjects. As someone who preferred to shoot lightning bolts at my enemies, I wasn't well practiced in sleep spells.

The faces of the mob were even more twisted with fury than before as they watched the door begin to give way. And they relished the thought of shedding the blood of those they feared and hated.

Marge pointed her hands at the door.

"My spell on the door just broke," Cory said.

I finished my incantation and sent my energy outside. Though my view was distorted by the fisheye lens, the men holding the battering ram stopped moving, set it on the ground, and collapsed on top of it.

Other people outside sat down slowly, then toppled over, or leaned against the house next door and slid to the alley floor.

My spell worked.

But not on everyone. Marge was completely awake, as were two other women and a man.

That my spell didn't work on Marge meant it was ineffective against faeries. Which meant the other three awake members of the mob were faeries, too.

Four faeries could be just as dangerous as a full mob.

Marge surveyed the ruination of her mob, then looked back at the door and smiled. I realized she hadn't needed the mob to capture or kill us. She was merely training the clueless humans to use violence against their perceived enemies.

Now, she could eliminate us much more effectively.

The metal of the door whined, and I jumped to the side just in time to miss being flattened as it popped loose and sailed past me, clattering against the concrete wall on the opposite side of the room.

Cory disappeared into the laundry alcove. I set my crossbow on the counter and unsheathed my sword. Marge Moosebacher strode confidently into our home.

The purple lightning that shot from my sword bounced off an invisible bubble around Marge. It was a Fae-magic protection spell.

We were so screwed.

"You're not a very formidable witch, are you?" Marge sneered. "We've been surveilling you for quite some time now.

One of our operatives, a Mr. Humphrey, stayed here and reported you as a grave danger. It looks like he was wrong."

A spy! He must have been the one who added me to the Monster Monitor app. On the night he attacked me, he acted like he had simply discovered me in the app. That jerk not only reported me, but also wanted to get a bounty for turning me in.

"You should add yourself to your monster database," I said. "You're more dangerous than I am."

"This is not about public safety. This is about having power over the public."

She gestured for the three other faeries to come inside. "Search the inn for supernaturals," she told them.

"All we have are a few ghosts."

"We don't care about ghosts," Marge said.

"The ghost of the Elvis impersonator in room 202 is a real hoot. You'll love him."

She walked closer to me. I stepped back.

"I don't sense the presence of the psychic who has the Goddess in her. Where is she?"

"You haven't been reading your internal memos. The Fae abducted her on the orders of your Queene."

"We're not subjects of her court."

"You're clearly on the same side as her court."

"Regarding conquering humans, yes, we have the same goal."

Marge moved aggressively toward me, and I thrust the sword at her. It hit the invisible barrier about a foot from her skin. She tried to circle around me, but I followed her with my blade.

We were in a standoff. I braced myself for her to attack with different magic.

Before she did, I felt a cool breeze of human magic blow around me. It came from the laundry alcove.

Cory! He was casting a protection spell around me, something I would have done myself had I not been so focused on attacking. I couldn't see him in there, and apparently neither could Marge.

A second later, Marge flung something at me. It was a small patch of solid black, like an inkblot, that went straight for my eyes. A blinding spell.

It turned into black dust when it hit my new protection bubble and sifted to the floor.

Impulsively, I swung my sword at her, putting my entire body into it. It struck her protection bubble so forcefully she staggered to the side and almost lost her footing.

With her off balance, I hacked at her again and again but couldn't break through her protection spell. I fed more energy into my sword, as if I were going to shoot lightning, hoping it would give the steel power to penetrate her bubble.

She spun away from me and fled past me into the main hallway.

I was pleased that I had fended off her attacks on me, but now she was running amok inside the inn, and I feared for the safety of our guests.

Most of all, I feared for my beloved supernatural residents.

"Thank God you're safe," Cory said, emerging from the laundry alcove.

"Four faeries are loose inside," I said. "Please take my sword and do whatever you have to do to stop them from hurting anyone. I'll be right behind you."

I handed him Alfie, and he raced after her. When I turned to retrieve my crossbow from the counter, I hesitated. In the quiver attached to the stock were only two steel bolts. The other four were carved from ash wood and tipped with steel, designed specifically for firing into vampire hearts to destroy them.

I wondered if the steel bolts, fired at such a greater velocity and force than my sword thrusts, could penetrate a faerie's magical protection bubble. Maybe, but I doubted it.

As I picked up the crossbow, I remembered an esoteric fact about faeries and gripped the crossbow's stock with a bit of hope.

Jogging down the main hallway, I headed for the kitchen, worried about Roderick. A commotion coming from inside made me break into a sprint.

Two female faeries had pushed the refrigerator aside, and one was attempting to pry the crawlspace door open with a kebab skewer. Its ultimate use would be to stake Roderick.

The other faerie was fighting off Cory. He slashed at her with Alfie, but to the same useless effect I had experienced with Marge. This faerie, too, had conjured a protection bubble around herself.

Using magic of some sort, she advanced toward Cory and tossed him onto the kitchen table in the corner.

Pointing the crossbow at the floor, I put my foot in the stirrup and used the crank to draw the powerful string. I lifted the cocked bow and placed an ash bolt in the flight groove.

The blonde faerie looked at me with curiosity and arrogance as I walked casually up to her. Encased in her protection spell, why would she worry about me?

She walked toward Cory to attack him before he got off the table.

I followed her, pressed the crossbow close to her, until it met the resistance of her protection bubble.

Then I pulled the trigger.

The bolt plunged into her spine, and she dropped to the kitchen floor.

I had remembered that not only was ash deadly to vampires, but also to faeries. So deadly, in fact, that it wasn't affected by their magic and could pass easily through their protection spells.

The faerie trying to get to Roderick shrieked and charged at me with the kebab skewer. She hadn't conjured a protection spell yet.

I kicked her in the stomach, and she doubled over, gasping.

As you probably know, crossbows are hardly quick firing. With no time for cocking the weapon, I lunged toward Cory and grabbed my sword, which he'd dropped on the floor.

I'm very good about regularly sharpening my steel. Let's just say the faerie with the skewer was skewered thoroughly.

"Wow," Cory said. "How did you get through the first one's protection spell?"

I explained about the ash.

"Not to complain," he said, "but we have two dead women on our kitchen floor. Not a good look when you're under police investigation."

"Look at them."

The women, now fully expired, had shifted back to their natural faerie forms. The police would not consider the knee-high creatures with the hideous doll-like faces to be human homicide victims.

"According to the Supernatural Criminality Act, the recently passed law in our great state of Florida, I killed illegal supernatural creatures. I don't believe I need to worry about getting arrested for this, Cory."

He laughed. It was more of an act of letting off steam than jocularity. But he understood the point I was making.

"There are still others in the inn," he said.

"On it."

I hurried to the front parlor. The male faerie was attempting to chip away at the fireplace mantel with a hammer, specifically targeting Archibald, who had returned to his usual perch. He remained as inanimate stone despite the hammer blows.

The faeries were remarkably good at locating supernaturals. I guess being supernatural creatures themselves helped. This one must have heard the tussle in the kitchen, because his protection shield was activated.

"I'm sorry to break the news," I said to him, "but your spell isn't as good as you think it is."

He looked confused by my statement until the ash bolt plunged into his chest. Then, he just looked sad.

I turned away as he went through the ugly transformation on the floor to his actual body. Archibald showed no signs of interest, despite the divot in his head from the hammer.

I thought I had abandoned this kind of killing when I quit being an enforcer. I thought my becoming an empath would make it impossible. But my anger issues had taken over when the faeries invaded my home—especially after the Fae of the Unseelie Court had kidnapped Mom.

I had reverted to the killing machine I abhorred.

But I didn't care. My job wasn't yet complete.

Where was Marge? I stalked from the parlor back to the kitchen to make sure Cory was safe.

He wasn't there.

It occurred to me that the faerie instinct for sniffing out supernatural energy would lead Marge to him.

I headed to the courtyard and the cottage.

CHAPTER 23

SOPHIE

I crept quietly into the courtyard. The only illumination came from the light in the fountain near the tiny swimming pool off to my right, and the ambient light from the windows of the cottage straight ahead.

The cottage door was ajar. The shadow of someone inside moved across a window. As quietly as I could, I cocked the crossbow and loaded a bolt made of ash.

I pressed myself against the wall of the cottage, just to the side of the door, and listened.

Footsteps. A heavy sigh. At least one person was alive in there, and I hoped it was Cory.

Leaving my cover, I yanked the door open, my crossbow in firing position. The living room was empty.

I walked in and saw movement in the master bedroom door.

"Don't shoot," Cory said.

"Is Marge in here?"

"No. But she was. Look at this."

I followed him into the bathroom.

Die witches was scrawled on the mirror in red lipstick.

"So," I said, "she's not just a political activist who's a faerie. She's a psycho, too."

"I'm guessing she sensed the lingering energy of the witch and psychic who live here and came in to see if you'd lied about Darla, thinking she might be home after all."

"Do you think she's still on the property somewhere?"

"She's gone," Cory replied. "I logged onto the security system and saw video of her leaving through the courtyard gate."

"I feel so violated."

"Our guests surely feel the same way. I saw two keycards on the front desk from people who checked out while the mob was trying to break in."

"Wonderful."

"Knock-knock," called a voice across the courtyard. It was Samson standing in the doorway of the inn.

"No disrespect, Detective," I said, "but you took your sweet time getting here."

He smiled bitterly. "It turns out tonight has been a big night for social unrest. Your mob wasn't the only one out there. The department has been overwhelmed, and I had to put in extra duty for crowd control."

"All because of the new law?"

"Yeah. And people—including certain politicians—are fanning the flames on social media."

"Well, our mob was special. It was led by the president of Moms Against Monsters."

"Marge Moosebacher?"

"Yep. She's a faerie, by the way."

"That explains the three dead faeries I found inside the inn. Is she one of them?"

"She left," Cory said. "She wrote a threatening note on our mirror in lipstick before she went."

"I'll explain everything," I said. "But there are some loose ends to tie up first. To be exact, there are a dozen or so citizens sleeping in the alley who made up the mob that attacked the inn."

"Sleeping spell?" Samson asked.

"Yeah. It probably won't last much longer."

"Let me get some officers here to arrest them." He sighed. "The jail is going to be full tonight."

"The new law is a travesty," Cory said, leading the way to the utility room and alley. "It's designed to pit neighbors against each other. I mean, what were they thinking when they added protections for people to make citizens' arrests? It's encouraging vigilantism. It's still illegal to break into someone's home and attack them, right?"

"Yes," Samson replied. "The laws are supposed to protect you if a 'monster' attacks you and you capture or kill it. But try telling that to the rabble-rousers."

"How are the police going to protect us?" I asked. "Think of all the supernaturals who will be harmed along with the regular people accused of being supernatural."

We entered the utility room with its missing door and the people sleeping just outside.

"I think the idea is the police will simply give up trying to protect supernaturals and the falsely accused," Samson said.

"There will be massacres," Cory whispered.

"Except the state won't kill anyone," Samson replied. "Only arrest them. The citizens, and whatever militias they form—will do the killing."

"But why?" I asked. "What's the point of it all?"

"Our fear gives them the power to rule us."

"Who's *them?*"

"For now, it's the governor and her toadies. Later, it will be someone else. Let's not dwell on this. Help me move the faerie bodies to the alley, so fewer questions will be asked of you."

Fortunately, the bodies were small. We carried them wrapped in towels and put them by the exterior door of the utility room. It was grim work. According to the new laws, we had every right to kill them to protect ourselves, and that's exactly what I had done—protect my extended family of supernaturals.

Samson answered a call on his portable radio, telling the arriving police officers where to park. I returned to the main part of the inn for some privacy. I needed to think. There was too much darkness hanging over me.

I checked on Archibald in the front room. He remained in a stony slumber. The piece the hammer had chipped from his forehead was minor and looked more like the ravages of time than the vandalism of a faerie.

"Archibald, you've been around for nearly a thousand years, right?"

I didn't expect an answer, but the stone shimmered, and Archibald's face became flesh-like.

"Yes, love."

"How were you born, exactly?"

"I was hatched into the piece of limestone that became this mantel. Gargoyles and grotesques were more common back then. Our mums would lay their eggs where masons were already working. You see my three brethren with me beneath the mantel?"

I nodded. He was referring to the other gargoyles who resembled him but were not supernatural.

"My mum laid an egg beside them, and I hatched overnight. When the mason began work the next day, he found four of us instead of three. He believed it was a divine message to him, and he gave up drinking."

Archibald chuckled.

"With all your time on earth," I said, "what wisdom do you have for me in times like this, when humans are under threat from the Fae, and from their own inhumanity?"

"What are you going on about?" he asked. "Aside from the one trying to bash my head in, are the Fae trying to conquer humans again?"

I explained the complicated situation as simply as possible.

"Humans go through periods of madness from time to time," he said. "They treat each other with cruelty and have horribly destructive wars. There are always groups who are scapegoated and oppressed. But they persevere. They fight for their rights. They overcome. Humans and the Fae won't grow out of their savagery, I'm afraid. However, it can be kept in check. And things will improve. Humans are much less savage these days compared to the Middle Ages when I was young, though their technology makes them more destructive. All wars end. You simply must wait them out."

"I'm not immortal like you. I can't wait forever."

"Then you must fight for justice."

I realized then what must be done. Just like the groups of humans throughout history who had been mistreated and fought to improve their standing, the supernaturals could do the same.

We did not choose to be unmasked. The Equilibrium had been working. But the hateful humans who unmasked us left us with no choice but to assert our right to exist.

With supernatural creatures and magic out in the open, we'd seem more normal and less scary. And if we were less scary, there would be little gained by abusing us.

Sure, we'd still face prejudice, but our lives would be relatively normal, and the fever of fear and hatred would break.

I would fight for supernatural rights. That would be my purpose.

But first, we had to stop the Fae. The indigenous faeries living among us who had now betrayed us, and the Fae of the Unseelie Court, who had more numbers and resources, but who couldn't seem to get their act together.

IT WAS AFTER MIDNIGHT, AND MY ADRENALINE WAS FINALLY wearing off. The police had left with the mob members in custody (after I released the sleep spell). I was still feeling guilty about killing the faeries and expected I would never get over it, however necessary it had been.

Cory put up a sheet of plywood to cover the utility room's missing door. It wouldn't keep out another mob, but it made me feel a little more secure than an open doorway.

Maybe, if I was lucky, I could get some sleep.

I wasn't lucky.

The chime went off on my phone, telling me someone was ringing the doorbell at the main entrance. I hoped it wasn't someone with hostile intentions.

I checked the camera and didn't see anyone. Then there was some movement. Was that an upright bird feather moving across the bottom of the screen?

Rushing downstairs, I approached the safety-glass door. I realized I hadn't seen anyone because the camera was oriented for a human's height.

Not gnome height.

A dozen of them stood at the door, looking at me expectantly. They wore felt hats, each with a feather stuck in the band. Aside from that, they looked like cute ornamental garden gnomes. Except with weapons. They carried spears, bows, and short stabbing swords, perfect for fighting in confined spaces like tunnels.

There were both male and female gnomes. You could tell their gender because the females had sparser beards than the males.

Gorkee stood behind them in her natural faerie form.

"I present to you the gnome special forces," she said.

She rattled off their names, none of which I would remember, thanks to their odd pronunciations. They chattered what sounded like friendly greetings to me. You'd think little folk only a foot and a half tall would have high-pitched voices, but theirs were deep.

"I'm afraid I don't speak Gnomish," I said.

"Of course," Gorkee said. "I prepared a spell for you. Wear this and you'll be fluent in Gnomish and Faerie."

She handed me a cloth pouch tied to a leather cord. I placed the amulet around my neck, my nose crinkling at its foul, cheese-like odor.

Gorkee now spoke in Gnomish, and I could understand it.

"These are the shock troops who will go into the tunnels with you to extract the prisoners. I will command them. Have you found a sorcerer to shrink you?"

"A human arch mage. Well, technically, he's a vampire now. He's been to the Queene's Winter Palace before and can guide us. My stepfather, a witch, will also come, but he'll stay above ground to provide security."

"Excellent. When and where will we brief our forces on the battle plan?"

That was a good question. I volunteered Bob's surf shop the

following night after it closed. There weren't too many choices of venues for hosting gnomes, vampires, and a faerie out of the public eye.

"Dude," Bob said to me the next night, "could you ask the gnomes to stop playing with the flip-flops, unless they're going to pay for them?"

Pagan Surf Shop displayed its surf and boogie boards, with related gear, in a back room. Here, up front, was the stuff the tourists loved: T-shirts, bathing suits, footwear, sunglasses, etc. The gnomes were chattering and laughing, trying on the ridiculously large rubber sandals and slapping each other on the head with them.

I told them in Gnomish to knock it off. They snapped to attention, their military training shining through.

Diego was nowhere to be seen. I had called and texted him with no response. I didn't blame him for not wanting to go on a perilous raid, especially in this new era when vampires were endangered by just existing.

Lethia, I suspected, was the more likely reason he was blowing me off. She probably had forbidden him to have anything to do with me. Why was I so disappointed he hadn't replied to me?

For this mission, I was focused on freeing Mom, and Gorkee would be the overall commander of the entire operation, above and below ground. The faerie cleared her throat and hopped atop a display counter in her diminutive natural form.

"Listen up. Our mission is solely to free a human prisoner, the mother of Sophie here." She gestured toward me. "Consequently, we will not take and hold the mansion where the Faerie

Queene lives. The primary force will advance on the residence as a diversion."

A few of the gnomes grumbled. There was no love lost between gnomes and the Unseelie Court.

"Sophie will help us locate the approximate position of where her mother is held, and we will burrow directly into the adjacent tunnels. The assault squad will neutralize the guards. The rest of you will maintain a perimeter around where we make our descent into the tunnels. Cory here"—she pointed to him—"will provide defensive magic."

He gave a worried smile.

Gorkee continued, "Vans will pick us up tomorrow night at nineteen hundred hours so that we can travel to Palm Beach and complete the operation before dawn. Any questions?"

"Are there restrictions on lethal violence?" the leader of the gnome assault squad asked.

"No," Gorkee replied. "Treat the soldiers of the Unseelie Court with maximum prejudice."

The gnomes cheered. Bob glanced at me with concern. I wanted to rescue Mom alive, so I would allow Gorkee to do what she believed was best. After all, her motivation for helping me was a fondness for Mom, but more so, an enmity for the Fae of the Unseelie Court.

"I hope I didn't make a mistake agreeing to help you," Bob whispered to me.

"We shall see." It was the only answer I could truthfully give.

CHAPTER 24

SOPHIE

I t was strange riding in a van on the highway at night with a vampire, a faerie, and a dozen gnomes. But this was I-95 in Florida, so chances were that most of the other vehicles carried passengers even weirder than us. Right?

At one point, I fell asleep. When I woke up, my head was resting on the pointy cap worn by the gnome beside me. He graciously didn't complain.

As we progressed southward, we passed fewer stretches of trees and farmlands, and the landscape became more urban. When we cut through West Palm Beach, my pulse quickened.

We crossed a bridge over the Intracoastal Waterway and entered Palm Beach. Some of the world's richest people lived here, with no idea that one of their neighbors was the Faerie Queene. And many of them had mansions bigger than hers.

We passed Mar-a-Lago and drove south along the beach on A1A. Before long, we came upon the Queene's sprawling home, built in the 1920s. There was no place to pull over nearby, but doing so would have been foolish.

We turned onto the next street, a quiet residential lane perpendicular to the ocean. It was shaded by palms and giant banyan trees. Bob directed the driver to a home one and a half blocks to the west.

The home had a for-sale sign out front, and the fact that it was small and older meant that it would be knocked down so a bigger, gaudier home could replace it. I sent out magic, searching for signs of life, and found none. The home was empty and would be a great base of operations.

It was time for me to use my blood and my locator spell to find precisely where Mom was.

Most of the home's furniture had been removed, but the musty living room still had a couch and an old-fashioned TV. I crouched on the dusty parquet floor and began drawing a magic circle.

Bob entered the room, nostrils flaring.

"There's someone who's been staying in this house," he said.

"My magic found no signs of life."

"Yeah, no signs of life. Whoever's staying here isn't alive. I smell vampires."

That was a wild card we didn't need.

"Hopefully, they'll spend the rest of the night out hunting and won't bother us," I said.

"Let's hope so. 'Cause the scent I'm picking up isn't from a normal vampire. Make that vampires. There's more than one."

"Well, please guard this room while I do my locator spell. We can't begin the operation until I get a more precise location for Mom."

Pots clattered in the kitchen, followed by gnomes giggling. Time was a-wasting.

I entered the circle, lit the candles, and proceeded with the ritual of drawing my blood and mixing it with Mom's hair that I had brought with me. I intoned the incantation. When the candle flames erupted, a vision came to me.

Mom slept on the floor of a cavern. Tears had carved runnels through the dirt that covered her face. And there was someone else in the cavern I hadn't noticed the last time I had used this spell.

A man sat chained to the wall opposite her. He was awake, his eyes darting back and forth as if searching for something.

He must be aware of my magic. No surprise: studying him more closely, I realized he was an elf.

That meant our workload had doubled—two prisoners to extract.

I zoomed out on the vision my magic was sending me, raising the view out of the cavern, rising above ground to see where the cavern was.

Now, I was looking down at a large swimming pool, as if I were floating above it. Did faeries use swimming pools? Maybe in their human forms. Or, I supposed, the pool was a mandatory feature of a Palm Beach estate, whether it was utilized or not.

This was disappointing. The rescue party couldn't dig straight down to the cavern because it was beneath the swimming pool. I hoped they could reach it by digging a tunnel sideways.

But how long would that take?

After I released the spell, I told Bob what I'd seen.

"Under the swimming pool?" he asked.

"Yeah. About fifteen feet beneath it."

"I was kinda hoping it would be further away from the palace. And the guards."

I found Gorkee outside the house, speaking to a gnome.

"My scouts confirm what I expected. The palace is guarded by magical wards around the perimeter of the property," she told me. "It's lightly guarded by security personnel, but it's impossible to know how many soldiers are stationed on the estate."

I reported the cavern's location to her.

She frowned. "We'll have to dig a lateral tunnel to reach it. And we'll have to do it from here to maintain privacy."

"How long would that take? Humans would need days to cover that distance."

"Worry not. As a faerie, I know my way underground, and the gnomes are fast workers."

"Even so, we're a block and a half away."

"Faeries don't dig straight tunnels from Point A to Point B like you humans would. We can sense natural fissures and pockets underground. The limestone substratum is very porous. What we do is follow pathways, carved by water, that already exist, digging only here and there to connect them. And our basic magic makes it even faster."

I glanced at my watch. It was already past midnight.

"Worry not, Sophie."

Gorkee barked orders in Gnomish, and our diminutive soldiers came running, armed with picks, shovels, and five-gallon plastic buckets for removing soil.

She searched the lawn of the home we had thought was unoccupied, staring at the ground. Several times, she dropped to her knees and pressed an ear to the grass. Finally, she stopped and pointed to a spot near a hedge.

The gnomes raced over and got to work. They used a complicated choreography, taking turns digging out a shovel-full of dirt, then jumping out of the way as another gnome plunged their shovel, dumping the dirt in buckets, and plunging back in. Five would be inside the growing hole at one time, while the others ferried the dirt-filled buckets away.

The diggers disappeared as they burrowed downward,

gnomes easily climbing up and down the sides of the hole without collapsing it.

A shout of triumph came from the hole. Thanks to Gorkee's translating magic, I understood they had reached a horizontal fissure in the limestone.

Gorkee jumped into the hole, followed by a handful of gnomes with picks and shovels. I heard the clanging of steel against rock, which receded as they moved eastward. Soon, it was quiet, and the rest of us could only wait.

Bob had left the house and joined us.

"Any idea of what kind of vampires live there?" I asked.

"I think they're sin eaters. A very rare type of psychic vampire."

"Say what?"

"Sin eaters. Humans in Appalachia and similar regions had a folk-magic tradition of sin eating. Like, if you're a rich dude about to die, you pay a sin eater to consume your sins, so they don't weigh down your soul when you go to the pearly gates."

"I think I've heard of them," I said. "But didn't they transfer the sins to cakes, which the sin eaters would eat?"

"Yeah. But sin-eating vampires just eat the sins. No cake. The negative energy of the sins is their sustenance. No blood required. And they get the most energy from the Seven Deadly Sins, which you find a lot of here in Palm Beach, especially pride, greed, and envy."

"Are these vampires dangerous? Frankly, I wouldn't mind giving away my sins."

"They'll be dangerous if they're pissed off that we're on their lawn."

Gorkee climbed out of the hole beside the hedge and waved for us to come over to her. Glancing at my watch, I was surprised to see that it had only been forty-five minutes since the first shovel hit the ground.

"We've created a passage to the edge of the palace grounds," she said. "I need your magic to defeat the wards so we can go the final distance to the cavern. It's time for Sophie to get small."

"Let's go inside," Bob said to me. "You'll want some privacy for this."

"You can shrink my clothes, too, right?" I asked as I followed him. "I don't want to be naked."

"I'll shrink your clothes, crossbow, and sword. Don't worry."

Before entering the house, Bob stopped at the van we had ridden in and retrieved his wooden staff. I'd rarely seen him use his staff. He needed it for only his most powerful magic.

We returned to the living room where my magic circle remained, drawn on the wood floor with a dry-erase marker.

"Step inside the circle with me," he said.

After I did so, he redrew the part of the circumference I had erased when I released my previous spell.

"Should I kneel?" I asked.

"Nope. Just stand there. Gather your energies and clear your mind. This might hurt just a bit."

"What?" My concentration was broken.

"This is, like, a major physiological transformation, dude. Relax and go with the flow."

I tried to do as he said. Finally, I felt the warmth of my energies coalescing in my solar plexus. I closed my eyes and cleared my mind while my skin danced with magic coming from Bob.

The polished wood of the staff touched my left, then right, shoulder. It was extremely hot, but I didn't flinch.

Bob chanted in an unfamiliar language. The staff pressed against the top of my head.

And pressed harder and harder.

Pain spread through my skull and ran down my spine, an aching, hollow pain that was like a toothache but worse. I made no sound as the staff pressed ever harder, and I worried my neck would snap.

Finally, the pain ended. Bob's chanting ceased.

"Open your eyes," he said.

Everything looked normal. No, I take that back. I saw the room from a slightly different perspective than before. I turned my head, and instead of looking at Bob's face, I was staring at his legs, hairy and scarred, extending beneath his long surfer shorts.

I looked up to find his face towering above me. He smiled.

"My God, I've shrunk," I whispered.

"You have, but your magic is just as strong as always. You must leave the circle now while I stay inside it to maintain the spell. Careful, don't wipe away any of the marker."

I stepped out.

"Use your psychic-empath stuff to stay connected to me," he said. "I'll need to feed magic continually to you to keep you small. Good luck with your mission, dude."

I thanked him and walked outside, my steps quicker to compensate for my shorter legs. I felt the reassuring weight of Alfie strapped to my back, proportionally smaller now to fit my size.

Gorkee grinned when she saw me. "Welcome to the world of the wee people."

Cory laughed. "You look like a little doll. Except your head is the correct proportion."

Unlike faeries in their natural sizes. Fortunately, Gorkee didn't catch the reference.

I admit I felt a little self-conscious about my tiny new size. And the world looked a lot different from two feet high. Striding across the lawn felt like passing through the tall grass of a meadow.

"Follow me," Gorkee said. "I'll lead you to the first ward. After you defeat it, we'll connect the tunnel to the cavern beneath the estate."

The tunnel was tall enough that I didn't have to bend as I walked through it, though at times my head brushed against hanging roots or pieces of limestone. Gorkee illuminated our path with a glowing orb that floated just ahead of her.

For short stretches, the tunnel was like I had imagined— similar to a coal mine burrowed through the earth. But most of the time, it followed natural passageways through the limestone, zigging and zagging right and left, up and down, but always proceeding eastward.

After quite some distance, I felt the negative magic of the ward, making me feel slightly nauseous. Gorkee stopped, and I squeezed around her to the invisible barrier of the ward. It stretched from above ground to a point deeper underground than we were, probably to the water table.

The water table wasn't much deeper than we were, which pleased me. Its presence, along with the nearby ocean, would boost my magical powers.

I went into a semi-trance and probed the ward with my mind. Soon I could picture its structure. Though Fae magic was built on a different framework than human magic, this ward was essentially very similar to the kind I would have created.

I conjured up a deconstruction spell and focused it on the ward, painstakingly picking apart the strands of Fae magic. The ward loosened gradually, then fell apart all at once. The oppressive weight of its magic was gone.

"Okay," I said. "We're good to go."

My voice was more high-pitched than normal, kind of squeaky. It was going to take a lot of getting used to.

I pressed against the wall of the tunnel and allowed Gorkee and the gnomes to pass by. I followed as they wound through fissures and holes in the limestone. Occasionally, we stopped as they dug through earth or pulverized rock to make a passage larger.

We reached a solid wall of stone and stopped.

"We faeries learn simple blasting spells at an early age," Gorkee said. "I haven't used one tonight, because it would have been detected by the Queene's guards. Thorgrun, go tell the others to begin the diversionary attack."

A gnome pushed past me and scurried back the way we had come.

"Once the Queene's guards are distracted by the attack, I'll blast through the wall of the cavern. We'll go inside, get the prisoners, and get them to a van as quickly as possible."

"Could the blast injure the prisoners?" I asked.

"No, it's not like an explosion. More of an implosion. The rock simply crumbles downward."

We waited in the dark underground for what felt like an eternity. In addition to my nervousness about pulling off the rescue, the claustrophobia of being down here was getting to me. The approaching footsteps behind us were a relief.

Thorgrun chattered in Gnomish. I loosely translated it as *the attack has begun.*

"Brace yourselves," Gorkee said. She placed her palms on the rock wall, and it suddenly fell apart in small chunks and dust. We entered the chamber.

"Sophie!" Mom said, surprise and delight animating her face in the orb's light. "Gorkee!"

I put my finger to my lips to shush her, gave her a quick kiss, and withdrew my sword from its scabbard on my back. After filling it with energy, I hacked apart the chains that attached her and the elf to the walls.

Gorkee and I helped them to their feet and ushered them toward the opening we'd made in the wall.

Then the wooden door burst open, and faeries swarmed into the cavern to stop us.

CHAPTER 25

SOPHIE

"I thought the palace guards were being diverted," I said to Gorkee as I hacked at the faeries' thrusting spears.

"They *are* being diverted. Just not all of them."

The small cavern was packed now with faeries and gnomes. The crossbow was too slow of a weapon. And there was no room for me to shoot lightning from my sword, so I was forced to use it for hacking and stabbing. The same with Gorkee. The gnomes, smaller even than us, were adept at squeezing between us, or even between our legs, to puncture faeries with their spears.

I had conjured a protection bubble around myself, but because of the close-quarter fighting, I couldn't protect our entire force.

"We need to get the freed prisoners out of here," I shouted.

"The Divine One and the elf have already been escorted back through the tunnel we made," Gorkee said. "They should be safe now."

I hoped Bob would return Mom to her normal size once she

was out of the tunnel. I assumed the elf had the ability to restore himself.

Here in the cavern, several faeries were down. The attacking horde dragged their wounded from the cavern, but the dead lay where they were, making it difficult for both sides to move.

A gnome dropped to the ground, wounded.

"Take him out," Gorkee ordered another gnome.

We were greatly outnumbered, but thanks to the confined space in here, and the small door the faeries came through, we held our ground. For now.

"We need to retreat," I said to Gorkee.

"They'll follow us through the tunnel."

Just then, a faerie commander shouted something, and their fighters dropped to the cavern floor.

Behind them, a squad of faerie archers pushed through the doorway and loosed a flight of arrows.

Two arrows bounced off my protection bubble, but another gnome went down and Gorkee was grazed.

Since I had room now, I aimed my sword and shot purple lightning at the archers, blowing them away.

"You need to withdraw!" I shouted at Gorkee. "If they capture you, you'll be tortured for collaborating with humans."

"But—"

"Go now! I'll hold the entrance to our tunnel just outside of the cavern and the Fae magic field. When all but the last van has left, tell Darla to contact me telepathically, and I'll retreat. We'll use magic to collapse the tunnel behind me when I'm out."

While my team slipped out of the cavern, I spent a huge amount of energy blasting away the faeries. The ground was covered with their bodies.

But still, they kept coming.

It would have been nice if we'd had intelligence that the

Queene had such a large fighting force stationed at her palace. I didn't know what was going on with the above-ground diversionary attack, but I knew we had way too few gnomes to hold back all the faeries. I hoped they had managed to disengage and were escaping in the vans.

I backed into our tunnel entrance. In its tight confines, only one faerie could reach me at a time. And none lived very long afterward.

They finally changed their tactics and stayed out of my sword's reach. I knelt in the tunnel's entrance, my protection bubble shaking from the arrows and spears that struck it.

My spell was weakening. I had expended so much energy on my lightning bolts that I was having difficulty keeping the spell going at maximum strength while it was being continually tested like this.

Mom, can you hear me? I projected my thoughts to her.

Sophie! How are you able to reach me through the Fae magic?

It only covers the cavern. I guess it was meant only to isolate you. Is our team leaving Palm Beach yet? I need to retreat and have Cory use magic to collapse the tunnel behind me. I'm weakening.

A van with the wounded has left, but the rest of us are still here, trying to get away from the Fae army.

You said army?

Yes. There are so many faeries here. No one expected it.

An ominous rumbling came from behind me. Cold air buffeted my back, dust clouding around me. The roar of falling rock and earth shook the ground.

The tunnel had collapsed.

I jumped out of the tunnel just in time, but had no way to escape, except through the Fae's own tunnels. Which were continuing to disgorge soldiers into the cavern.

Now, they had to climb over their fallen comrades, which

made them highly vulnerable to my blasts of lightning. Yet I couldn't continue fighting this way. My stock of energy, both internal and elemental, was running out.

The spells I knew for disabling people, such as my sleep spell, only worked on subjects who were right in front of me. I wished I could pump poison gas into the faerie tunnels and clear them out, allowing me to escape.

But wait. I knew a spell to pump something *out* of the tunnels.

Oxygen.

As an elemental witch, I harvested the energy for my magic from the five elemental powers: earth, water, air, fire, and spirit. I was a water witch because I had the greatest affinity with that element. But I could work with the other four.

With my sword, I drew a rough circle around me on the dirt and stone floor. I gathered what little of my personal energy I had left. Next, I created a void of energy that needed to be filled —air energy, to be exact. It was a vacuum of sorts.

And when I activated the void inside me, opening it to the external world, something incredible happened.

Air swept from the faerie tunnels into the cavern. It smelled like the air that had come in after our tunnel collapsed behind me—stale air from underground pockets redolent of damp earth and minerals.

It also had the smell of the living creatures who had been breathing it before I sucked it all down here. There were no fresh scents of the air from above ground. This was semi-stale tunnel air.

Losing pressure in the tunnels would eventually draw in the air from above ground, but for a brief period before that, any faeries in the tunnels would be unable to breathe.

Now was my moment to escape. I strengthened my protection spell and took several deep breaths, almost hyperventilat-ing, as if I were preparing to free dive.

I raced from the cavern, stepping over the fallen Fae soldiers. To my left, the tunnel went downhill. To my right, it ascended. Naturally, I went to the right.

Along the way, I passed or jumped over faeries who had passed out from lack of oxygen. They would wake up, but hope-fully only after I was out of here. I had to hurry before I, too, passed out.

Other tunnel openings appeared as I traveled uphill, but the passage I was in appeared to be the main one, so I stayed in it. Soon, the natural limestone walls transitioned to limestone blocks quarried by the Fae. I must be near ground level.

Yes, I was, because my breathing became easier. And the two faeries charging at me were as healthy as could be.

Until Alfie made quick work of them.

I continued running up the tunnel, which abruptly ended in a wall of limestone blocks with an illumination orb attached. Two wooden, steel-reinforced doors were to my left and right. The one on the left showed only darkness in the gap between the door and the floor. On the right, faint light appeared below the door, as well as the scent of ocean air.

I was about to open the door to my right, which obviously led outside, when the heavy iron handle rattled. I jumped to the door to my left, thankfully found it unlocked, and passed into a dark space, closing the door behind me.

The stomping feet and rattling weapons of several faeries passed by on the other side of the closed door.

I sensed I was in a tiny room, perhaps a closet, but I couldn't see anything except a sliver of light coming from beneath another door. There was no option other than opening it.

It led to a long hall that was dimly lit by orbs—a normal hallway, not a tunnel. It was built to human scale, so it probably dated from the construction of the original estate, located within the palace or one of the adjacent buildings. This was a utilitarian hall, devoid of decorations, most likely used by staff and servants.

At the far end was a window through which moonlight streamed inside. A table sat beneath it. Even though I was still in my shrunken form, I believed I could climb onto the table and break through the window to escape.

I was halfway down the hall when another door opened just ahead of me. An elderly faerie in his natural state rolled a faerie-sized cart into the hall. It was covered by a tablecloth topped with platters of fruits, cheeses, and unidentifiable foods.

Why was he in his natural faerie form here above ground? Were they always like this in the palace when they couldn't be seen by humans?

I stopped and pressed myself into a shadowy doorway. Though he was so close I could nearly touch him, he didn't notice me.

The servant pushed the cart across the hallway, stopped, walked ahead of the cart, and opened another door.

I was waiting for him to go into the room when the door I was pressed against began to open.

Purely out of instinct, I tiptoed across the hall, dropped to the floor, and crawled beneath the tablecloth draped over the cart. There was a bottom shelf on the cart that was blessedly empty, and I got on it, hidden by the tablecloth hanging around me.

The cart resumed rolling and passed into a room. I couldn't see anything, but the echoes of voices told me this was a large, high-ceilinged space.

And the voices told me that being here put me into deep doo-doo.

THE CART, WITH ME ON IT, ROLLED INTO THE LARGE ROOM, amid reverberating voices—male and female—and awkward laughter. They were speaking in Fae. I clutched Gorkee's translation amulet, hoping to understand what they were saying.

The platters of food were removed from the top of the cart, and it was rolled to a place farther from the voices. I could still hear them, though, and finally, the nonsensical Faerie words became English to my ears.

"I ask you again," said a cultured male voice, sounding a bit elderly, "won't your strategy backfire on you if the public discovers that you're Fae?"

"How would they discover that?" replied an older-sounding woman.

Her voice was familiar. Although she spoke in Fae, I noted a slight Southern drawl that slowed down the normally rapid Fae consonants. Her tone was relaxed, but arrogant. Why was it so familiar?

"We're not going after faeries, anyway," said a different male voice, but in stilted Fae. "Just the usual creatures that scare humans. Most of them wouldn't believe faeries exist, and if they did, they'd think we're cute."

"Cute?" This female voice was quite old and very cultured. Regal, even.

"There's not much folklore about faeries in the US," said the southern-sounding woman. "Mostly cartoons and stuff."

"After you win reelection, what would become of your proposed alliance?" asked the male faerie.

"Our alliance would stay strong," replied the confident woman with the slight drawl.

"Our goal is to eradicate the humans," said the cultured male faerie. "Your goal is to rule them. If no humans remain, whom would you rule?"

"Let's be clear," said the woman with the drawl. "Your goal is not realistic, unless you want centuries of devastating war."

Someone gasped with surprise at her frankness.

"Wouldn't you prefer to rule the humans instead?" asked the male speaker with the awkward pronunciations. "And reap trillions of dollars in tribute while enjoying the humans' powerful weapons of war? Your Majesty, don't you think so?"

Your Majesty?

I carefully lifted the bottom of the tablecloth enough to see out. The room was enormous, with marble floors and a tall arched ceiling covered with frescos. Ornately carved wood accents, painted gold, bordered wall panels adorned with oil paintings. The style, I'd say, was Mediterranean Renaissance.

At the far end of the room was a fireplace over six feet tall. Arranged before it were several chairs and sofas. I gulped in surprise when I recognized the individuals sitting there.

The Faerie Queene was in her natural state, with a human-like head and upper torso. The rest of her was abnormally large and covered in elaborate robes.

Sitting across from her was our governor, Ada Witlessin. She was a faerie.

I almost didn't recognize the woman in her natural, diminutive faerie form with her freakish, doll-like head. But it was she, all right.

Beside her was Senator Poxton, also in faerie form. He and the governor wore human-style business suits, shrunken to faerie size. The sight was incongruous and almost silly.

Dressed in aristocratic Fae garb was the fourth individual, an elderly male faerie who I assumed was an advisor to the Queene.

My mind was reeling with the revelation that Witlessin and Poxton were faeries. They were imposters, posing as humans and using the naivete of our community to move their own agenda forward. I felt betrayed, as would all supernaturals once they learned that these two were negotiating an alliance with the Unseelie Court.

I couldn't resist continuing to peek at the faeries, though it was risky.

"As you desire, we will be clear," said the Faerie Queene in a voice that was old and somewhat gravelly, but musical at the same time. "The court's policy regarding humans is to get rid of them." She made a brushing motion with the back of her hand. "That is what our people want. For centuries, we've used the same strategy on my subjects that you are using on your voters, to make them fear and hate the other, while promising that only we can save them from the object of their fear. Humans."

Governor Witlessin smiled and nodded.

"In reality," said the Queene, "we realize the human population has grown too large, infesting every habitable part of Florida and the world. Eradicating them is not realistic now."

"An alliance between your court and us, the indigenous faeries, would help you conquer the humans and cement your rule for all time," the governor said.

"You understand there is a great deal of suspicion among our people of you native faeries," said the Queene's advisor. "You've coexisted with the humans for too long. Some of you are even rumored to be working with the humans."

"No one knows human behavior better than we do," said Poxton. "You'll benefit from our expertise. And those collaborators will be tracked down and eliminated."

"We're not convinced we need an alliance to achieve our goals," the advisor said.

"No offense, but your court hasn't conquered Florida, or any other part of the country, after all these years," Poxton said with attitude.

The advisor gave an angry smile. "Not yet. We have a powerful weapon in the works."

"We've heard of it," the governor said. "It's very encouraging."

"Perhaps that is why you are here?" asked the Queene. "To align yourselves with the predestined conquerors?"

"Yes, Your Majesty," the governor said. "We want to help you with your historic triumph."

"You need us," Poxton said. "We're making Florida a soft target for you. Even if your secret weapon is effective against humans, you will still have to conquer the supernaturals who oppose you. Our unmasking campaign is eliminating them before you invade."

"As I mentioned before, your campaign could make faeries, like you, targets," the Queene's advisor said.

"Only if they find out we're faeries," the governor replied. "Which is highly unlikely."

"I'm still trying to get to the bottom of why you and your team want to be our allies, Governor. Yes, you want to be safe when we come marching into Tallahassee. But there must be something more," probed the advisor.

"Not just safe," Governor Witlessin said. "Remaining in command. I have the legislature in the palm of my hand. No governor has had as firm a control of the state as I do. And if I win—*when* I win—reelection, we have plans to make my power nearly absolute. I want to keep it that way."

"I'm beginning to understand," the advisor said.

"When the Unseelie Court conquers Florida and the rest of the country, I want to rule the state of Florida in your name. And, eventually, all the southern states."

The Queene chuckled. "Oh, do you?"

"I do. And I will prove my worth to you. So much so that you will happily anoint me as your viceroy."

"We shall see," the Queene said.

"Governor, Senator, thank you for coming," said the advisor. "We will continue this conversation soon."

Large double doors opened, near the one I had been rolled through, and I dropped the edge of the tablecloth. Several faeries entered the room and passed my cart. When they returned in my direction, I ventured another peek beneath the tablecloth and saw footmen carrying a litter with the Queene upon it.

After the Queene departed, there was a hum of conversation as the others left the room, and I wondered if it was safe to try again to escape.

I heard more footsteps as others entered the room, and the clinking of china and pewter came to me as servants cleaned up the refreshments. Perhaps when the cart was wheeled back to the kitchen, I could slip away.

The door nearest me opened, and a chill came over me. Someone with serious magic had entered the room. Suddenly, terror seized me as I felt as if I had been caught in the beams of searchlights, and hundreds of eyes were on me, though I was crouched in the darkness beneath the cart.

The tablecloth was yanked away. A stern faerie in a sorcerer's red robes leaned over to look at me.

"You! I heard about the trouble you gave us beneath the palace," he said. "I destroyed your tunnel to flush you out into the open, but you were crafty. Until my magic found you right here in our home."

CHAPTER 26

DARLA

Mom, can you hear me?

I was resting on the disgusting couch of the empty home near the palace when Sophie's words came to me telepathically. After she discovered she was an empath, it seemed as if our psychic connection has grown stronger with each passing day. And that included our telepathy.

Where are you, Sophie? I'm worried sick. The tunnel collapsed, so we couldn't send anyone through it to rescue you.

I'm in the palace, locked up in some closet. A faerie sorcerer caught me. I think he's the same one who kept you captive.

Oh, no. My torturer, who had never told me his name, had taken her. We had to free Sophie before he tortured her.

Outside of the house, gnomes were readying for a new offensive. The mission to rescue me was turning into a debacle. Gorkee had wanted to whisk me out of Palm Beach, but I refused to go until I knew Sophie was safe.

Now she was a captive, and I might become one again as the Fae closed in on us.

Cory burst into the room. "I've found a ley line!"

His face fell when he saw I wasn't impressed.

"Sophie contacted me telepathically," I said. "She's been captured."

"Oh, no. We'll be lucky enough to get off this island alive. How can we possibly rescue her?"

"With luck. And magic. How did you find the ley line?"

"I've been super sensitive to them ever since I harvested the ones in San Marcos. I took one of the vans and let my magic direct me. I ended up at a freshwater spring near one of the first churches built here during South Florida's pioneer days. It's a minor ley line, but it juiced me up."

"That was risky. The Fae are everywhere looking for us."

"If they want to attack us with magic, I'm ready. If they're using conventional arms, we're doomed. We're massively outnumbered. But it's only a couple of hours before dawn, and I don't see how the Queene would allow her soldiers to run around in the billionaires' backyards in daylight."

A gnome sentry whistled outside.

Gorkee appeared in the living room, her mouth a tight, straight line.

"Divine One, you must escape now," she said. "The Fae are blocking the roads."

"You can just call me Darla. And no, I'm not leaving this town while Sophie is in captivity."

"Have you heard from her?"

"Yes. They're holding her in the palace somewhere. We need to rescue her."

"With all due respect, I'm the commander of this mission. And I strongly advise you to escape Palm Beach while you still can."

"Well, I have a goddess in me, so I outrank you. And I'm staying until we free Sophie."

"The Fae are blocking the road?" Bob asked, still sitting in his magic circle on the living room floor. "Why didn't I get out of here before it was too late?"

"That settles it," I said. "I can't escape. All we can do now is fight."

Another whistle came from the yard, and Gorkee went outside.

"The only reason I came here was to shrink Sophie so she could fit in the tunnels," Bob complained.

"You turned me normal sized again," I said. "Got to give you credit for that."

"Now you can use your magic for fighting," Cory said.

"I still need to keep Sophie small, unless I hear otherwise. Anyway, fighting's not my thing," Bob said.

"It is now. Put a protection spell over this house so I can use my magic offensively."

Cory and I went from room to room, peering out the windows. Cory used a spell that enhanced his distance vision and enabled him to see in the dark. My goddess powers were dormant now, so I was useless.

"I can see faerie scouts fanning out throughout the neighborhood," Cory said.

"It's only a matter of time before they find this house."

"Bob's magic should protect us, at least for a while. And Gorkee has placed a small detachment of guards around the house. Ah, I see what she's doing. She's leading a frontal attack!"

"But we're outnumbered."

From the window of a dark bedroom, I saw a phalanx of gnomes, bristling with spears, marching away from the house and onto a neighboring lawn, heading straight toward the palace.

A dog barked. Man, I hoped the neighbors were heavy sleepers.

"The faeries are scattered all over the place," Cory said. "Gorkee's tight formation can push right through them. She might even make it all the way to the palace."

"And then what? Get wiped out?"

"I'm going with them," Cory said. "They'll need any magic I can provide to help them."

"Um, excuse me. Why are you in our home?" asked an unfamiliar voice.

I jumped. Two young men in clubbing clothes stood in the bedroom with us. I sensed they were supernatural.

"I thought the house was empty and for sale," I said.

"We're squatting—"

"—renting," his companion interjected.

These must be the psychic vampires Bob told me he believed were living here.

"Sorry," Cory said. "Did you know the oceanfront mansion at the end of your street is full of faeries?"

"Yes," the first vampire said. "Horrible neighbors. All sorts of weird creatures trooping in and out of that place. There's even the occasional execution."

"Executions the neighbors can see?"

"People have tall hedges here."

"Worst of all, we've been trying to sell the old lady annuities ever since we moved in," said the second one. "She just laughs at us."

"You work in finance?" I asked.

He smiled. "No better place than Palm Beach to make money from money."

"I understand you're psychic vampires. Sin eaters. You feed upon the humans' greed, pride, and envy."

"Yes," the first one said. "And lust, gluttony, etcetera. You can find all seven deadly sins here in Palm Beach."

"How did you know about us?" asked his partner.

"We have a vampire with us. He detected your presence. I'm Darla, by the way. This is my husband, Cory."

"Pleased to meet you," said the first one. "I'm Bill and this is Javier."

"Sorry to break into your home," I said, "but a bunch of friends came here to rescue me. The old lady—the Faerie Queene—was holding me prisoner in the mansion. And torturing me."

"How horrible!" Javier exclaimed. "Why would they do that?"

"Long story. Let's just say the Fae are evil."

"I'm not at all surprised," Bill said.

"My daughter, who rescued me, has been captured by them. We're trying to rescue her."

"That sounds absolutely fascinating," said Javier. "We wish you the best of luck."

"Thank you," Cory said. "I'm going to follow our soldiers."

"Can we go with you?" Bill asked. "Perhaps we can help."

"I'm going with you, too," I said. "I'm not just going to sit here while Sophie is locked up in there."

"Whoa, dudes, the vampires are back," Bob called from the living room.

The sin eaters went to the living room, and the three vampires looked each other up and down.

"We need you to make your protection spell mobile," I told him. "We're heading to the palace."

"That's not a good idea," Bob said.

"None of this mission is a good idea. But we're doing it anyway. Come on."

"I told you I need to stay inside the magic circle to keep Sophie small."

"Let your spell fade. It's okay if she returns to normal size," I said. "She needs any advantage she can get to fight the faeries. If they want to put her in the tunnels again, they can shrink her themselves."

Bob muttered an incantation before standing and wiping away part of the circle with his foot.

I headed out the front door with the rest of the gang following. A gnome jabbered at me and tried to block my way.

"Let us go," I ordered him. "We're needed on the front lines."

So, full of eagerness and foolishness, we trooped through the hedge the gnome battle column had cut through, past a very attractive swimming pool, and on into the next yard. We continued trespassing through yards until we heard the unmistakable clatter of a hand-to-hand battle.

Elves, faeries, gnomes, and other species frowned upon using gunpowder. They preferred their ancient traditions of using edged weapons when fighting each other. Guns, they believed, were only for weakling humans. Also, faeries were too small in their natural forms to handle guns. They thought it was silly to manufacture their own tiny firearms, so they stuck with old-school weaponry. However, should a Fae army ever face a human one, believe me, they would do so in human form, using modern arms.

Not on this pre-dawn morning. I beheld the same kind of battlefield Julius Caesar or King Henry V would have seen: infantry using brute force to cut and clobber each other, while archers picked off their targets from afar.

The battle column of gnomes had punched through a thin line of faerie defenders and had now changed formation into a battle line, led by Gorkee, advancing across the palace grounds toward the swimming pool.

Yes, the swimming pool ruined the illusion that this was taking place hundreds of years ago.

"I can't believe neighbors haven't woken up and called the police about this racket," I said.

"The faeries use magic to dampen the noise coming from their property," Bill said. "It lets them get away with their barbaric activities."

"Like karaoke," Javier said.

Gorkee and her troops reached a row of French doors facing the pool patio, but the gnomes couldn't wrench them open. They must have been magically sealed.

This left the gnomes trapped with their backs against the doors, holding their shields high to shelter themselves from the rain of arrows. Fae infantry began flooding the grounds—from where, I didn't know.

I'd thought we were at a safe distance from the fighting, but we had followed the gnomes all the way to the palace grounds, and the faeries were surrounding us.

"We must get inside the palace," I shouted. "Cory?"

Cory pointed both arms toward the French doors, less than a hundred yards away from us. The air around him felt supercharged as he drew upon the energy of the ley lines, as well as his own magical energy.

A *whoosh* of power flew from his hands, and the French doors blew open as if from an explosion.

"Not bad, if I do say so myself," Cory crowed.

The gnomes rushed into the palace, but the influx of Fae soldiers would only follow them inside and slaughter them if we didn't stop them.

Bob brandished his staff, and with a crackling energy, cast a sleeping spell on the faeries. They dropped to the pool patio before they could reach the doors.

But more were coming. And some of them were coming toward us.

I realized they had emerged from the tunnels beneath the pool, the ones that connected to the cavern where I'd been held. There must be a giant barracks underground.

Sophie, are you still in the closet above ground? I asked telepathically.

Yes. Where are you?

We're on our way.

Strangely, I could see the tunnels now, as if I had x-ray vision. I smelled the water of the swimming pool—saltwater with no chlorine—and its dense molecules. The water felt like it belonged to me.

The Goddess was coming to life within me, changing my perspective, filling me with power and the urge for victory.

I went away.

And became Danu, goddess of not just the earth but of all its waters, mother of the rivers, streams, marshes, oceans, aquifers, and underground water tables.

A vengeful goddess who abhorred the puny human attempts to tame her waters. I hated dams. I despised drainage canals. More than anything, I couldn't stand swimming pools.

Power surged inside me and flowed outward.

The giant, Olympic-sized pool showed cracks in its bottom. And then, with the ground rumbling, the concrete broke apart and all the water drained from the pool like a flushed toilet.

Flooding all the tunnels and spaces below.

The fresh faerie troops stopped arriving in the backyard.

"Good, you're back," Cory said to me. "Good job with the swimming pool. But we need to go inside now and find Sophie. The gnomes are still outnumbered."

I was still a bit disoriented now that the Goddess had left me. Cory led me by the hand. We circled the massive crater that used to be the pool and entered a giant room that looked like it belonged in a Renaissance palace. Bob and the two psychic vampires were just behind us.

The clanging of swords upon swords and shields came from other parts of the palace, and I didn't know which way to go.

Sophie, we've made it into the palace, I thought, reaching out psychically to my daughter. *Do you know where the closet is?*

No. But I smell food, so I must be near the kitchen. There's fighting going on nearby.

That didn't help. There seemed to be fighting everywhere.

"I think she's near the kitchen," I said. "How do we find it?"

"Dude, that's right up my alley," Bob said. "Heightened vampire olfactory glands, plus some magic to make them even more sensitive. I'm better than a hound dog."

And, like a hound dog, he began sniffing. Not with his nose to the ground, but with it raised, his head tilted backward.

"Follow me."

We left the large room and went down a corridor.

Something screeched behind us, and I turned to find a faerie servant armed with a dagger rushing toward me.

I was unarmed. But I was also in my full human size. I swung my leg and kicked the little faerie, sending him bouncing off a wall and sliding, unconscious, along the polished floor.

"The kitchen is just ahead," Bob said.

"Sophie!" I shouted at the top of my lungs. "Can you hear me?"

"I'm in here," came her muffled voice. She pounded on the door of her closet.

It was behind us. We had run past it.

The door was locked, of course. Cory used an unlocking spell. I admired his prowess at magic after having abandoned it for so long.

When the door opened, Sophie leaped into my arms like a spider monkey. In fact, that's how big she was. The magic that had shrunk her was still working.

"Are you okay, sweetie?" I asked.

"Yes. Ignore the blood on me. It's faerie blood."

"Are you strong enough to run, or should I carry you?"

"I'm fine." She noticed Bob among us. "Bob, can you restore me to my proper size?"

"Yeah." He glanced around. "Keep an eye out for guards. Sophie and I will be very vulnerable for a bit."

The rest of us turned away as Bob went into a trance and Sophie went through the awkward metamorphosis into her normal size. It wasn't as painful a process as some shifters go through, but I didn't want to watch.

"Okay, let's get the heck out of here," Sophie said, pointing in the other direction. "Away from the tunnels."

We jogged down the hall, heading back to the room with the French doors.

"It's time for Gorkee's forces to retreat from the palace before they're all killed or captured," Sophie said. "Mom, can you contact her?"

It had been easy to communicate telepathically with Leighnel, an elf. I hoped that would be the case with a faerie.

It worked.

"Gorkee said we should make our way back to the vans and

leave immediately," I reported. "She'll follow us after she does 'a little mopping up.'"

We rushed through the double doors of the large room.

And collided with a faerie in human form, wearing red robes.

It was the sorcerer who had tortured me.

CHAPTER 27

SOPHIE

The faerie, who had captured me from the food cart, was larger than they usually were in human form. And he was brimming with power.

During the brief moment we all stood there stunned, he exchanged glances with Mom. She instinctively cringed, then pushed her face forward in defiance.

I was certain now that he was the sorcerer who had tortured her. I pulled my now full-sized sword from the scabbard on my back and lunged at him without a second thought.

An invisible force that felt like a King-Kong grip around my body picked me up and threw me across the hallway, slamming me against the wall behind the others. I dropped my sword, and it clanged atop the tile floor.

We had an arch mage and a witch on our side, though they weren't into attack magic like I was. Bob waved his staff, and I glimpsed a haze fill the doorway in front of the sorcerer before it disappeared. A barrier spell.

The problem with that was it prevented Cory from sending

any magic at the sorcerer. A problem that proved not to matter as soon as the sorcerer broke through the barrier and strode into the hallway.

He didn't attack Bob or Cory. He went straight for Mom.

As I gathered my wits, I cast a protection spell around her. The sorcerer reached for her, and his hands bounced off the bubble. I didn't doubt he had the power to defeat it, but it gave me a few valuable seconds to retrieve my sword.

I crouched on the opposite side of the hall and sent lightning bolts at the sorcerer. The first one took him unawares, and he staggered backward, wisps of smoke rising from his red robe.

Then, he came after me again.

I lifted my sword above my head, as if I were going to chop him, then spun my body and swung the sword in a sideways arc. Just before it struck his abdomen, he blocked it with his hand.

Yeah, his bare hand. The impact stung my hands as if my sword had hit an iron bar. And there was not a drop of blood on his palm.

I tried again, thrusting the sword point straight toward his heart.

He batted it away with his hand like I was using a foam toy.

"Your human magic is so pathetic," he said in English with the slight Eastern European accent faeries affected. "I'm going to stomp you to a pulp like a cockroach."

Meanwhile, my other teammates with magic were hovering in the background. Bob aimed his staff at the sorcerer, and Cory waved his hands, with no effect. Either their magic was useless, or they couldn't even figure out what to do.

I was lucky the sorcerer hadn't taken my sword—why, I had no idea. But I gave a silent *thank you* and swung it at his neck. As I expected, he blocked it with his hand. But this time, I sent a magical bolt through the blade at exactly the right moment, and the sorcerer jerked as if electrocuted.

He still gripped the blade, and I sent more and more power through it, making him stagger backward. Now on the offensive, I advanced as he retreated.

Finally, my comrades came through. Cory sent a massive wave of power that hit the sorcerer like a freight train, smashing him against the wall. He released my sword, looking dazed.

I moved in for the kill.

Or so I thought.

Fire coursed through my entire body. I knew it wasn't actual fire, but that's what it felt like. A shriek escaped me, and I fell to the floor, writhing and kicking in agony.

"Put the fire out!" I screamed.

Mom rushed to my side and knelt over me. Bob and Cory kept the sorcerer away from us with alternating blasts of power. Even Bill and Javier had joined the battle, moving faster than the eye as they slashed at the sorcerer. Too bad psychic vampires didn't have fangs.

"Mom, you need to escape," I said, panting with pain.

"Nonsense," she said.

She stroked my body and hummed a low tune. I recognized what was happening. It was that ancient Celtic song that meant the Goddess was rising in her.

The sensation of cold water flowed over and through me, soothing the burning. Eventually, it erased the pain entirely.

"Thank you," I whispered, "but please save yourself. The rest of us will keep this jerk busy while you escape."

"I can't leave you. You're my only child."

I felt like I was going to get all weepy, but I couldn't pick a worse time to do so.

I was wrong. The time got even worse. Two Fae soldiers

wandered into the hallway. They must have been escaping the mayhem elsewhere in the palace, but as soon as they saw three humans and three vampires fighting the sorcerer, they joined the fray.

The soldiers were in their natural forms, but they were archers, so they attacked us without engaging in physical contact. Rapidly fired arrows streaked toward us.

Bill was struck in the neck, but the vampire plucked out the small arrow, no worse for wear. Before I could get myself together, one pierced my jacket, but didn't touch my skin.

Cory yelped and dropped to his knees with an arrow in his thigh.

Finally, I regained my focus and sent lightning bolts at the faeries. Each exploded in a shower of fire.

Mom had gone to Cory's side to tend to his wound with her goddess powers, and Bob cast a binding spell on the sorcerer. Fibers of an invisible magic twine wrapped the faerie like a standing-rib roast. You couldn't see the fibers, but his robe and flesh were indented by them.

He broke through them in seconds.

I prepared for another painful attack as the sorcerer sprinted toward us, but he did what I hadn't expected yet should have.

He scooped up Mom in his arms and took off running.

EVEN IF YOU'RE A POWERFUL SORCERER, YOU CAN'T OUTRUN vampires, especially if you're carrying a woman over your shoulder. Bill and Javier quickly caught up with the faerie and tried to take Mom from him. This lifted my desperate spirits.

But even if you're a vampire, you can't prevent yourself from getting knocked to the ground by mega-ton magic. Seeing the two young vamps bounce across the floor like bowling pins promptly lowered my spirits again.

I'm no vampire, but I was in good shape and wasn't carrying anybody. Still, I was having trouble keeping up with the faerie as he ran through the cavernous foyer of the mansion and up a curving grand staircase.

Bob, the rare combination of a magician and a vampire, was my only hope. He wasn't as fast as the psychic vampires, but he was right behind me. Though his binding spell hadn't worked, he tried a magical version of a lariat, meant to tangle around the sorcerer's legs and trip him.

The faerie did, in fact, stumble, almost dropping Mom as he reached the second floor. Bob and I gained ground on him. Bob passed me. I was huffing and puffing as I reached the top of the stairs and turned the corner.

My heart dropped. There was no sign of the sorcerer or of Bob. At the far end of the long hall, two gnomes and three faeries were engaged in hand-to-hand combat. But no one else was in sight.

Where are you, Mom? I asked telepathically.

I'm in a bedroom. My legs are frozen, and I can't move. I don't know where the sorcerer went.

I heard grunting nearby. Where was it coming from? A loud boom came from my right, making me jump. A big dent appeared in the wall plaster underneath the old-fashioned wallpaper.

Directly in front of me, the Persian carpet was sliding and scrunching. My skin tingled with magic when I finally figured out what was going on.

Bob and the sorcerer had made themselves invisible, each hoping it would give them an advantage. Instead, it only gave them a wrestling match.

Someone screamed. Then came another scream that I recognized as Bob's. Two thuds of bodies hitting the floor. And finally, their invisibility wore off.

Both Bob and the sorcerer were lying on the floor, convulsing in pain. They must have attacked each other with spells like the one that had made me feel on fire.

Two of the most powerful magicians in the world, and just look at them.

I stood over the sorcerer with the point of my sword touching his throat. That was when my empathy kicked in.

Great. Perfect timing, Empathy.

But there was nothing redeemable about the sorcerer based on his emotions. There was lots of pride, greed, and ambition, tons of hatred for humans and elves, numerous grievances against the other sorcerers of the court. And, most of all, frustration that he couldn't get rid of us and return to torturing Mom to make her convert Danu to his side.

"How interesting," Bill said.

"Quite a bit of pride, greed, envy, and wrath," Javier said. "More than I've ever sensed in one individual."

The two psychic vampires had appeared at my side.

"Do you mind if we feed on his deadly sins?" Bill asked me.

"Go right ahead."

The two vampires did nothing other than stand above the sorcerer. I guessed they were absorbing the energies of the sinful emotions.

Sure enough, my empathy didn't detect them in the sorcerer anymore.

"Hey guys, he has some random lust in him, too," I said.

"Oh, good," Javier said. "Let's get second helpings."

The vampires continued their absorbing.

"Could you please consume his hatred?" I asked.

"Technically, that's not one of the seven deadly sins," Bill replied. "Though, we ate all his wrath, which is a big part of hatred. But some hatred comes from fear, too."

There wasn't much left to define the sorcerer, now that his sins had been eaten by the vampires. He was basically just a jerk who knew lots of magic.

The spell that was torturing Bob dissipated, and the vampire mage got to his feet.

"Are you going to kill him?" Bob asked me. He hadn't yet released his spell that was tormenting the sorcerer, who still writhed in pain.

"It's not like I'm fighting for my life at the moment. I'm changing as a person, you know. I'm less inclined to kill someone in cold blood."

"Okay. You can put 'less inclined to kill someone in cold blood' in your dating app profile. Let's see what Darla wants to do, because she was tortured by this dude."

We found her in a nearby bedroom on the bed. Bob broke the spell that had bound her.

"Mom, should we kill the sorcerer?" I asked. "The psychic vampires consumed a lot of his negative energy, so it's a little less appealing to kill him now."

She left the bedroom and stared down at her persecutor, who was still undergoing torture from Bob's spell. She seemed to struggle with herself before coming to a decision.

"No. They have other sorcerers. Only defeating them all would make a difference. Let's go."

We went downstairs and found Cory standing, thanks to Danu's healing of his arrow wound. We returned to the big room and went outside, past the destroyed pool. That's when Mom got a message from Gorkee.

"Gorkee said they're beginning an orderly retreat," Mom

reported. "The Queene is barricaded in a wing of the palace, and her forces still outnumber ours. Even if we captured the palace, we couldn't hold it. Gorkee begged us to leave Palm Beach."

We were only too happy to oblige. But a truck driven by faeries tried to block our van from entering the causeway to the mainland.

Fortunately, this happened shortly before dawn, when the roads were empty. After Cory blew up the Fae truck, it would probably be a while before anyone noticed the fire. By then, we should be well on our way along I-95.

"There's something I need to tell you guys," I said to Cory and Mom in the back seat of the van.

I explained the conversation I had overheard between the Queene, Governor Witlessin, and Senator Poxton.

"You've got to be kidding me," Cory said. "They're faeries? And they want to sell us all out to the Queene?"

"Yep."

"Nothing surprises me anymore," Mom said.

"I'd figured their campaign of fear and hatred was all about consolidating their power," Cory said. "But I never imagined it was this sinister."

"You realize they need to keep all of this secret," I said. "Especially the fact that they're faeries. If they knew that I know, they'd kill me in an instant."

Everyone was silent for a few miles.

"I'm tempted to take them down," I said.

"You will *not* risk your life to do that," Mom said.

The violence the governor had unleashed might kill me anyway. And it had never been like me to listen to my mother.

CHAPTER 28

SOPHIE

We slept most of the way back to San Marcos and returned to our family inn exhausted, traumatized, and really, really hungry. Mom had refused to stop for fast food. Sausage-and-egg biscuits must give goddesses heartburn or something. But we arrived in the middle of breakfast service at the inn, so all was well.

Mom wrinkled her nose the moment we walked inside.

"Scones? Who's baking scones?"

"I told you we hired a temporary cook to handle breakfast and the food for Afternoon Tea," I said. "Her name is Pinky."

Mom could have headed straight for the shower. After all, she'd been held prisoner for days in an underground cavern and was smelling pretty ripe. But no, she marched straight into the kitchen. I hurried after her.

"Pinky, meet Darla Chesswick," I said.

"Pleased to meet you, ma'am," Pinky said, offering her hand. "Thanks for the opportunity—"

"Scones. where are the scones?" Mom demanded.

"I just brought a fresh batch to the buffet."

Mom turned on her heels and strode into the dining room, Pinky and me following behind her. Only one table was occupied. The elderly couple looked up at Mom, their eyes widening as they took in her disheveled state.

Mom grabbed a scone from the basket and took a bite. She closed her eyes and frowned.

"Not bad. It tastes like my recipe."

"It is your recipe," Pinky said.

"Good job, Pinky."

"Pinky has some good scone recipes of her own," I added, "but I told her to use yours."

"I always thought you were a smart child." She surveyed the room. "Where is everybody?"

"We're at very low occupancy at the moment. Let's take this conversation elsewhere."

We returned to the kitchen.

"The anti-supernatural mobs have targeted the inn," I explained. "It's not good for business, to put it mildly."

"What do you mean by 'targeted'?"

"Attacked. It wasn't pretty. If I were you, I'd avoid the utility room."

I gave her a summary of what had happened, as well as the threat Marge Moosebacher had made to us.

"It's clear now that some of the local faeries are behind the Great Unmasking," Mom said. "But I'm disappointed humans succumbed to the fear and hatred so thoroughly."

"It's our lizard brain, a remnant of our primitive origins," Pinky said.

Mom and I looked at her with our mouths slightly open. Who would have expected Pinky to be so deep?

"Long before modern humans, if you encountered someone

different from you, it meant they were from another tribe," she continued. "And chances were this person meant you harm. Suspicion of the other is embedded in our genes. We simply must get past it. Just like toddlers must be taught to share."

"Wow," I said.

"And if I can change topics, do I still have a job now that Mrs. Chesswick is back?"

"Yes, you do. And you can call me Darla. I can't keep up with my workload anymore, especially because of my 'moments.'"

Pinky looked quizzical.

"It's a long story," Mom said. "I'll fill you in later."

Cervantes strolled into the kitchen, his tail sticking straight up. He rubbed against Pinky's leg.

"Sophie's familiar agrees with my decision," Mom said.

She's a keeper, Cervantes said to me telepathically. *She wears too much perfume, and I'm not a big fan of skunks, but she'll make a fierce ally.*

What he meant was an ally in the fights to come. As if to emphasize that point, my phone gave an unfamiliar alert tone. I pulled it from my pocket and glanced at the screen.

"What was that?" Mom asked.

"The Mothers Against Monsters app just sent me a notification about an event." I clicked on the alert. "They're having a rally on the waterfront this weekend."

"We can't miss that," Mom said.

"You're being sarcastic, right?"

"Nope. We're going to attend that rally and create some mayhem."

"That's crazy. We're the ones they want to harm."

"Sophie, war is breaking out. Citizens against their fellow citizens, and the Fae against all of us. There's nothing we can do but fight, and never stop, until this is over. And the good guys win."

"Heckling at a rally. Is that a way to win a war?"

"No, but we have to defy them every step of the way."

"Then we should join the insurrection," I said.

"What insurrection?"

"Diego is organizing to take down the Executive Council. They're not doing anything to protect the supernaturals, and I believe some of them, like Baldric, are collaborating with the governor. We need new leadership that unites the supernaturals to fight back."

"I'm all in," Mom replied. "Pinky, are you a member of the Shifters Guild?"

"Um, no."

She looked uncomfortable with the question, so we let it slide.

"I'll go with you to cause trouble at the rally," she added.

IT WASN'T MUCH OF A RALLY, IN MY OPINION. THERE WERE 100 people at the most, though they behaved like hardcore supporters. A couple of dozen people, like us, stood apart from the crowd at its fringes. I couldn't tell if they were simply curious or opposed to the movement.

Marge Moosebacher stood on a small plywood stage next to the waterfront promenade that lined the Sangre River and the bay it formed beside the city, just inside of the ocean inlet. The police had probably told Marge she couldn't block the promenade, so occasional joggers passed by behind the stage. It was rather funny seeing them distract from Marge's bombastic speech shouted into a bullhorn.

Several people held up signs and banners with the Mothers Against Monsters logo, and others called for mass incarceration of supernaturals or made crude insults I won't repeat.

A couple of police officers watched the rally. You'd think, based on the violent nature of the anti-supernatural mobs, that there would have been more of a police presence. Maybe they'd simply grown tired of all this drama.

Marge's speech began like the one she'd given to the Skunk Ape Society, but after she'd gotten the crowd all worked up, she sounded like a maniac. Her magic spread through the crowd, increasing her malignant influence over them.

She was screaming about witches and werewolves, and how they must be killed if America were to survive.

I was getting very uncomfortable knowing that my picture was in the app, standing there with a psychic-goddess and a shifter beside me.

The sun was setting behind us, giving the bay a purple sheen, broken by whitecaps as the wind picked up. The banners of hate fluttered and strained in the breeze, while the fading sun gave Marge's face a demonic glow.

The crowd, already agitated, was pulsing with a restlessness that was about to erupt.

"They're everywhere!" Marge screamed through her bullhorn. "Your coworkers could be monsters! Your neighbors could be monsters! Even your teammates in your bowling league could be monsters! You'll never know until it's too late, unless you scrutinize everyone. Look for something strange, something suspicious. If anything bothers you about them, report them to the police and to our app. Before it's too late!"

A tussle broke out in the center of the tightly packed crowd.

"He's a shifter!" a woman shouted.

"Stop him before he shifts!" several voices insisted.

The crowd converged on a man, kicking, throwing punches.

Icy fear trickled through my gut. I've faced many evil creatures in my life, but there's nothing scarier than an irrational, unpredictable mob.

I focused on my empathy, repulsed by the emotions of hate, fear, and sadism. I fed energy into my empathy, trying to use my magic to persuade.

A third cop strolled over and joined the two who had been watching the rally. They strained to see what was going on but made no effort to stop the violence.

"See?" Marge bellowed. "One is in our very midst!"

The man went down, and the mob grew tighter as they kicked and stomped on him in his vulnerability.

"Someone should do something," Mom said, looking at me.

"I can't make any magic that's obvious. Marge will know a witch did it, and I'll be spotted. I'm trying to control their emotions."

"Whatever works and can save that man."

"Can't Danu help?"

"For some reason, she's not responding."

I poured magic into my empathy, but there were too many people, too many conflicting emotions. How could I control the entire crowd of more than 100 people?

A teenaged boy was on the edge of the crowd, trying to force his way into the center where he could attack the victim. I focused on him, picking up fear, insecurity, and the desire to prove he was masculine.

I pumped confidence and sympathy into him, along with the notion that a real man wouldn't attack a defenseless victim.

A few seconds later, the teenager backed off. His desire to hurt the victim had fled. Now, he decided to go to the police officers and urge them to intervene.

My empathy had worked—but only on one person. There was no time to persuade the crowd one by one.

"Can't you cast a sleep spell on them?" Mom asked.

"I don't know if it would work on so many people. I'll try it, but Marge will spot me right away."

"Guys, stand close to me, so I won't be seen," Pinky said.

I thought I knew what she had in mind. Mom and I huddled over her as she crouched on the grass behind a park bench.

And then, quickly and relatively painlessly, shifted into a skunk.

This was a first for me.

I gathered the pile of Pinky's clothing as the skunk scurried bravely through the crowd and disappeared into the melee.

A few people looked down at their feet, startled. But the full effect of her charge happened a moment later.

People shrieked, and the crowd surged outward like water from a rock dropped in a pond.

The eye-watering reek of skunk spray filled the air, worse even than tear gas. Everyone was freaking out.

As the crowd dispersed, it revealed the victim lying on the grass beside the promenade. Despite his face being covered in blood, he looked familiar.

It was Mr. Humphrey, the guest at the inn who had been spying on us for Marge.

How on earth did one of her most fanatic followers get accused of being a shifter? Having come in close contact with him before, I knew he was just a normal human being, aside from his faith-healing abilities.

Jeez Louise, this was the kind of atrocity a mob full of hate and fear was capable of. It was exactly what Marge was encouraging.

The people who looked like they had been hit directly by

Pinky's spray staggered away. One of them jumped into the bay, hoping to be cleansed. The mob had disintegrated, but at least half the crowd remained.

I caught a glimpse of a skunk darting between parked cars, heading back toward the inn.

The police, wearing surgical masks, checked on Mr. Humphrey. But instead of caring for him, they put him in hand-cuffs and dragged him away.

Marge watched with glee.

"You see what I mean?" she bellowed into her bullhorn. "They're in our midst always. We must be vigilant!"

The remaining audience approached her and closed ranks, despite the lingering reek of skunk.

I was beyond angry. If I'd had my crossbow with me, a bolt made of ash would shoot toward her heart right now.

What magic could I use to hurt her?

What would that even accomplish? She would sic the crowd on me.

Then, I thought of a better idea. I took a journey through Hell—a plunge into her emotions.

The Fae species is different from humans, but being highly intelligent apex predators like we are, they have similar kinds of emotions. However, they are more brutal and cunning, less prone to mercy. They feel pride, like we do, but much more of it.

Her pride was what I manipulated as I used my empathy.

She was pleased with herself for whipping this crowd into a frenzy. And ecstatic about how well the campaign against super-naturals was going. She was confident humans would destroy themselves without any help from the Faerie Queene's armies.

Yeah, she was proud of herself and felt vastly superior to humans. In fact, she disliked being in human form—a big, lumbering creature that was too hairy and sweaty and stupid.

Being in human form was the price she had to pay to coexist with us, and to run this campaign against the supernaturals.

I detected another strong emotion that was intertwined with her pride. Envy. She envied humans for dominating the planet, despite being an inferior species.

Could envy explain why the Fae hated us so much?

And boy, she hated being in the guise of a creature she scorned.

I leveraged this hatred by concentrating on it and feeding it magic, heightening it.

Wouldn't it feel great to shift out of this disgusting human body? Wouldn't it be liberating to be in my beautiful, magnificent faerie form during this moment of triumph? I am the master of these bleating sheep standing before me. Let them see my true self and how superior I am to them.

I felt these feelings myself, and fed them into her, boosted by magic. I repeated them over and over until her caution and common sense were overcome.

And soon, I felt these very same feelings coming from her, as she experienced them intensely.

"You have so many monsters among you because humans are monsters," she told the crowd. "You're flawed and weak. That's what monsters are—defects spawned by you miserable creatures. You're not beautiful and perfect like the Fae."

And just like that, she shifted into her faerie form. Which, believe me, was not beautiful.

The crowd gasped.

She lifted the bullhorn in both hands and continued to speak, though now in a squeaky, raspy voice.

"Faeries are superior to humans. We are not like the monsters among you that must be destroyed."

Too late, Marge, or whatever your Fae name is.

279

The crowd, frightened by her sudden transformation into a creature they had never seen before, did what she had trained them to do.

They attacked. They swarmed the little plywood stage, and their numbers swallowed her.

The bullhorn amplified her scream, which was abruptly cut off as the crowd beat her with more savagery than they had used on Mr. Humphrey. The bullhorn went flying and landed near Mom and me, rolling in the grass.

We left the scene before the crowd had finished with Marge. I didn't want to see what they had done to her.

Mom and I walked with an arm around each other's shoulders, but it was not enough to make me feel better. I had a sudden urge to speak with Diego, not so much thinking he would comfort me, but to tell him I would join the insurrection. I needed to move forward.

He'd been ignoring my texts and calls, but later that evening, he finally returned a text.

Yes, he texted, *come by my place at nine tonight.*

CHAPTER 29

SOPHIE

I sensed Diego's presence in his apartment before I even began climbing the stairs. My supernatural sensitivity had increased over the years, and then practically flooded me when my abilities as an empath awakened.

My sword was strapped to my back, and my crossbow hung from a harness over one shoulder, as was the case now whenever I went out at night.

Was it rude to visit his home carrying weapons? Should I have brought a gift, like a plant, too?

When I reached the top of the stairs, he opened the door before I'd even knocked. Our eyes met. There was something in his look, but I couldn't be sure what.

"Good to see you again," he said, with an innocent peck on my cheek.

"Yes, you've finally stopped avoiding me." I surveyed the living and dining rooms. They looked the same. "Thank you for letting me stay here before. If anything was out of place when you came home, it was your ghost's fault."

He smiled. "Would you like a bottled water?"

"Yes, please."

I sat on his couch's armrest. My sword would make it too awkward to sit on the couch properly, and I didn't feel safe enough to remove it yet.

Diego returned from the kitchen with a bottle of spring water and handed it to me with a glass. I drank straight from the bottle.

"It looks like you're doing some work downstairs," I said. "Are you going to reopen the restaurant?"

"Yes. In a month or two. I've invested too much time and money in it to just walk away, especially with so many loyal customers."

"It's Lethia's fault you had to close it."

"Yes." He sat in an antique chair across from me but looked away. "I returned to her, so I don't have to fear for my life anymore."

I said nothing.

He returned his gaze to me, then smiled. "Pathetic, I know."

"None of my business," I said. "Except when she vowed to kill me, too. I have to ask, is she in league with Baldric?"

"What do you mean?"

"I've decided to join your insurrection, and it's clear now that the local faeries have corrupted the Executive Council. And our state government, too."

I told him the long, complicated story about the connections between Baldric, Senator Poxton, and Marge Moosebacher. I wasn't ready to share the knowledge that could get me killed: that Poxton and the governor were faeries. But I did mention that they visited the Faerie Queene's palace.

"Her court and the indigenous Fae have never gotten along," I said. "But they both want to conquer humans and rule the state, the country, the world. The local faeries are using the Great Unmasking to make humans help them get rid of supernaturals who would be difficult foes."

"What do they need from the Queene?"

"She's always wanted to conquer us, and she has armies. Plus, a magical secret weapon that's in development based on a substance produced by the forests. The reason they kidnapped Mom was to convince Danu to help them."

"I apologize for not helping you. Lethia wouldn't allow me to speak to you, let alone go on a raid in Palm Beach."

"Now the truth comes out. I suppose I'm lucky you're even allowed to be here."

He was growing angry. He'd been humiliated by Lethia in front of me and my teasing wasn't helping his pride.

"Your relationship with her is not my concern," I said. "But you need to find out how closely allied she is with Baldric if you're going to lead an insurrection against the Council."

"The insurrection must be wider. We must topple Baldric, and all the guild leaders allied with him, to bring integrity back to the Council. And we also have to fight the local Fae and the corrupted members of the state government."

I agreed. Yet it was a massive undertaking.

"What about Lethia?" I pressed.

Diego hesitated. "She must prove her loyalty is to our guild, not to Baldric's machinations."

The stairs creaked. The front door flew open.

If you speak of the devil too much, sometimes the devil hears you.

"Why are you here?" Lethia asked me, trembling with rage.

"I need Diego's help to, protect my mother." It was the best excuse I could think of.

Before I could blink, she had crossed the floor and grabbed me with one hand by the neck. She lifted me from the floor.

"Protect her from what?"

"The Fae." I could barely speak through my constricted throat. "From the Faerie Queene. And Baldric, too. He's betraying the guilds."

"Nonsense."

"Baldric is allied with the politicians who passed the anti-supernatural laws," Diego said. He'd gotten up from the couch and moved closer to us. "The people who want to eliminate vampires."

"Why would he do that?" Lethia asked with derision. "He's supernatural himself."

I wished she would put me down already.

"The indigenous faeries believe they will not be unmasked," I said with difficulty, since my jaw was about to pop out. "They want the other supernaturals arrested or killed, and humans to destroy themselves. That way, it will be easy for the Fae to take over."

"I have existed for three thousand years," Lethia said. "I don't care about petty politics."

"I think we should take this seriously," Diego said.

The next thing I knew, I was flying across the apartment, landing with my butt in the kitchen sink. Good thing vampires don't eat food, so there were no dirty dishes in there.

I realized with despair that I had dropped my crossbow. Alfie was still strapped to my back, but the scabbard had twisted into an awkward position. *Please, don't let the blade be bent.*

Lethia stood face to face with Diego. He didn't retreat.

"Why do you care what this silly human thinks?" She bared her fangs at him. "Are you attracted to her?"

"Lethia, you're being unreasonable."

Any man, especially one who has existed for five hundred years, should know better than to say that to his girlfriend.

She slapped him across the face with a crack like the bough of a tree breaking.

"You will respect and honor me." Her words were quiet but deadly. "And obey me. I am wiser and more powerful than you—more than any other vampire."

"Don't you ever strike me again," Diego said. His words, too, were calm but full of rebellion.

She slapped him with her other hand.

"Leave my home," he said. "Our relationship has ended."

They both moved so quickly I saw little more than blurs as they fought like two tigers. Biting and slashing, they rose into the air until they hit the ceiling, then dropped to the floor and wrestled. Blood flew everywhere.

I couldn't do anything to stop them. Physically, I couldn't restrain them, nor could I use a weapon against Lethia without endangering Diego.

I cast my sleep spell.

"Cease your magic, you stupid witch! Or I will kill your mother after I kill you."

Before the spell was completed, Lethia threw Diego, and he slammed into me, knocking me out of the sink. My head struck a cabinet, and everything went black.

WHEN I CAME TO, I WAS LYING ON MY STOMACH ON THE tiled floor, head throbbing, eyes blurry. I was dizzy and disoriented.

Sucking and slurping sounds came from nearby. Painfully

moving my head, I saw Lethia sitting astride Diego, her mouth over his throat, gulping his blood, gorging on it.

She was going to drain him to death.

And I couldn't do anything to stop her. I could barely move and was too groggy to cast a spell.

But we weren't entirely alone in this building.

"Acora," I whispered. "Help Diego. Please, help him."

My empathy, so sensitive to spirits, reached out to the ghost of the Timucuan woman who haunted this place. I had comforted her before. Would she remember me? Would a ghost have the focus and agency to save Diego?

"Acora, please help him. The other vampire is killing him."

Spiritual energy was brewing. I could sense it. She was here, invisible, but present.

A kitchen chair suddenly flew across the room and struck Lethia hard enough to knock her off Diego.

She snarled and crawled back on top of him, resuming her feast. She was so focused on feeding and destroying him that I don't believe she realized what had happened.

Another chair slammed into her, again sending her onto the floor. But this time, the kitchen table rose into the air and shot across the room, smashing on top of the prone Lethia.

Then the refrigerator shimmied out from its nook, rolled across the floor to Lethia, and tipped over, dropping onto the upended table that was still on her.

Lethia groaned. The fridge and table rocked as she struggled to get out from under them. Diego lay unmoving on the floor, not yet destroyed, but close to it.

Lethia was simply too strong to be incapacitated by blunt force. I had to do something fast before she freed herself, finished draining Diego, and came after me.

My head was clearer now, but magic would not save us.

I wasn't sure if I could even reach around to remove my sword from its scabbard, let alone have the strength to use it to decapitate Lethia or pierce her heart. I definitely couldn't conjure blasts of lightning right now.

I glanced around the kitchen. And then I saw it. My crossbow lay on the floor beside the kitchen island.

It was painful to crawl across the floor, but finally I had my hands on the smooth wood of the stock. I cocked the bow, which was a challenge, as I was on all fours. The bolts were still in the quiver attached to the stock.

I placed an ash bolt, notching it to the string, and crawled toward Lethia just as the refrigerator slid off the table and landed on the floor with a boom.

When Lethia crawled from beneath the upended table, I was standing, ready for her. I stepped closer and aimed my crossbow.

"You've been on this planet long enough," I said and pulled the trigger.

The crossbow bolt made a loud thump after passing through her heart and hitting the tile beneath her.

She dissolved into dust, faster than other vampires because of her extreme longevity. The millennia during which her body had defied the effects of aging and decay had caught up with her.

Surprisingly for me, I didn't feel any regret or guilt for what I'd done. Her thousands of years in this world had turned Lethia into a metaphorical, as well as a literal, monster. It had warped her personality and turned her heart as black as a chunk of coal.

Diego lay on his back, staring at the pile of dust that had been his lover. His expression was blank. His preternatural healing abilities were at work, bringing him back from the edge of his destruction.

"I'm sorry." I didn't know what else to say.

The monster had attacked both of us, but I was the one who

had destroyed her. I watched him carefully, searching his face for emotions, trying in vain to sense them.

He slowly got to his feet, moving stiffly and gingerly in a very un-vampire-like manner. He was still weakened and not yet fully healed.

"I must go now," he said.

"Diego, please don't be angry at me. I had to do it."

He looked at me with sadness. "I understand. Even if I was willing to be destroyed, it didn't mean you had to die as well. And you would have."

He still loved her—even after all the abuse and assassination attempts—to the point of accepting his destruction?

"Stay safe," he said.

He walked out of the kitchen. The front door opened and closed, and I was left alone in his apartment with the pile of ancient dust.

CHAPTER 30

DARLA

C ory and I snuggled in bed. Our lovemaking had seemed more desperate than any other time before.

"Wow," I said. "Maybe I should be kidnapped by the Fae and rescued by you more often."

"Maybe you should enjoy a simple life of running an inn and baking scones."

"I think Pinky is eclipsing me in the scone arena."

"What I mean is, you don't have to be involved with fighting the Fae anymore. You've done it before. Let someone else do it now."

"Danu refused to help them. But that doesn't mean they won't ask her again, by going through me."

"Just curious. Why wouldn't Danu help them?"

"The only creatures worse for the earth than humans are faeries."

"How could they be worse?" Cory asked. "I don't see any Fae strip mines or power plants."

"The Fae damage the earth in more insidious ways, deep

underground. And unlike we humans, they know they can escape to their homeland if they destroy the earth."

"Maybe rich humans will be able to go somewhere else after a little more technical innovation in space travel."

I grunted in agreement. "I wish I knew more about Danu's intentions. She only tells me the bare minimum."

"She's in your life too much as it is."

"I told you about this evening at the MAM rally, what the crowd did."

"Yeah. Disgusting."

"Why didn't Danu come into me and allow me to end the mob violence? I was able to do that before, when the tourist trolley attacked the jogger."

"I don't know. Could it be because the crowd tonight was larger and more frenzied?"

"I don't know."

"And they had that Moosebacher woman egging them on. Maybe it all was too much for even Danu to quell."

"Maybe."

"It could be that she knew Sophie was going to break up the rally."

"Yes, but Mr. Humphrey was severely beaten. And Marge Moosebacher was, too. I think she was killed, but I'm not sure. Why did Danu allow that to happen?"

"They weren't good characters, Darla."

"Yeah. I guess you're right."

"Let's hope that from now on, we can stay out of all this mess."

"Sophie is still in the app. And let's face it, we're not a normal family. We have three witches, including my mother, and two of them are living here in the same house. I'm a psychometrist and the human vessel of an ancient goddess. Plus, we have a living gargoyle, a vampire, and several ghosts. We even have a skunk shifter working here. This inn deserves its reputation as a supernatural haven."

"Only the real kooks believe that. Let's hope they fade away."

Cory drifted off to sleep, comforted by his naïveté. I got out of bed and put on a nightgown, then went into the bathroom to brush my teeth.

Only, it wasn't the bathroom anymore as soon as I closed the door behind me. I was in Ehrendil, my hand on the doorknob of a door to the interior of their tree world.

"Thank you for coming," Leighnel said, approaching me along the hollowed interior of a tree root.

"I didn't have a choice. Somehow, I just ended up here."

"Yes, it's a power we have with our people and our allies. Sorry for not alerting you first."

Thank God I had put on a nightgown before I was transported here, even though my body didn't come with me, only my spiritual essence manifested as me in my nightgown. It was like when the Goddess summoned me—a type of astral travel. I hoped Cory wouldn't discover my inert body was in the bathroom. He got so concerned whenever I "went away."

"I brought you here because I've had a major breakthrough with my research," Leighnel said. "I've discovered what the purpose of phytolucine is. Its purpose for the trees, that is, not whatever twisted aim the Fae have for it."

"Okay. Are you going to tell me?"

"In due time, in due time. First, I need to leave my body like you did, and we're going to take a little tour."

He took my hand—a gorgeous, slender, blond Elf holding hands with a short, middle-aged woman in a nightgown. Suddenly, the visual manifestations of our bodies were gone, and we were speeding down a hallway, inside a root, that grew progressively smaller.

And then we were outside of the root, in the soil deep beneath the tree, following the roots as they spread downward and outward, growing tinier and tinier as they branched out.

The roots wove through the soil, around rocks and the roots of other trees. And soon they joined a stringy, tangled mass of white fibers. It seemed to stretch forever through this underground world.

The mycorrhiza fungus, Leighnel said in my head. *The trees use it as a communication network. They can send messages to each other over many miles.*

Though I wasn't in my psychic's body, I detected a hum of energy spreading through the fungi.

Trees obviously don't have brains, Leighnel said. *But through my years of research, I've found trees to be sentient, though not in a way we elves or humans would understand. There is a consciousness in each tree and in the forest as a whole.*

Yes, I replied. *I've sensed it before.*

Our spirits raced through the soil, along the expanse of the mycorrhiza. I noted where the roots of different trees intersected with it.

When there is a drought, trees tell each other to conserve water and where to find moister soil, Leighnel said. *They can even share water and nutrients via the mycorrhizal networks.*

We stopped at a particularly complex web of threads intertwined with tree roots.

There are many more examples of the ways trees communicate and adapt to their environment, Leighnel continued. *But the way most pertinent to us right now is how they fight insects or animals that are damaging and dangerous to the trees.*

Our spirit selves shot upward through the soil and the

progressively larger roots closer to the surface. Then, we broke through and rose along the trunk of an oak, out along a limb to the branches and leaves.

"There are many species of insects that swarm and travel through forests, devouring leaves and killing trees," Leighnel said, speaking audibly now. "But the trees have a remedy for that. They can produce toxins that harm the insects so they go away, or hormones that make the leaves taste terrible for, say, a giraffe. Over the last few centuries, a deadly pest, or predator if you will, has become a serious problem. It is the most dangerous of all to the forests."

"Let me guess," I said. "Humans."

"Yes, humans. Wiping out forests on a grand scale to build their shopping malls and subdivisions. Faeries are destructive to trees, too, but not as much since they've been driven underground by the ascendancy of human beings."

"And that's why the trees produce phytolucine?"

"Yes. It's a naturally produced substance that is meant to repel humans. I finally came to that discovery the other day, after decades of research, after learning how to communicate rudimentarily with the trees myself. I believe phytolucine also has a greater purpose beyond protecting trees from humans, but we don't understand yet what that is."

"Is phytolucine a poison?"

"I don't know. It might not be toxic at all. I'm still trying to figure out how it works. I've only been able to acquire the smallest samples. It's as if the trees are hiding and protecting it from the various hominid species. For all I know, it may be intended to repel us in a harmless way, like making us love the trees too much to kill them."

"It turns humans into tree-huggers?"

"Perhaps. But its significant effect on your species must be why the Fae want it for their magic. As you can well imagine, their magic would not be harmless."

"No," I said. "It's meant to wipe us out."

"Yes. That is probably true."

"You didn't mention if the phytolucine affects elves."

"The sample I obtained was too small to produce sufficient data on that point, but the short answer is no. It does not affect elves. Our species is a protector of the trees and forests. They would have no reason to repel us."

We flew quickly back down the tree and returned to the inside of the trunk where I had first appeared, the astral projection of myself, that is. Me standing in my nightgown.

"So, what do we do?" I asked, while knowing that Cory didn't want me to do anything at all.

"We must get more phytolucine for me to study and learn exactly how it affects humans. Somehow, we must learn if the trees will deploy it against humans or if that could be prevented. And, in any event, we must keep it away from the Fae."

"How would we prevent the trees from deploying it?"

"Convince them somehow by communicating with them. Or"—he smiled at me—"Danu could convince them."

"I've already learned I can't get Danu to do anything, so don't look at me."

"Danu will do what's best for the forests and the earth. And the humans, too, if she believes they deserve it."

The next thing I knew, I was in my bathroom again. Unfortunately, Cory was there, too, staring into my face with grave concern.

"You froze again," he said.

"How would you know? I was in here with the door closed."

"Darla, you know very well that I'm long past the age when I can get through the night without multiple visits to the bath-room. You didn't answer when I knocked, so I came in."

"Sorry. I was summoned by Leighnel, you know, the elf who was imprisoned with me."

"Oh, man. What did he want?"

I explained to him about the phytolucine.

"That's the same stuff the faeries want?"

"Yeah. We want the Elves to get it, but not the Fae."

He covered his face with his hands and sighed theatrically.

"What do you mean by *we*?" he whined. "Why do *we* have to do anything?"

"*We,* as in the good guys. The knights in shining armor. The gallant protectors of San Marcos and the free world."

"Why can't we just run an inn and have a simple life?"

"Cory, that ship sailed a long, long time ago."

CHAPTER 31

SOPHIE

When I returned home, the inn showed no lights on in any bedrooms. Only the cheery lamp above the main entrance glowed. Cory and Mom had obviously gone to bed, as had the guests in our only two occupied rooms.

I was feeling low. Really low. My new vow of not killing anyone anymore had been broken repeatedly. My latest assassination was only fifteen minutes ago.

The allegedly new, empathetic Sophie was still a brutal enforcer.

But I didn't want to be! What happened to my purpose to do good and fight for the rights of the oppressed supernaturals?

Instead, it seemed like all I was doing was fighting and killing faeries. And now, executing one of the world's oldest vampires. My friend's lover.

I climbed the stairs to my room, the crossbow bouncing against my thigh, reminding me of the faeries and vampires it had taken out. When I entered my bedroom, I put my weapons in the back of the closet, next to my art supplies, hoping the weapons would be forgotten, like my paintbrushes and sketch pads.

I turned on the TV.

"Rally attendees claim that Ms. Moosebacher turned into a monster during her speech," droned the reporter, Meghan Whortle. "The paramedics dispute this and insist they treated a normal human being with severe injuries. She was taken to the ER in critical but stable condition. No charges have been filed in the incident."

She must have shifted back to her human form to save herself from the mob after it attacked her. I hit the power button so forcefully I almost broke the remote.

I wanted to go to bed, but guilt about Lethia haunted me. Destroying her had been necessary, I told myself yet again. She was seconds away from ending Diego's existence, and she would have killed me, too.

I couldn't have had Lethia arrested. The police would have staked her. She was a psycho and no one, not even an empath, would have been able to convince her not to murder people whenever she had the whim.

There had been no option other than to do what I had done. Whatever jealousy I felt for her had nothing to do with it. Honest.

So, why did I feel so rotten?

Because of Diego.

I felt sorry for his loss. Yeah, I empathized with the grief he felt. And I guess I didn't want him to hate me for what I did.

Why did I care if Diego hated me? Because we'd been friends.

And because maybe I'd wanted us to be a bit more than friends.

Well, that was out of the question now. I killed his girlfriend, after all. He had been in an abusive relationship, and I knew he wanted to end it. But not in this way.

Would he ever forgive me?

I went into the bathroom, clicked on the light, and screamed.

As I stared at the mirror, a crazy woman was standing behind me.

I turned around. No one was there. But when I looked in the mirror, she was still behind me. A freaky woman, kind of Goth. With a triskelion tattooed on her cheek, braided red hair with different varieties of leaves stuck in each braid, and mascara smudged around her eyes.

"Ye better get used to seein' me around," she said.

She also had blackened teeth.

"Who are you?"

"I'm Birog. I was a druid back in the day. Back when I was alive. Now, I serve the earth-mother, Danu."

"Oh. You know my mother, Darla?"

"'Course I do. I used to visit her and give her guidance. Now it's yer turn."

"Um, why is it my turn?"

"Because before long, yer mum will become Danu. They'll be one and the same."

"Will Mom have to die?"

She snorted. "'Course not. She will ascend to the heights of the goddess realm. I don't know what that means, but it sounded good."

"But will Mom still be here for me?"

"She won't be cookin' yer holiday feasts, that's for sure."

"So, what kind of guidance are you here to give me?"

"Have you heard of the Tuatha Dé Danann?"

"Um, not exactly."

"The name means the Children of Danu. They're a magical race of demigods who ruled Ireland."

"And what does that have to do with me?"

"You will soon be the literal daughter of Danu. And that means you've got a lot of work to do. You've already got magic and psychic powers, but you'll need to ramp them up."

"Why?"

"To lead your people. And fight off the Fomorians."

"The who?"

"Long story. I'll tell ye another time."

"Will I have to fight the Fae?"

"Ye've already begun that, I see. And ye'll need to defeat them."

"How?" I felt like crying. "I don't want to do any more fighting."

"Oh, yes, you do. Ye have a lot of greatness ahead of you. Get some sleep, and ye'll feel better. I'll visit ye again soon."

Her image disappeared. I opened the bathroom door to make sure she wasn't lurking in the bedroom.

"Why me?" I said aloud. "I don't deserve all this trouble."

Oh, yes you do, said the telepathic words of Cervantes, who had appeared out of nowhere to rub against my leg. *You deserve all the power and glory that will come to you.*

"No."

But first, you deserve a good night's sleep. Sleeping fixes everything. Take it from a cat. I know of what I speak.

"I want to wake up in a different life."

Oh, you will. Someday soon. Just not tomorrow. You'll need to help with breakfast tomorrow. And give me treats. Priorities, Sophie.

PLEASE LEAVE A REVIEW

Dear reader, thank you in advance:
Please give my book a better chance.
Success and sales depend on you,
So kindly post a book review.

WHAT'S NEXT

Book 2 of the Goddess's Daughter: Of Fear and Fae

It's open season for supernaturals. After The Great Unmasking, the state has passed a bill outlawing supernatural creatures and magical activity. Vigilantism is on the rise. A militia roams the streets committing violence.

I'm a witch, an empath, and now, an outlaw. Not just because of the Supernatural Criminality Act, but because the governor wants me dead. You see, I know her secrets.

All my family wants to do is run our historic inn. But it's in danger of being shut down because of supernatural activity.

My life is also threatened by the corrupt leader of the super-natural guilds who should have been protecting us. I need help from the vampire Diego, but I must suppress my growing attraction and regain his trust. And he must win a lethal combat ritual to become the next leader of the vampire guild.

Meanwhile, Mom is working with the Elves to prevent a Fae invasion. But she keeps going into catatonic states when she is summoned by the Goddess Danu.

Is the Goddess taking Mom away from us?

Get swept up by the Goddess's Daughter series (a sequel to the Memory Guild): urban fantasy with magic and monsters, secrets and treachery, a touch of humor, and a slow-burn romance.

Visit your favorite e-retailer or wardparker.com

INTERESTED IN THE BOOKS THAT SPAWNED THE GODDESS'S DAUGHTER?

Check out the Memory Guild Midlife Paranormal Mystery Thrillers

Visit wardparker.com

GET A FREE BOOK

GET A FREE E-BOOK

Sign up for my newsletter and get *A Ghostly Touch*, a Memory Guild novella, for free, offered exclusively to my newsletter subscribers. Darla reads the memories of a young woman, murdered in the 1890s, whose ghost begins haunting Darla, looking for justice. As a subscriber, you'll be the first to know about my new releases and lots of free book promotions. The newsletter is delivered only a couple of times a month. No spam at all, and you can unsubscribe at any time. Get your free book for all e-readers at wardparker.com

ACKNOWLEDGMENTS

I wish to thank my loyal readers, who give me a reason to write more every day. I'm especially grateful to Shelley Holloway and Elizabeth Thurmond for all your editing and proofreading brilliance. To my A Team (you know who you are), thanks for reading and reviewing my ARCs, as well as providing good suggestions. And to my wife, Martha, thank you for your love and moral support.

ABOUT THE AUTHOR

Ward is the author of the Memory Guild midlife paranormal mystery thrillers. The Goddess's Daughter urban fantasy series continues the adventures.

He also writes the Monsters of Jellyfish Beach paranormal mysteries, set in the same world as his Freaky Florida series.

Ward lives in Florida with his wife, several cats, and a demon who wishes to remain anonymous.

Connect with him on Facebook (wardparkerauthor), Book-Bub, Goodreads, Bluesky (wardparker.bsky.social), or Threads (wardparker2223). Check out his books and sign up for his newsletter at wardparker.com.

PARANORMAL BOOKS BY WARD PARKER

Freaky Florida Humorous Paranormal Novels

Snowbirds of Prey
Invasive Species
Fate Is a Witch
Gnome Coming
Going Batty
Dirty Old Manatee
Gazillions of Reptilians

Hangry as Hell (novella)
Books 1-3 Box Set

The Memory Guild Midlife Paranormal Mystery Thrillers

A Magic Touch (also available in audio)
The Psychic Touch (also available in audio)
A Wicked Touch (also available in audio)
A Haunting Touch
The Wizard's Touch
A Witchy Touch
A Faerie's Touch
The Goddess's Touch
The Vampire's Touch
An Angel's Touch
A Ghostly Touch (novella)
Books 1-3 Box Set (also available in audio)

The Goddess's Daughter

(Continuing the Memory Guild Series.)
Of Envy and Empaths
Of Fear and Fae
Of Valor and Vampires

Monsters of Jellyfish Beach Paranormal Mystery Adventures

The Golden Ghouls
Fiends With Benefits

Get Ogre Yourself
My Funny Frankenstein
Werewolf Art Thou?
In Sprite of Herself
Worms of Endearment